J. G. BALLARD was born in Shanghai in 1930, interned in a Japanese prison camp from 1943 to 1945 and arrived in England in 1946. He published his first novel, *The Drowned World*, in 1962, and his latest, *Kingdom Come*, in 2006. His autobiography, *Miracles of Life*, was published in [illegible] in Shepperton.

By the same author

The Drowned World
The Voices of Time
The Terminal Beach
The Drought
The Crystal World
The Day of Forever
The Disaster Area
The Atrocity Exhibition
Vermilion Sands
Concrete Island
High-Rise
Low-Flying Aircraft
The Unlimited Dream Company
Hello America
The Venus Hunters
Myths of the Near Future
Empire of the Sun
The Day of Creation
Running Wild
War Fever
The Kindness of Women
Rushing to Paradise
A User's Guide to the Millennium
Cocaine Nights
Super-Cannes
The Complete Short Stories
Millennium People
Kingdom Come
Miracles of Life

J. G. BALLARD

Crash

HARPER PERENNIAL
London, New York, Toronto, Sydney and New Delhi

This edition produced for The Book People Ltd,
Hall Wood Avenue, Haydock, St Helens, WA11 9UL

Harper Perennial
An imprint of HarperCollins*Publishers*
77–85 Fulham Palace Road
Hammersmith
London W6 8JB

www.harperperennial.co.uk
Visit our authors' blog at www.fifthestate.co.uk

This Harper Perennial edition published 2008
1

First published in Great Britain by Jonathan Cape in 1973
Published by Vintage in 1995 and 2004

A catalogue record for this book is available from the British Library

ISBN 978-0-00-785197-3

Printed and bound in Great Britain by Clays Ltd, St Ives plc

FSC
Mixed Sources
Product group from well-managed forests and other controlled sources
www.fsc.org Cert no. SW-COC-1806
© 1996 Forest Stewardship Council

FSC is a non-profit international organisation established to promote the
responsible management of the world's forests. Products carrying the FSC
label are independently certified to assure consumers that they come
from forests that are managed to meet the social, economic and
ecological needs of present and future generations.

Find out more about HarperCollins and the environment at
www.harpercollins.co.uk/green

Introduction

THE MARRIAGE OF reason and nightmare that has dominated the 20th century has given birth to an ever more ambiguous world. Across the communications landscape move the spectres of sinister technologies and the dreams that money can buy. Thermo-nuclear weapons systems and soft-drink commercials coexist in an overlit realm ruled by advertising and pseudo-events, science and pornography. Over our lives preside the great twin leitmotifs of the 20th century – sex and paranoia.

Increasingly, our concepts of past, present and future are being forced to revise themselves. Just as the past, in social and psychological terms, became a casualty of Hiroshima and the nuclear age, so in its turn the future is ceasing to exist, devoured by the all-voracious present. We have annexed the future into the present, as merely one of those manifold alternatives open to us. Options multiply around us, and we live in an almost infantile world where any demand, any possibility, whether for life-styles, travel, sexual roles and identities, can be satisfied instantly.

In addition, I feel that the balance between fiction and reality has changed significantly in the past decades. Increasingly their roles are reversed. We live in a world ruled by fictions of every kind – mass-merchandizing, advertising, politics conducted as a branch of advertising, the pre-empting of any original response to experience by the television screen. We live inside an enormous novel. It is now less and less necessary for the writer to invent the fictional content of his novel. The fiction is already there. The writer's task is to invent the reality.

In the past we have always assumed that the external world around us has represented reality, however confusing or uncertain, and that the inner world of our minds, its dreams, hopes, ambitions, represented the realm of fantasy and the imagination. These roles, it seems to me, have been reversed. The most prudent and effective method of dealing with the world around us is to assume that it is a complete fiction – conversely, the one small node of reality left to us is inside our own heads. Freud's classic distinction between the latent and manifest content of the dream, between the apparent and the real, now needs to be applied to the external world of so-called reality.

Given these transformations, what is the main task facing the writer? Can he, any longer, make use of the techniques and perspectives of the traditional 19th century novel, with its linear narrative, its measured chronology, its consular characters grandly inhabiting their domains within an ample time and space? Is his subject matter the sources of character and personality sunk deep in the past, the unhurried inspection of roots, the examination of the most subtle nuances of social behaviour and personal relationships? Has the writer still the moral authority to invent a self-sufficient and self-enclosed world, to preside over his characters like an examiner, knowing all the questions in advance? Can he leave out anything he prefers not to understand, including his own motives, prejudices and psychopathology?

I feel myself that the writer's role, his authority and licence to act, have changed radically. I feel that, in a sense, the writer knows nothing any longer. He has no moral stance. He offers the reader the contents of his own head, a set of options and imaginative alternatives. His role is that of the scientist, whether on safari or in his laboratory, faced with an unknown terrain or subject. All he can do is to devise various hypotheses and test them against the facts.

Crash is such a book, an extreme metaphor for an extreme situation, a kit of desperate measures only for use in an extreme crisis. *Crash*, of course, is not concerned with an imaginary disaster, however imminent, but with a pandemic cataclysm that kills hundreds of thousands of people each year and injures millions. Do we see, in the car crash, a sinister portent of a nightmare marriage between sex and technology? Will modern technology provide us with hitherto undreamed-of means for tapping our own psychopathologies? Is this harnessing of our innate perversity conceivably of benefit to us? Is there some deviant logic unfolding more powerful than that provided by reason?

Throughout *Crash* I have used the car not only as a sexual image, but as a total metaphor for man's life in today's society. As such the novel has a political role quite apart from its sexual content, but I would still like to think that *Crash* is the first pornographic novel based on technology. In a sense, pornography is the most political form of fiction, dealing with how we use and exploit each other, in the most urgent and ruthless way.

Needless to say, the ultimate role of *Crash* is cautionary, a warning against that brutal, erotic and overlit realm that beckons more and more persuasively to us from the margins of the technological landscape.

J. G. Ballard
1995

I

VAUGHAN DIED YESTERDAY in his last car-crash. During our friendship he had rehearsed his death in many crashes, but this was his only true accident. Driven on a collision course towards the limousine of the film actress, his car jumped the rails of the London Airport flyover and plunged through the roof of a bus filled with airline passengers. The crushed bodies of package tourists, like a haemorrhage of the sun, still lay across the vinyl seats when I pushed my way through the police engineers an hour later. Holding the arm of her chauffeur, the film actress Elizabeth Taylor, with whom Vaughan had dreamed of dying for so many months, stood alone under the revolving ambulance lights. As I knelt over Vaughan's body she placed a gloved hand to her throat.

Could she see, in Vaughan's posture, the formula of the death which he had devised for her? During the last weeks of his life Vaughan thought of nothing else but her death, a coronation of wounds he had staged with the devotion of an Earl Marshal. The walls of his apartment near the film studios at Shepperton were covered with the photographs he had taken through his zoom lens each morning as she left her hotel in London, from the pedestrian bridges above the westbound motorways, and from the roof of the multi-storey car-park at the studios. The magnified details of her knees and hands, of the inner surface of her thighs and the left apex of her mouth, I uneasily prepared for Vaughan on the copying machine in my office, handing him the packages of prints as if they were the instalments of a death warrant. At his apartment I watched him matching the details of her body with the photographs of grotesque wounds in a textbook of plastic surgery.

In his vision of a car-crash with the actress, Vaughan was obsessed by many wounds and impacts – by the dying chromium and collapsing bulkheads of their two cars meeting head-on in complex collisions endlessly repeated in slow-motion films, by the identical wounds inflicted on their bodies, by the image of windshield glass frosting around her face as she broke its tinted surface like a death-born Aphrodite, by the compound fractures of their thighs impacted against their handbrake mountings, and above all by the wounds to their genitalia, her uterus pierced by the heraldic beak of the manufacturer's medallion, his semen emptying across the luminescent dials that registered for ever the last temperature and fuel levels of the engine.

It was only at these times, as he described this last crash to me, that Vaughan was calm. He talked of these wounds and collisions with the erotic tenderness of a long-separated lover. Searching through the photographs in his apartment, he half turned towards me, so that his heavy groin quietened me with its profile of an almost erect penis. He knew that as long as he provoked me with his own sex, which he used casually as if he might discard it for ever at any moment, I would never leave him.

Ten days ago, as he stole my car from the garage of my apartment house, Vaughan hurtled up the concrete ramp, an ugly machine sprung from a trap. Yesterday his body lay under the police arc-lights at the foot of the flyover, veiled by a delicate lacework of blood. The broken postures of his legs and arms, the bloody geometry of his face, seemed to parody the photographs of crash injuries that covered the walls of his apartment. I looked down for the last time at his huge groin, engorged with blood. Twenty yards away, illuminated by the revolving lamps, the actress hovered on the arm of her chauffeur. Vaughan had dreamed of dying at the moment of her orgasm.

Before his death Vaughan had taken part in many crashes. As I think of Vaughan I see him in the stolen cars he drove and damaged, the surfaces of deformed metal and plastic that for ever embraced him. Two months earlier I found him on the lower deck of the airport flyover after the first rehearsal of his own death. A taxi driver helped two shaken air hostesses from a small car into which Vaughan had collided as he lurched from the mouth of a concealed access road. As I ran across to Vaughan I saw him through the fractured windshield of the white convertible he had taken from the car-park of the Oceanic Terminal. His exhausted face, with its scarred mouth, was lit by broken rainbows. I pulled the dented passenger door from its frame. Vaughan sat on the glass-covered seat, studying his own posture with a complacent gaze. His hands, palms upwards at his sides, were covered with blood from his injured knee-caps. He examined the vomit staining the lapels of his leather jacket, and reached forward to touch the globes of semen clinging to the instrument binnacle. I tried to lift him from the car, but his tight buttocks were clamped together as if they had seized while forcing the last drops of fluid from his seminal vesicles. On the seat beside him were the torn photographs of the film actress which I had reproduced for him that morning at my office. Magnified sections of lip and eyebrow, elbow and cleavage formed a broken mosaic.

For Vaughan the car-crash and his own sexuality had made their final marriage. I remember him at night with nervous young women in the crushed rear compartments of abandoned cars in breakers' yards, and their photographs in the postures of uneasy sex acts. Their tight faces and strained thighs were lit by his polaroid flash, like startled survivors of a submarine disaster. These aspiring whores, whom Vaughan met in the all-night cafés and supermarkets of London Airport, were the first cousins of the patients illustrated in his surgical textbooks. During his studied courtship of injured women, Vaughan was obsessed with the buboes of gas bacillus infections, by facial injuries and genital wounds.

Through Vaughan I discovered the true significance of the automobile crash, the meaning of whiplash injuries and roll-over, the ecstasies of head-on collisions. Together we visited the Road Research Laboratory twenty miles to the west of London, and watched the calibrated vehicles crashing into the concrete target blocks. Later, in his apartment, Vaughan screened slow-motion films of test collisions that he had photographed with his cine-camera. Sitting in the darkness on the floor cushions, we watched the silent impacts flicker on the wall above our heads. The repeated sequences of crashing cars first calmed and then aroused me. Cruising alone on the motorway under the yellow glare of the sodium lights, I thought of myself at the controls of these impacting vehicles.

During the months that followed, Vaughan and I spent many hours driving along the express highways on the northern perimeter of the airport. On the calm summer evenings these fast boulevards became a zone of nightmare collisions. Listening to the police broadcasts on Vaughan's radio, we moved from one accident to the next. Often we stopped under arc-lights that flared over the sites of major collisions, watching while firemen and police engineers worked with acetylene torches and lifting tackle to free unconscious wives trapped beside their dead husbands, or waited as a passing doctor fumbled with a dying man pinned below an inverted truck. Sometimes Vaughan was pulled back by the other spectators, and fought for his cameras with the ambulance attendants. Above all, Vaughan waited for head-on collisions with the concrete pillars of the motorway overpasses, the melancholy conjunction formed by a crushed vehicle abandoned on the grass verge and the serene motion sculpture of the concrete.

Once we were the first to reach the crashed car of an injured woman driver. A middle-aged cashier at the airport duty-free liquor store, she sat unsteadily in the crushed compartment, fragments of the tinted windshield set in her forehead like jewels. As a police car approached, its emergency beacon pulsing along the overhead motorway, Vaughan ran back for his camera and flash equipment. Taking off my tie, I searched helplessly for the woman's wounds. She stared at me without speaking, and lay on her side across the seat. I watched the blood irrigate her white blouse. When Vaughan had taken the last of his pictures he knelt down inside the car and held her face carefully in his hands, whispering into her ear. Together we helped to lift her on to the ambulance trolley.

On our way to Vaughan's apartment he recognized an airport whore waiting in the forecourt of a motorway restaurant, a part-time cinema usherette for ever worrying about her small son's defective hearing-aid. As they sat behind me she complained to Vaughan about my nervous driving, but he was watching her movements with an abstracted gaze, almost encouraging her to gesture with her hands and knees. On the deserted roof of a Northolt multi-storey car-park I waited by the balustrade. In the rear seat of the car Vaughan arranged her limbs in the posture of the dying cashier. His strong body, crouched across her in the reflected light of passing headlamps, assumed a series of stylized positions.

Vaughan unfolded for me all his obsessions with the mysterious eroticism of wounds: the perverse logic of blood-soaked instrument panels, seat-belts smeared with excrement, sun-visors lined with brain tissue. For Vaughan each crashed car set off a tremor of excitement, in the complex geometries of a dented fender, in the unexpected variations of crushed radiator grilles, in the grotesque overhang of an instrument panel forced on to a driver's crotch as if in some calibrated act of machine fellatio. The intimate time and space of a single human being had been fossilized for ever in this web of chromium knives and frosted glass.

A week after the funeral of the woman cashier, as we drove at night along the western perimeter of the airport, Vaughan swerved on to the verge and struck a large mongrel dog. The impact of its body, like a padded hammer, and the shower of glass as the animal was carried over the roof, convinced me that we were about to die in a crash. Vaughan never stopped. I watched him accelerate away, his scarred face held close to the punctured windshield, angrily brushing the beads of frosted glass from his cheeks. Already his acts of violence had become so random that I was no more than a captive spectator. Yet the next morning, on the roof of the airport car-park where we abandoned the car, Vaughan calmly pointed out to me the deep dents in the bonnet and roof. He stared at an airliner filled with tourists lifting into the western sky, his sallow face puckering like a wistful child's. The long triangular grooves on the car had been formed within the death of an unknown creature, its vanished identity abstracted in terms of the geometry of this vehicle. How much more mysterious would be our own deaths, and those of the famous and powerful?

Even this first death seemed timid compared with the others in which Vaughan took part, and with those imaginary deaths that filled his mind. Trying to exhaust himself, Vaughan devised a terrifying almanac of imaginary automobile disasters and insane wounds – the lungs of elderly men punctured by door handles, the chests of young women impaled by steering-columns, the cheeks of handsome youths pierced by the chromium latches of quarter-lights. For him these wounds were the keys to a new sexuality born from a perverse technology. The images of these wounds hung in the gallery of his mind like exhibits in the museum of a slaughterhouse.

Thinking of Vaughan now, drowning in his own blood under the police arc-lights, I remember the countless imaginary disasters he described as we cruised together along the airport expressways. He dreamed of ambassadorial limousines crashing into jack-knifing butane tankers, of taxis filled with celebrating children colliding head-on below the bright display windows of deserted supermarkets. He dreamed of alienated brothers and sisters, by chance meeting each other on collision courses on the access roads of petrochemical plants, their unconscious incest made explicit in this colliding metal, in the haemorrhages of their brain tissue flowering beneath the aluminized compression chambers and reaction vessels. Vaughan devised the massive rear-end collisions of sworn enemies, hate-deaths celebrated in the engine fuel burning in wayside ditches, paintwork boiling through the dull afternoon sunlight of provincial towns. He visualized the specialized crashes of escaping criminals, of off-duty hotel receptionists trapped between their steering wheels and the laps of their lovers whom they were masturbating. He thought of the crashes of honeymoon couples, seated together after their impacts with the rear suspension units of runaway sugar-tankers. He thought of the crashes of automobile stylists, the most abstract of all possible deaths, wounded in their cars with promiscuous laboratory technicians.

Vaughan elaborated endless variations on these collisions, thinking first of a repetition of head-on collisions: a child-molester and an overworked doctor re-enacting their deaths first in head-on collision and then in roll-over; the retired prostitute crashing into a concrete motorway parapet, her overweight body propelled through the fractured windshield, menopausal loins torn on the chromium bonnet mascot. Her blood would cross the over-white concrete of the evening embankment, haunting for ever the mind of a police mechanic who carried the pieces of her body in a yellow plastic shroud. Alternatively, Vaughan saw her hit by a reversing truck in a motorway fuelling area, crushed against the nearside door of her car as she bent down to loosen her right shoe, the contours of her body buried within the bloody mould of the door panel. He saw her hurtling through the rails of the flyover and dying as Vaughan himself would later die, plunging through the roof of an airline coach, its cargo of complacent destinations multiplied by the death of this myopic middle-aged woman. He saw her hit by a speeding taxi as she stepped out of her car to relieve herself in a wayside latrine, her body whirled a hundred feet away in a spray of urine and blood.

I think now of the other crashes we visualized, absurd deaths of the wounded, maimed and distraught. I think of the crashes of psychopaths, implausible accidents carried out with venom and self-disgust, vicious multiple collisions contrived in stolen cars on evening freeways among tired office-workers. I think of the absurd crashes of neurasthenic housewives returning from their VD clinics, hitting parked cars in suburban high streets. I think of the crashes of excited schizophrenics colliding head-on into stalled laundry vans in one-way streets; of manic-depressives crushed while making pointless U-turns on motorway access roads; of luckless paranoids driving at full speed into the brick walls at the ends of known culs-de-sac; of sadistic charge nurses decapitated in inverted crashes on complex interchanges; of lesbian supermarket manageresses burning to death in the collapsed frames of their midget cars before the stoical eyes of middle-aged firemen; of autistic children crushed in rear-end collisions, their eyes less wounded in death; of buses filled with mental defectives drowning together stoically in roadside industrial canals.

Long before Vaughan died I had begun to think of my own death. With whom would I die, and in what role – psychopath, neurasthenic, absconding criminal? Vaughan dreamed endlessly of the deaths of the famous, inventing imaginary crashes for them. Around the deaths of James Dean and Albert Camus, Jayne Mansfield and John Kennedy he had woven elaborate fantasies. His imagination was a target gallery of screen actresses, politicians, business tycoons and television executives. Vaughan followed them everywhere with his camera, zoom lens watching from the observation platform of the Oceanic Terminal at the airport, from hotel mezzanine balconies and studio car-parks. For each of them Vaughan devised an optimum auto-death. Onassis and his wife would die in a recreation of the Dealey Plaza assassination. He saw Reagan in a complex rear-end collision, dying a stylized death that expressed Vaughan's obsession with Reagan's genital organs, like his obsession with the exquisite transits of the screen actress's pubis across the vinyl seat covers of hired limousines.

After his last attempt to kill my wife Catherine, I knew that Vaughan had retired finally into his own skull. In this overlit realm ruled by violence and technology he was now driving for ever at a hundred miles an hour along an empty motorway, past deserted filling stations on the edges of wide fields, waiting for a single oncoming car. In his mind Vaughan saw the whole world dying in a simultaneous automobile disaster, millions of vehicles hurled together in a terminal congress of spurting loins and engine coolant.

I remember my first minor collision in a deserted hotel car-park. Disturbed by a police patrol, we had forced ourselves through a hurried sex-act. Reversing out of the park, I struck an unmarked tree. Catherine vomited over my seat. This pool of vomit with its clots of blood like liquid rubies, as viscous and discreet as everything produced by Catherine, still contains for me the essence of the erotic delirium of the car-crash, more exciting than her own rectal and vaginal mucus, as refined as the excrement of a fairy queen, or the minuscule globes of liquid that formed beside the bubbles of her contact lenses. In this magic pool, lifting from her throat like a rare discharge of fluid from the mouth of a remote and mysterious shrine, I saw my own reflection, a mirror of blood, semen and vomit, distilled from a mouth whose contours only a few minutes before had drawn steadily against my penis.

Now that Vaughan has died, we will leave with the others who gathered around him, like a crowd drawn to an injured cripple whose deformed postures reveal the secret formulas of their minds and lives. All of us who knew Vaughan accept the perverse eroticism of the car-crash, as painful as the drawing of an exposed organ through the aperture of a surgical wound. I have watched copulating couples moving along darkened freeways at night, men and women on the verge of orgasm, their cars speeding in a series of inviting trajectories towards the flashing headlamps of the oncoming traffic stream. Young men alone behind the wheels of their first cars, near-wrecks picked up in scrap-yards, masturbate as they move on worn tyres to aimless destinations. After a near collision at a traffic intersection semen jolts across a cracked speedometer dial. Later, the dried residues of that same semen are brushed by the lacquered hair of the first young woman who lies across his lap with her mouth over his penis, one hand on the wheel hurtling the car through the darkness towards a multi-level interchange, the swerving brakes drawing the semen from him as he grazes the tail-gate of an articulated truck loaded with colour television sets, his left hand vibrating her clitoris towards orgasm as the headlamps of the truck flare warningly in his rear-view mirror. Later still, he watches as a friend takes a teenage girl in the rear seat. Greasy mechanic's hands expose her buttocks to the advertisement hoardings that hurl past them. The wet highways flash by in the glare of headlamps and the scream of brake-pads. The shaft of his penis glistens above the girl as he strikes at the frayed plastic roof of the car, marking the yellow fabric with his smegma.

The last ambulance had left. An hour earlier the film actress had been steered towards her limousine. In the evening light the white concrete of the collision corridor below the flyover resembled a secret airstrip from which mysterious machines would take off into a metallized sky. Vaughan's glass aeroplane flew somewhere above the heads of the bored spectators moving back to their cars, above the tired policemen gathering together the crushed suitcases and handbags of the airline tourists. I thought of Vaughan's body, colder now, its rectal temperature following the same downward gradients as those of the other victims of the crash. Across the night air these gradients fell like streamers from the office towers and apartment houses of the city, and from the warm mucosa of the film actress in her hotel suite.

I drove back towards the airport. The lights along Western Avenue illuminated the speeding cars, moving together towards their celebration of wounds.

2

I BEGAN TO understand the real excitements of the car-crash after my first meeting with Vaughan. Propelled on a pair of scarred and uneven legs repeatedly injured in one or other vehicle collision, the harsh and unsettling figure of this hoodlum scientist came into my life at a time when his obsessions were self-evidently those of a madman.

As I drove home from the film studios at Shepperton on a rain-swept June evening, my car skidded at the intersection below the entrance to the Western Avenue flyover. Within seconds I was moving at sixty miles an hour into the oncoming lane. As the car struck the central reservation the off-side tyre blew out and whirled off its rim. Out of my control, the car crossed the reservation and turned up the high-speed exit ramp. Three vehicles were approaching, mass-produced saloon cars whose exact model-year, colour schemes and external accessories I can still remember with the painful accuracy of a never-to-be-eluded nightmare. The first two I missed, pumping the brakes and barely managing to steer my car between them. The third, carrying a young woman doctor and her husband, I struck head-on. The man, a chemical engineer with an American foodstuffs company, was killed instantly, propelled through his windshield like a mattress from the barrel of a circus cannon. He died on the bonnet of my car, his blood sprayed through the fractured windshield across my face and chest. The firemen who later cut me from the crushed cabin of my car assumed that I was bleeding to death from a massive open-heart wound.

I was barely injured. On my way home after leaving my

secretary Renata, who was freeing herself from an unsettling affair with me, I was still wearing the safety belt I had deliberately fastened to save her from the embarrassment of embracing me. My chest was severely bruised against the steering wheel, my knees crushed into the instrument panel as my body moved forwards into its own collision with the interior of the car, but my only serious injury was a severed nerve in my scalp.

The same mysterious forces that saved me from being impaled on the steering wheel also saved the young engineer's wife. Apart from a bruised upper jawbone and several loosened teeth, she was unharmed. During my first hours in Ashford Hospital all I could see in my mind was the image of us locked together face to face in these two cars, the body of her dying husband lying between us on the bonnet of my car. We looked at each other through the fractured windshields, neither able to move. Her husband's hand, no more than a few inches from me, lay palm upwards beside the right windshield wiper. His hand had struck some rigid object as he was hurled from his seat, and the pattern of a sign formed itself as I sat there, pumped up by his dying circulation into a huge blood-blister – the triton signature of my radiator emblem.

Supported by her diagonal seat belt, his wife sat behind her steering wheel, staring at me in a curiously formal way, as if unsure what had brought us together. Her handsome face, topped by a broad, intelligent forehead, had the blank and unresponsive look of a madonna in an early Renaissance icon, unwilling to accept the miracle, or nightmare, sprung from her loins. Only once did any emotion cross it, when she seemed to see me clearly for the first time, and a peculiar rictus twisted the right side of her face, as if the nerve had been pulled on a string. Did she realize then that the blood covering my face and chest was her husband's?

Our two cars were surrounded by a circle of spectators, their silent faces watching us with enormous seriousness. After this brief pause everything broke into manic activity. Tyres singing, half a dozen cars pulled on to the verge and mounted the central reservation. A massive traffic jam formed along Western Avenue, sirens wailed as police headlamps flared against the rear bumpers of stalled vehicles tailing back along the flyover. An elderly man in a transparent plastic raincoat was pulling uneasily at the passenger door behind my head, as if frightened that the car might throw a powerful electric charge into his thin hand. A young woman carrying a tartan blanket lowered her head to the window. Only a few inches away, she stared at me with pursed lips, like a mourner peering down at a corpse laid out in an open coffin.

Unaware of any pain at that time, I sat with my right hand holding a spoke of the steering wheel. Still wearing her seat belt, the dead man's wife was coming to her senses. A small group of people – a truck driver, an off-duty soldier in uniform and a woman ice-cream attendant – were pressing their hands at her through the windows, apparently touching parts of her body. She beckoned them away, and freed the harness across her chest, her capable hand fumbling with the chromium release mechanism. For a moment I felt that we were the principal actors at the climax of some grim drama in an unrehearsed theatre of technology, involving these crushed machines, the dead man destroyed in their collision, and the hundreds of drivers waiting beside the stage with their headlamps blazing.

The young woman was helped from her car. Her awkward legs and the angular movements of her head appeared to mimic the distorted streamlining of the two cars. The rectangular bonnet of my car had been wrenched off its seating below the windshield, and the narrow angle between the bonnet and fenders seemed to my exhausted mind to be repeated in everything around me – the expressions and postures of the spectators, the ascending ramp of the flyover, the flight paths of the airliners lifting from the distant runways of the airport. The young woman was carefully steered from her car by an olive-skinned man in the midnight-blue uniform of an Arab airline pilot. A thin stream of urine trickled involuntarily between her legs, running down on to the roadway. The pilot held her shoulders reassuringly. Standing beside their cars, the spectators watched this puddle forming on the oil-stained macadam. In the fading evening light, rainbows began to circle her weak ankles. She turned and stared down at me, a peculiar grimace on her bruised face, a clear confusion of concern and hostility. However, all I could see was the unusual junction of her thighs, opened towards me in this deformed way. It was not the sexuality of the posture that stayed in my mind, but the stylization of the terrible events that had involved us, the extremes of pain and violence ritualized in this gesture of her legs, like the exaggerated pirouette of a mentally defective girl I had once seen performing in a Christmas play at an institution.

I gripped the steering wheel in both hands, trying to keep still. A continuous tremor shook my chest, and almost stopped me from breathing. A policeman's strong hands held my shoulder. A second policeman placed his flat-peaked cap on the bonnet of the car beside the dead man and began to wrench at the door. The frontal impact had compressed the forward section of the passenger compartment, jamming the doors on to their locks.

An ambulance attendant reached across me and cut the sleeve from my right arm. A young man in a dark suit drew my hand through the window. As the hypodermic needle slid into my arm I wondered if this doctor, who seemed no more than an overlarge child, was old enough to have qualified professionally.

An uneasy euphoria carried me towards the hospital. I vomited across the steering wheel, half-conscious of a series of unpleasant fantasies. Two firemen cut the door from its hinges. Dropping it into the road, they peered down at me like the assistants of a gored bullfighter. Even their smallest movements seemed to be formalized, hands reaching towards me in a series of coded gestures. If one of them had unbuttoned his coarse serge trousers to reveal his genitalia, and pressed his penis into the bloody crotch of my armpit, even this bizarre act would have been acceptable in terms of the stylization of violence and rescue. I waited for someone to reassure me as I sat there, dressed in another man's blood while the urine of his young widow formed rainbows around my rescuers' feet. By this same nightmare logic the firemen racing towards the burning wrecks of crashed airliners might trace obscene or humorous slogans on the scalding concrete with their carbon dioxide sprays, executioners could dress their victims in grotesque costumes. In return, the victims would stylize the entrances to their deaths with ironic gestures, solemnly kissing their executioners' gun-butts, desecrating imaginary flags. Surgeons would cut themselves carelessly before making their first incisions, wives casually murmur the names of their lovers at the moment of their husbands' orgasms, the whore mouthing her customer's penis might without offence bite a small circle of tissue from the upper curvature of his glans. That same painful bite which I once received from a tired prostitute irritated by my hesitant erection reminds me of the stylized gestures of ambulance attendants and filling station personnel, each with their repertory of private movements.

Later, I learned that Vaughan collected the grimaces of casualty nurses in his photographic albums. Their dark skins mediated all the sly sexuality which Vaughan aroused in them. Their patients died in the interval between one rubber-soled step and the next, in the shifting contours of their thighs as they touched each other in the doors of emergency theatres.

The policemen lifted me from the car, their firm hands steering me on to the stretcher. Already I felt isolated from the reality of this accident. I tried to sit up on the stretcher, and swung my legs from the blanket. The young doctor pushed me back, hitting my chest with the palm of his hand. Surprised by the irritation in his eyes, I lay back passively.

The draped body of the dead man was lifted from the bonnet of my car. Seated like a demented madonna between the doors of the second ambulance, his wife gazed vacantly at the evening traffic. The wound in her right cheek was slowly deforming her face as the bruised tissues gorged themselves on their own blood. Already I was aware that the interlocked radiator grilles of our cars formed the model of an inescapable and perverse union between us. I stared at the contours of her thighs. Across them the grey blanket formed a graceful dune. Somewhere beneath this mound lay the treasure of her pubis. Its precise jut and rake, the untouched sexuality of this intelligent woman, presided over the tragic events of the evening.

3

THE HARSH BLUE lights of police cars revolved within my mind during the next three weeks as I lay in an empty ward of the casualty hospital near London Airport. In this quiet terrain of used-car marts, water reservoirs and remand centres, surrounded by the motorway systems that served London Airport, I began my recovery from the accident. Two wards of twenty-four beds – the maximum number of survivors anticipated – were permanently reserved for the possible victims of an air-crash. One of these was temporarily occupied by car-crash injuries.

Not all the blood which covered me had belonged to the man I killed. The Asian doctors in the emergency theatre found that both my knee-caps had been fractured against the instrument panel. Long spurs of pain reached along the inner surface of my thighs into my groin, as if fine steel catheters were being drawn through the veins of my legs.

Three days after the first surgery on my knees I caught some minor hospital infection. I lay in the empty ward, taking up a bed that belonged by rights to an air-crash victim, and thinking in a disordered way about the wounds and pains he would feel. Around me, the empty beds contained a hundred histories of collision and bereavement, the translation of wounds through the violence of aircraft and automobile crashes. Two nurses moved through the ward, tidying the beds and radio headphones. These amiable young women ministered within a cathedral of invisible wounds, their burgeoning sexualities presiding over the most terrifying facial and genital injuries.

As they adjusted the harness around my legs, I listened

to the aircraft rising from London Airport. The geometry of this complex torture device seemed in some way related to the slopes and contours of these young women's bodies. Who would be the next tenant of this bed – some middle-aged bank cashier en route to the Balearics, her head full of gin, pubis moistening towards the bored widower seated beside her? After a runway accident at London Airport her body would be marked for years by the bruising of her abdomen against the seat belt stanchion. Each time she slipped away to the lavatory of her provincial restaurant, weakened bladder biting at a worn urethra, during each sex act with her prostatic husband she would think of the few seconds before her crash. Her injuries fixed for ever this imagined infidelity.

Did my wife, when she visited the ward each evening, ever wonder what sexual errand had brought me to the Western Avenue flyover? As she sat beside me, her shrewd eyes itemizing whatever vital parts of her husband's anatomy were left to her, I was certain that she read the answer to her unspoken questions in the scars on my legs and chest.

The nurses hovered around me, carrying out their painful chores. When they replaced the drainage tubes in my knees I tried not to vomit back my sedative, strong enough to keep me quiet but not to relieve the pain. Only their sharp tempers rallied me.

A young, blond-haired doctor with a callous face examined the wounds on my chest. The skin was broken around the lower edge of the sternum, where the horn boss had been driven upwards by the collapsing engine compartment. A semi-circular bruise marked my chest, a marbled rainbow running from one nipple to the other. During the next week this rainbow moved through a sequence of tone changes like the colour spectrum of automobile varnishes. As I looked down at myself I realized that the precise make and model-year of my car could have been reconstructed by an automobile engineer from the pattern of my wounds. The layout of the instrument panel, like the profile of the steering wheel bruised into my chest, was inset on my knees and shinbones. The impact of the second collision between my body and the interior compartment of the car was defined in these wounds, like the contours of a woman's body remembered in the responding pressure of one's own skin for a few hours after a sexual act.

On the fourth day, for no evident reason, the anaesthetics were withdrawn. All morning I vomited into the enamel pail which a nurse held under my face. She stared at me with good-humoured but unmoved eyes. The cold rim of the kidney pail pressed against my cheek. Its porcelain surface was marked by a small thread of blood from some nameless previous user.

I leaned my forehead against the nurse's strong thigh as I vomited. Beside my bruised mouth her worn fingers contrasted strangely with her youthful skin. I found myself thinking of her natal cleft. When had she last washed this moist gulley? During my recovery, questions like this one obsessed me as I talked to the doctors and nurses. When had they last bathed their genitalia, did small grains of faecal matter still cling to their anuses as they prescribed some antibiotic for a streptococcal throat, did the odour of illicit sex acts infest their underwear as they drove home from the hospital, the traces of smegma and vaginal mucus on their hands marrying with the splashed engine coolant of unexpected car-crashes? I let a few threads of green bile leak into the pail, aware of the warm contours of the young woman's thighs. A seam of her gingham frock had been repaired with a few loops of black cotton. I stared at the loosening coils lying against the round surface of her left buttock. Their curvatures seemed as arbitrary and as meaningful as the wounds on my chest and legs.

This obsession with the sexual possibilities of everything around me had been jerked loose from my mind by the crash. I imagined the ward filled with convalescing air-disaster victims, each of their minds a brothel of images. The crash between our two cars was a model of some ultimate and yet undreamt sexual union. The injuries of still-to-be-admitted patients beckoned to me, an immense encyclopedia of accessible dreams.

Catherine seemed well aware of these fantasies. During

her first visits I had been in shock and she had made herself familiar with the layout and atmosphere of the hospital, exchanging good-humoured banter with the doctors. As a nurse carried away my vomit Catherine expertly pulled the metal table from the foot of the bed and unloaded on to it a clutch of magazines. She sat down beside me, casting a brisk eye over my unshaven face and fretting hands.

I tried to smile at her. The stitches in the laceration across my scalp, a second hairline an inch to the left of the original, made it difficult for me to change my expression. In the shaving mirror the nurses held up to my face I resembled an alarmed contortionist, startled by his own deviant anatomy.

'I'm sorry.' I took her hand. 'I must look rather sunk in myself.'

'You're fine,' she said. 'Absolutely. You're like someone's victim in Madame Tussaud's.'

'Try to come tomorrow.'

'I will.' She touched my forehead, gingerly peering at the scalp wound. 'I'll bring some make-up for you. I imagine the only cosmetic attention given to the patients here is at Ashford Mortuary.'

I looked up at her more clearly. Her show of warmth and wifely concern pleasantly surprised me. The mental distance between my work at the television commercial studios in Shepperton and her own burgeoning career in the overseas tours section of Pan American had separated us more and more during the past years. Catherine was now taking flying lessons, and with one of her boyfriends had started a small air-tourist charter firm. All these activities she pursued with a single mind, deliberately marking out her independence and self-reliance as if staking her claim to a terrain that would later soar in value. I had reacted to all this like most husbands, quickly developing an extensive repertory of resigned attitudes. The small but determined drone of her light aircraft crossed the sky over our apartment house each weekend, a tocsin that sounded the note of our relationship.

The blond-haired doctor walked through the ward, nodding to Catherine. She turned away from me, her bare legs revealing her thighs as far as her plump pubis, shrewdly summing up the sexual potential of this young man. I noticed that she was dressed more for a smart lunch with an airline executive than to visit her husband in hospital. Later I learned that she had been badgered at the airport by police officers investigating the road-death. Clearly the accident and any possible manslaughter charges against me had made her something of a celebrity.

'This ward is reserved for air-crash victims,' I told Catherine. 'The beds are kept waiting.'

'If I groundloop on Saturday you might wake up and find me next to you.' Catherine peered at the deserted beds, presumably visualizing each imaginary injury. 'You're getting out of bed tomorrow. They want you to walk.' She looked down at me solicitously. 'Poor man. Have you antagonized them in any way?'

I let this pass, but Catherine added, 'The other man's wife is a doctor – Dr Helen Remington.'

Crossing her legs, she began the business of lighting a cigarette, fumbling with an unfamiliar lighter. From which new lover had she borrowed this ugly machine, all too clearly a man's? Tooled from an aircraft cannon shell, it was more like a weapon. For years I had been able to spot Catherine's affairs within almost a few hours of her first sex act simply by glancing over any new physical or mental furniture – a sudden interest in some third-rate wine or film-maker, a different tack across the waters of aviation politics. Often I could guess the name of her latest lover long before she released it at the climax of our sexual acts. This teasing game she and I needed to play. As we lay together we would describe a complete amatory encounter, from the first chit-chat at an airline cocktail party to the sexual act itself. The climax of these games was the name of the illicit partner. Held back until the last moment, it would always produce the most exquisite orgasms for both of us. There were times when I felt that these affairs took place merely to provide the raw material for our sexual games.

Watching her cigarette smoke move away across the empty ward, I wondered with whom she spent the past few days. No doubt the thought that her husband had killed another man lent an unexpected dimension to their sex acts, presumably conducted on our bed in sight of the chromium telephone which had brought Catherine the first news of my accident. The elements of new technologies linked our affections.

Irritated by the aircraft noise, I sat up on one elbow. The bruises across my chest wall made it painful for me to breathe. Catherine peered down at me with a worried gaze, obviously concerned that I might die on the spot. She put the cigarette between my lips. I drew uncertainly on the geranium-flavoured smoke. The warm tip of the cigarette, stained with pink lipstick, carried with it the unique taste of Catherine's body, a flavour I had forgotten in the phenol-saturated odour of the hospital. Catherine reached for the cigarette, but I held on to it like a child. The grease-smeared tip reminded me of her nipples, liberally painted with lipstick, which I would press against my face, arms and chest, secretly imagining the imprints to be wounds. In a nightmare I had once seen her giving birth to a devil's child, her swollen breasts spurting liquid faeces.

A dark-haired student nurse came into the ward. Smiling at my wife, she pulled back the bedclothes and dug the urine bottle from between my legs. Inspecting its level, she flipped back the sheets. Immediately my penis began to dribble; with an effort I controlled the sphincter, numbed by the long succession of anaesthetics. Lying there with a weak bladder, I wondered why, after this tragic accident involving the death of an unknown young man – his identity, despite the questions I asked Catherine, remained an enigma to me, like an anonymous opponent killed in a pointless duel – all these women around me seemed to attend only to my most infantile zones. The nurses who emptied my urinal and worked my bowels with their enema contraption, who steered my penis through the vent of my pyjama shorts and adjusted the drainage tubes in my knees, who cleansed the pus from the dressings on my scalp and wiped my mouth with their hard hands – these starched women in all their roles reminded me of those who attended my childhood, commissionaires guarding my orifices.

A student nurse moved around my bed, shy thighs under her gingham, eyes fixed on Catherine's glamorous figure. Was she calculating how many lovers Catherine had taken since the accident, excited by the strange posture of her husband in his bed, or – more banal – the cost of her expensive suit and jewellery? By contrast, Catherine gazed frankly at this young girl's body. Her assessment of the contours of thigh and buttock, breast and armpit, and their relationship with the chromium bars of my leg harness, an abstract sculpture designed to show off her slim figure, was open and interested. An interesting lesbian streak ran through Catherine's mind. Often as we made love she asked me to visualize her in intercourse with another woman – usually her secretary Karen, an unsmiling girl with silver lipstick who spent the entire office party before Christmas staring motionlessly at my wife like a pointer in rut. Catherine often asked me how she could allow herself to be seduced by Karen. She soon came up with the suggestion that they visit a department store together, where she would ask Karen's help in choosing various kinds of underwear. I waited for them among the racks of nightdresses outside their cubicle. Now and then I glanced through the curtains and watched them together, their bodies and fingers involved in the soft technology of Catherine's breasts and the brassières designed to show them off to this or that advantage. Karen was touching my wife with peculiar caresses, tapping her lightly with the tips of her fingers, first upon the shoulders along the pink grooves left by her underwear, then across her back, where the metal clasps of her brassière had left a medallion of impressed skin, and finally to the elastic-patterned grooves beneath Catherine's breasts themselves. My wife stood through this in a trance-like state, gabbling to herself in a low voice, as the tip of Karen's right forefinger touched her nipple.

I thought of the bored glance which the assistant, a middle-aged woman with the small face of a corrupt doll, had given me as the two young women had left, flicking back the curtain as if some little sexual playlet had ended. In her expression was the clear assumption that not only did I know what had been going on, and that these booths were often used for these purposes, but that Catherine and I would later exploit the experience for our own complex pleasures. As I sat in the car beside my wife, my fingers moved across the control panel, switching on the ignition, the direction indicator, selecting the drive lever. I realized that I was almost exactly modelling my responses to the car on the way in which Karen had touched Catherine's body. Her sullen eroticism, the elegant distance she placed between her fingertips and my wife's nipples, were recapitulated in the distance between myself and the car.

Catherine's continuing erotic interest in her secretary seemed an interest as much in the idea of making love to her as in the physical pleasures of the sex act itself. Nonetheless, these pursuits had begun to make all our relationships, both between ourselves and with other people, more and more abstract. She soon became unable to reach an orgasm without an elaborate fantasy of a lesbian sex-act with Karen, of her clitoris being tongued, nipples erected, anus caressed. These descriptions seemed to be a language in search of objects, or even, perhaps, the beginnings of a new sexuality divorced from any possible physical expression.

I assumed that she had at least once made love to Karen, but we had now reached the point where it no longer mattered, or had any reference to anything but a few square inches of vaginal mucosa, fingernails and bruised lips and nipples. Lying in my hospital ward, I watched Catherine summing up the student nurse's slim legs and strong buttocks, the deep-blue belt that outlined her waist and broad hips. I half expected Catherine to reach out and put her hand on this young woman's breast, or slip it under her short skirt, the edge of her palm sliding between the natal cleft into the sticky perineum. Far from giving a squeal of outrage, or even pleasure, the nurse would probably continue folding her hospital corner, unmoved by this sexual gesture, no more significant than the most commonplace spoken remark.

Catherine pulled a manila folder from her bag. I recognized the treatment of a television commercial I had prepared. For this high-budget film, a thirty-second commercial advertising

Ford's entire new sports car range, we hoped to use one of a number of well-known actresses. On the afternoon of my accident I had attended a conference with Aida James, a freelance director we had brought in. By chance, one of the actresses, Elizabeth Taylor, was about to start work on a new feature film at Shepperton.

'Aida telephoned to say how sorry she was. Can you look at the treatment again? She's made a number of changes.'

I waved the folder away, gazing at the reflection of myself in Catherine's hand-mirror. The severed nerve in my scalp had fractionally lowered my right eyebrow, a built-in eyepatch that seemed to conceal my new character from myself. This marked tilt was evident in everything around me. I stared at my pale, mannequin-like face, trying to read its lines. The smooth skin almost belonged to someone in a science-fiction film, stepping out of his capsule after an immense inward journey on to the overlit soil of an unfamiliar planet. At any moment the skies might slide . . .

On an impulse I asked, 'Where's the car?'

'Outside – in the consultant's car-park.'

'What?' I sat up on one elbow, trying to see through the window behind my bed. '*My* car, not yours.' I had visualized it mounted as some kind of cautionary exhibit outside the operating theatres.

'It's a complete wreck. The police dragged it to the pound behind the station.'

'Have you seen it?'

'The sergeant asked me to identify it. He didn't believe you'd got out alive.' She crushed her cigarette. 'I'm sorry for the other man – Dr Hamilton's husband.'

I stared pointedly at the clock over the door, hoping that she would soon leave. This bogus commiseration over the dead man irritated me, merely an excuse for an exercise in moral gymnastics. The brusqueness of the young nurses was part of the same pantomime of regret. I had thought for hours about the dead man, visualizing the effects of his death on his wife and family. I had thought of his last moments alive, frantic milliseconds of pain and violence in which he had been catapulted from a pleasant domestic interlude into a concertina of metallized death. These feelings existed within my relationship with the dead man, within the reality of the wounds on my chest and legs, and within the unforgettable collision between my own body and the interior of my car. By comparison, Catherine's mock-grief was a mere stylization of a gesture – I waited for her to break into song, tap her forehead, touch every second temperature chart around the ward, switch on every fourth set of radio headphones.

At the same time, I knew that my feelings towards the dead man and his doctor wife were already overlaid by certain undefined hostilities, half-formed dreams of revenge.

Catherine watched me trying to catch my breath. I took her left hand and pressed it to my sternum. In her sophisticated eyes I was already becoming a kind of emotional cassette, taking my place with all those scenes of pain and violence that illuminated the margins of our lives – television newsreels of wars and student riots, natural disasters and police brutality which we vaguely watched on the colour TV set in our bedroom as we masturbated each other. This violence experienced at so many removes had become intimately associated with our sex acts. The beatings and burnings married in our minds with the delicious tremors of our erectile tissues, the spilt blood of students with the genital fluids that irrigated our fingers and mouths. Even my own pain as I lay in the hospital bed, while Catherine steered the glass urinal between my legs, painted fingernails pricking my penis, even the vagal flushes that seized at my chest seemed extensions of that real world of violence calmed and tamed within our television programmes and the pages of news magazines.

Catherine left me to rest, taking with her half the flowers she had brought. As the elder of the Asian doctors watched her from the doorway she hesitated at the foot of my bed, smiling at me with sudden warmth as if unsure whether she would ever see me again.

A nurse came into the ward with a bowl in one hand. She was a new recruit to the casualty section, a refined-looking woman in her late thirties. After a pleasant greeting, she drew back the bedclothes and began a careful examination of my dressings, her serious eyes following the bruised contours. I caught her attention once, but she stared back at me evenly, and went on with her work, steering her sponge around the central bandage that ran from the waistband between my legs. What was she thinking about – her husband's evening meal, her children's latest minor infection? Was she aware of the automobile components shadowed like contact prints in my skin and musculature? Perhaps she was wondering which model of the car I drove, guessing at the weight of the saloon, estimating the rake of the steering column.

'Which side do you want it?'

I looked down. She was holding my limp penis between thumb and forefinger, waiting for me to decide whether I wanted it to lie to right or left of the central bandage.

As I thought about this strange decision, the brief glimmer of my first erection since the accident stirred through the cavernosa of my penis, reflected in a slight release of tension in her neat fingers.

4

THIS QUICKENING IMPULSE, my loins soon at full cock, lifted me almost literally from the sick-bed. Within three days I hobbled to the physiotherapy department, ran errands for the nurses and hung around the staff room, trying to talk shop to the bored doctors. The sense of a vital sex cut through my unhappy euphoria, my confused guilt over the man I had killed. The week after the accident had been a maze of pain and insane fantasies. After the commonplaces of everyday life, with their muffled dramas, all my organic expertise for dealing with physical injury had long been blunted or forgotten. The crash was the only real experience I had been through for years. For the first time I was in physical confrontation with my own body, an inexhaustible encyclopedia of pains and discharges, with the hostile gaze of other people, and with the fact of the dead man. After being bombarded endlessly by road-safety propaganda it was almost a relief to find myself in an actual accident. Like everyone else bludgeoned by these billboard harangues and television films of imaginary accidents, I had felt a vague sense of unease that the gruesome climax of my life was being rehearsed years in advance, and would take place on some highway or road junction known only to the makers of these films. At times I had even speculated on the kind of traffic accident in which I would die.

I was sent to the X-ray department, where a pleasant young woman who discussed the state of the film industry with me began to photograph my knees. I enjoyed her conversation, the contrast between her idealistic view of the commercial feature-film and the matter-of-fact way in which she operated her own bizarre equipment. Like all laboratory technicians, there was something clinically sexual about her plump body in its white coat. Her strong arms steered me around, arranging my legs as if I were some huge jointed doll, one of those elaborate humanoid dummies fitted with every conceivable orifice and pain response.

I lay back as she concentrated on the eye-piece of her machine. Her left breast rose inside the jacket of her white coat, the chest wall swelling below the collar bone. Somewhere within that complex of nylon and starched cotton lay a large inert nipple, its pink face crushed by the scented fabrics. I watched her mouth, no more than ten inches from mine as she arranged my arms in a new posture. Unaware of my curiosity about her body, she walked to the remote control switch. How could I bring her to life – by ramming one of these massive steel plugs into a socket at the base of her spine? Perhaps she would then leap into life, talk to me in animated tones about the latest Hitchcock retrospective, launch an aggressive discussion about women's rights, cock one hip in a provocative way, bare a nipple.

Instead, we faced each other in this maze of electronic machinery as if completely de-cerebrated. The languages of invisible eroticisms, of undiscovered sexual acts, lay waiting among this complex equipment. The same unseen sexuality hovered over the queues of passengers moving through airport terminals, the junctions of their barely concealed genitalia and the engine nacelles of giant aircraft, the buccal pouts of airline hostesses. Two months before my accident, during a journey to Paris, I had become so excited by the conjunction of an air hostess's fawn gaberdine skirt on the escalator in front of me and the distant fuselages of the aircraft, each inclined like a silver penis towards her natal cleft, that I had involuntarily touched her left buttock. I laid my palm across a small dimple in the slightly worn fabric, as this young woman, completely faceless to me, switched her weight from left thigh to right. After a long pause, she looked down at me with a knowing eye. I waved my briefcase at her and murmured something in pidgin French, at the same time going through an elaborate pantomime of falling down an upcoming escalator, nearly throwing myself off-balance. The flight to Orly took place under the sceptical gaze of two passengers who witnessed this episode, a Dutch businessman and his wife. During the short flight I was in a state of intense excitement, thinking of the strange tactile and geometric landscape of the airport buildings, the ribbons of dulled aluminium and areas of imitation wood laminates. Even my relationship with a young mezzanine bartender had been brought alive by the contoured lighting systems above his balding head, by the tiled bar and his stylized uniform. I thought of my last forced orgasms with Catherine, the sluggish semen urged into her vagina by my bored pelvis. Over the profiles of her body now presided the metallized excitements of our shared dreams of technology. The elegant aluminized air-vents in the walls of the X-ray department beckoned as invitingly as the warmest organic orifice.

'All right, you've finished.' She put a strong arm under my back and lifted me into a sitting position, her body as close to mine as it would have been in a sexual act. I held her arm above the elbow, my wrist pressing against her breast. Behind her was the X-ray camera on its high pivot, heavy cables trailing across the floor. As I shuffled away along the corridor I could still feel the pressure of her strong hands on various parts of my body.

Tired by the crutches, I paused near the entrance to the women's casualty ward, resting against the partition wall of the external corridor. An altercation was going on between the sister in charge and a young coloured nurse. Listening in a bored way, the women patients lay in their beds. Two of them were suspended with their legs in traction, as if involved in the fantasies of a demented gymnast. One of my first errands had been to collect the urine specimens of an elderly woman in this ward, who had been knocked down by a cycling child. Her right leg had been amputated, and she now spent all her time folding a silk scarf around the small stump, tying and retying the ends as if endlessly wrapping a parcel. During the day this senile old dear was the nurses' pride, but at night, when no visitors were present, she was humiliated over the bedpan and callously ignored by the two nuns knitting in the staff room.

The sister cut short her reprimand and turned on her heel. A young woman wearing a dressing-gown and a white-coated doctor stepped through the door of a private ward reserved for 'friends' of the hospital: members of the nursing staff, doctors and their families. I had often seen the man before, always bare-chested under his white coat, moving about on errands not much more exalted than my own. I assumed that he was a graduate student specializing in accident surgery at this airport hospital. His strong hands carried a briefcase filled with photographs. As his pock-marked jaws champed on a piece of gum I had the sudden feeling that he was hawking obscene pictures around the wards, pornographic X-ray plates and blacklisted urinalyses. A brass medallion swung on his bare chest from a black silk chord, but what marked him out was the scar tissue around his forehead and mouth, residues of some terrifying act of violence. I guessed that he was one of those ambitious young physicians who more and more fill the profession, opportunists with a fashionable hoodlum image, openly hostile to their patients. My brief stay at the hospital had already convinced me that the medical profession was an open door to anyone nursing a grudge against the human race.

He looked me up and down, taking in every detail of my injuries with evident interest, but I was more concerned with the young woman moving towards me on her stick. This aid was clearly an affectation, a postural disguise that allowed her to press her face into her raised shoulder and hide the bruise marking her right cheekbone. I had last seen her as she sat in the ambulance beside the body of her husband, staring at me with calm hatred.

'Dr Remington – ?' Without thinking, I asked her name.

She came up to me, changing her grip on the stick as if ready to thrash me across the face with it. She moved her head in a peculiar gesture of the neck, deliberately forcing her injury on me. She paused when she reached the doorway, waiting for me to step out of her way. I looked down at the scar tissue on her face, a seam left by an invisible zip three inches long, running from the corner of her right eye to the apex of her mouth. With the nasolabial fold this new line formed an image like the palm-lines of a sensitive and elusive hand. Reading an imaginary biography into this history of the skin, I visualized her as a glamorous but overworked medical student, breaking out of a long adolescence when she qualified as a doctor into a series of uncertain sexual affairs, happily climaxed by a deep emotional and genital union with her engineer husband, each ransacking the other's body like Crusoe stripping his ship. Already the skin picked in a palisade of notches from her lower lip marked the arithmetic of widowhood, the desperate calculation that she would never find another lover. I was aware of her strong body underneath her mauve bathrobe, her rib-cage partly shielded by a sheath of white plaster that ran from one shoulder to the opposite armpit like a classical Hollywood ball-gown.

Deciding to ignore me, she walked stiffly along the communication corridor, parading her anger and her wound.

During my last days in the hospital I did not see Dr Helen Remington again, but as I lay in the empty ward I thought constantly of the crash that had brought us together. A powerful sense of eroticism had sprung up between me and this bereaved young woman, almost as if I unconsciously wished to re-conceive her dead husband in her womb. By entering her vagina among the metal cabinets and white cables of the X-ray department I would somehow conjure back her husband from the dead, from the conjunction of her left armpit and the chromium camera stand, from the marriage of our genitalia and the elegantly tooled lens shroud.

I listened to the nurses arguing in the staff room. Catherine visited me. She would soap her hand from the toilet bar in its wet saucer inside my cupboard, her pale eyes staring through the flower-filled window as she masturbated me, left hand holding an unfamiliar brand of cigarette. Without any prompting, she began to talk about my crash, and the police inquiries. She described the damage to the car with the persistence of a voyeur, almost nagging me with her lurid picture of the crushed radiator grille and the blood spattered across the bonnet.

'You should have gone to the funeral,' I told her.

'I wish I had,' she replied promptly. 'They bury the dead so quickly – they should leave them lying around for months. I wasn't ready.'

'Remington was ready.'

'I suppose he was.'

'What about his wife?' I asked. 'The woman doctor? Have you visited her yet?'

'No, I couldn't. I feel too close to her.'

Already Catherine saw me in a new light. Did she respect, and perhaps even envy me for having killed someone, in almost the only way in which one can now legally take another person's life? Within the car-crash death was directed by the vectors of speed, violence and aggression. Did Catherine respond to the image of these which had been caught, like a photographic plate or the still from a newsreel, in the dark bruises of my body and the physical outline of the steering wheel? In my left knee the scars above my fractured patella exactly replicated the protruding switches of the windshield wipers and parking lights. As I moved towards my orgasm she began to soap her hand every ten seconds, her cigarette forgotten, concentrating her attention on this orifice of my body like the nurses who attended me in the first hours after my accident. As my semen jerked into Catherine's palm she held tightly to my penis, as if these first orgasms after the crash celebrated a unique event. Her rapt gaze reminded me of the Italian governess employed by a Milanese account executive with whom we had stayed one summer at Sestri Levante. This prim spinster had lavished her life on the sexual organ of the two-year-old boy she tended, for ever kissing his small penis, sucking the glans to engorge it, showing it off with immense pride.

I nodded sympathetically, my hand on her thigh below her skirt. Her pleasantly promiscuous mind, fed for years on a diet of aircraft disasters and war newsreels, of violence transmitted in darkened cinemas, made an immediate connection between my accident and all the nightmare fatalities of the world perceived as part of her sexual recreations. I stroked the warm belly of her thigh through a tear in the crotch of her tights, then slipped my forefinger around the coif of blonde pubic hair that curled like a flame from the apex of her vulva. Her loins seemed to have been furnished by an eccentric haberdasher.

Hoping to soothe away the hyper-excitement which my crash had generated in Catherine – now ever-larger in memory, more cruel and more spectacular – I began to stroke her clitoris. Distracted, she soon left, kissing me firmly on the mouth as if she barely expected to see me alive again. She talked on and on as if she thought that my crash had not yet occurred.

5

'YOU'RE GOING TO drive? But your legs – James, you can barely walk!'

As we sped along the Western Avenue clearway at over seventy miles an hour Catherine's voice sounded a reassuring note of wifely despair. I sat back in the leaping bucket seat of her sports car, watching happily while she fought her blonde hair out of her eyes, slim hands swerving to and from the leopard-skin glove of the miniature steering wheel. Since my accident Catherine's driving had become worse, not better, as if she were confident now that the unseen powers of the universe would guarantee her erratic passage down these high-speed concrete avenues.

I pointed at the last moment to a truck looming in front of us, its refrigerated trailer bounding from side to side on over-inflated tyres. Catherine drove her small foot on to the brake pedal, pulling us around the truck into the slow lane. I put away the rental-car company brochure and gazed through the perimeter fence at the deserted standby runways of the airport. An immense peace seemed to preside over the shabby concrete and untended grass. The glass curtain-walling of the terminal buildings and the multi-storey car-parks behind them belonged to an enchanted domain.

'You're renting a car – how long for?'

'A week. I'll be near the airport. You'll be able to keep an eye on me from your office.'

'I will.'

'Catherine, I've got to get out more.' I drummed at the windshield with both fists. 'I can't sit on the veranda for ever – I'm beginning to feel like a potted plant.'

'I understand.'

'You don't.'

For the past week, after being brought home in a taxi from the hospital, I had been sitting in the same reclining chair on the veranda of our apartment, looking down through the anodized balcony rails at the unfamiliar neighbourhood ten storeys below. On the first afternoon I had barely recognized the endless landscape of concrete and structural steel that extended from the motorways to the south of the airport, across its vast runways to the new apartment systems along Western Avenue. Our own apartment house at Drayton Park stood a mile to the north of the airport in a pleasant island of modern housing units, landscaped filling stations and supermarkets, shielded from the distant bulk of London by an access spur of the northern circular motorway which flowed past us on its elegant concrete pillars. I gazed down at this immense motion sculpture, whose traffic deck seemed almost higher than the balcony rail against which I leaned. I began to orientate myself again round its reassuring bulk, its familiar perspectives of speed, purpose and direction. The houses of our friends, the wine store where I bought our liquor, the small art-cinema where Catherine and I saw American avant-garde films and German sex-instruction movies, together realigned themselves around the palisades of the motorway. I realized that the human inhabitants of this technological landscape no longer provided its sharpest pointers, its keys to the borderzones of identity. The amiable saunter of Frances Waring, bored wife of my partner, through the turnstiles of the local supermarket, the domestic wrangles of our well-to-do neighbours in our apartment house, all the hopes and fancies of this placid suburban enclave, drenched in a thousand infidelities, faltered before the solid reality of the motorway embankments, with their constant and unswerving geometry, and before the finite areas of the car-park aprons.

As I drove home with Catherine from the hospital I was surprised by how much, in my eyes, the image of the car had changed, almost as if its true nature had been exposed by my accident. Leaning against the rear window of the taxi,

I found myself flinching with excitement towards the traffic streams on the Western Avenue interchanges. The flashing lances of afternoon light deflected from the chromium panel trim tore at my skin. The hard jazz of radiator grilles, the motion of cars moving towards London Airport along the sunlit oncoming lanes, the street furniture and route indicators – all these seemed threatening and super-real, as exciting as the accelerating pintables of a sinister amusement arcade released on to these highways.

Aware that I was over-exhilarated, Catherine helped me quickly into the elevator. The visual perspectives of our apartment had been transformed. Pushing her away, I stepped out on to the veranda. Cars filled the suburban streets below, choking the parking lots of the supermarkets, ramped on to the pavements. Two minor accidents had taken place on Western Avenue, causing a massive tail-back along the flyover which crossed the entrance tunnel to the airport. Sitting nervously on the veranda as Catherine watched me from the sitting-room, one hand on the telephone behind her back, I looked out for the first time at this immense corona of polished cellulose that extended from the southern horizon to the northern motorways. I felt an undefined sense of extreme danger, almost as if an accident was about to take place involving all these cars. The passengers in the airliners lifting away from the airport were fleeing the disaster area, escaping from this coming autogeddon.

These premonitions of disaster remained with me. During my first days at home I spent all my time on the veranda, watching the traffic move along the motorway, determined to spot the first signs of this end of the world by automobile, for which the accident had been my own private rehearsal.

I called Catherine to the veranda and pointed to a minor collision on the southern access road of the motorway. A white laundry van had bumped into the back of a saloon car filled with wedding guests.

'They *are* rather like rehearsals. When we've all rehearsed our separate parts the real thing will begin.' An airliner was coming in over central London, wheels lowered above the noise-driven rooftops. 'Another cargo of eager victims – one almost expects to see Breughel and Hieronymus Bosch cruising the freeways in their rental-company cars.'

Catherine knelt beside me, her elbow on the chromium arm of my chair. I had seen the same flashing light on the instrument binnacle of my car as I sat behind the broken steering wheel waiting for the police to cut me free. She explored with some interest the changed contours of the knee-cap. Catherine had a natural and healthy curiosity for the perverse in all its forms.

'James, I've got to leave for the office – are you going to be all right?' She knew full well that I was capable of any deceit where she was involved.

'Of course. Is the traffic heavier now? There seem to be three times as many cars as there were before the accident.'

'I've never really noticed. You won't try to borrow the janitor's car?'

Her care was touching. Since the accident she seemed completely at ease with me for the first time in many years. My crash was a wayward experience of a type her own life and sexuality had taught her to understand. My body, which she had placed in a particular sexual perspective within a year or so of our marriage, now aroused her again. She was fascinated by the scars on my chest, touching them with her spittle-wet lips. These happy changes I felt myself. At one time Catherine's body lying beside me in bed had seemed as inert and emotionless as a sexual exercise doll fitted with a neoprene vagina. Humiliating herself for her own perverse reasons, she would leave late for her office and hang about the apartment, exposing parts of her body to me, well aware that the last service I wanted from her was that blonde orifice between her legs.

I took her arm. 'I'll come down with you – don't look so defensive.'

From the forecourt I watched her leave for the airport in her sports car, her white crotch flashing a gay semaphore between her sliding thighs. The varying geometry of her pubis was the delight of bored drivers watching the rotating dials of filling station pumps.

When she had gone I left the apartment and wandered down to the basement. A dozen cars, mostly owned by the wives of the lawyers and film executives who lived in the apartment house, stood in the garage. The bay reserved for my own car was still empty, the familiar pattern of oil-stains marking the cement. I peered through the dull light at the expensive instrument panels. A silk scarf lay on a rear window sill. I remembered Catherine describing our own personal possessions scattered on the floor and seats of my car after the crash – a holiday route map, an empty bottle of nail varnish, a trade magazine. The isolation of these pieces of our lives, as if intact memories and intimacies had been taken out of doors and arranged by a demolition squad, was part of the same remaking of the commonplace which in a tragic way I had brought about in the death of Remington. The grey herringbone of his coat sleeve, the whiteness of his shirt collar, were held for ever within that accident.

Horns sounded from the trapped vehicles on the motorway, a despairing chorus. Staring at the oil stains in my parking bay, I thought about the dead man. The entire accident seemed to be preserved by these indelible markers, the police, spectators and ambulance attendants frozen in their postures as I sat in my crashed car.

A transistor radio played behind me. The janitor, a young man with almost waist-length hair, had returned to his office beside the basement elevator entrance. He sat on his metal desk, an arm around his child-like girlfriend. Ignoring their respectful stares, I walked back to the forecourt. The tree-lined avenue which led to the neighbourhood shopping centre was deserted, cars parked nose to tail under the plane trees. Glad to be able to walk without being knocked off my feet by some aggressive housewife, I strolled along the avenue, now and then resting against a polished fender. It was a minute before two o'clock, and the shopping centre was empty. Cars filled the main thoroughfare, double-parked in the side-streets while their drivers rested indoors out of the hot sunlight. I crossed the tiled piazza in the middle of the shopping mall, and climbed the staircase to the car-park on the roof of the supermarket. Each of the hundred parking spaces was filled, the lines of windshields reflecting the sunlight like a glass testudo.

As I leaned against the concrete balcony I became aware that an immense silence hung over the landscape around me. By a rare freak of flight control no aircraft were landing or taking off from the airport runways. The traffic along the motorway was stationary in a southward queue. Along Western Avenue the stalled cars and airline coaches sat in their lanes, waiting for the lights to change. A tailback carried three lines of vehicles up the ramp of the flyover, and beyond this on to the new southward extension of the motorway.

During my weeks in hospital the highway engineers had pushed its huge decks more than half a mile further south. Looking closely at this silent terrain, I realized that the entire zone which defined the landscape of my life was now bounded by a continuous artificial horizon, formed by the raised parapets and embankments of the motorways and their access roads and interchanges. These encircled the vehicles below like the walls of a crater several miles in diameter.

The silence continued. Here and there a driver shifted behind his steering wheel, trapped uncomfortably in the hot sunlight, and I had the sudden impression that the world had stopped. The wounds on my knees and chest were beacons tuned to a series of beckoning transmitters, carrying the signals, unknown to myself, which would unlock this immense stasis and free these drivers for the real destinations set for their vehicles, the paradises of the electric highway.

The memory of this extraordinary silence remained vivid in my mind as Catherine drove me to my office at Shepperton. Along Western Avenue the traffic sped and swerved from one jam to the next. Overhead, the engines of the airliners taking off from London Airport wearied the sky. My glimpse of an unmoving world, of the thousands of drivers sitting passively in their cars on the motorway embankments along the horizon, seemed to be a unique vision of this machine landscape, an invitation to explore the viaducts of our minds.

My first need was to end my convalescence and rent a car. When we reached the television-commercial studios Catherine drove aimlessly around the car-park, reluctant to let me out. Waiting by his car, the young rental-company driver watched us circle him.

'Is Renata going with you?' Catherine asked.

The shrewdness of this off-hand guess surprised me.

'I thought she might come along – handling a car again may be more tiring than I imagine.'

'I'm amazed that she'll let you drive her.'

'You're not envious?'

'Maybe I am a little.'

Sidestepping any local alliance that might be formed between the two women, I said goodbye to Catherine. I spent the next hour in the production offices, discussing with Paul Waring the contractual difficulties blocking the car commercial, in which we hoped to use the film actress Elizabeth Taylor. All this time, however, my real attention was fixed on the rental-company vehicle waiting for me in the car-park. Everything else – Waring's irritation with me, the cramped perspectives of the offices, the noisiness of the staff – formed a vague penumbra, unsatisfactory footage that would later be edited out.

I was barely aware of Renata when she joined me in the car.

'Are you all right? Where are we going?'

I stared at the steering wheel between my hands, at the padded instrument panel with its dials and control tabs.

'Where else?'

The aggressive stylization of this mass-produced cockpit, the exaggerated mouldings of the instrument binnacles emphasized my growing sense of a new junction between my own body and the automobile, closer than my feelings for Renata's broad hips and strong legs stowed out of sight beneath her red plastic raincoat. I leaned forward, feeling the rim of the steering wheel against the scars on my chest, pressing my knees against the ignition switch and handbrake.

We reached the foot of the flyover half an hour later. The afternoon traffic passed along Western Avenue and divided at the motorway interchange. I drove past the site of my accident to the roundabout half a mile to the north, circled and moved back along the path I had taken in the minutes before the crash. By chance the road ahead was empty. Four hundred yards ahead a truck climbed the overpass. A black saloon appeared on the shoulder of the slip road, but I accelerated past it. Within a few seconds we reached the impact point. I slowed and stopped the car on the concrete verge.

'Are we allowed to park here?'

'No.'

'All right – the police will make an exception in your case.'

I unbuttoned Renata's raincoat and placed my hand on her thigh. She let me kiss her throat, holding my shoulder reassuringly like an affectionate governess.

'I saw you just before the accident,' I told her. 'Do you remember? We made love.'

'Are you still involving me in your crash?'

I moved my hand along her thigh. Her vulva was a wet flower. An airline coach passed, the passengers bound for Stuttgart or Milan peering down at us. Renata buttoned her coat and took a copy of *Paris-Match* from the dashboard shelf. She turned the pages, glancing at the photographs of famine victims in the Philippines. This immersion in parallel themes of violence was a protective decoy. Her serious student's eyes barely paused at the photograph of a swollen corpse that filled a complete page. This coda of death and mutilation passed below her precise fingers as I stared at the road junction where, fifty yards from the car in which I now sat, I had killed another man. The anonymity of this road junction reminded me of Renata's body, with its polite repertory of vents and cleavages, which one day would become as strange and meaningful to some suburban husband as these kerb-stones and marker lines were to myself.

A white convertible approached, the driver flashing his headlamps as I stepped from my car. I stumbled, my right knee giving way after the effort of driving. At my feet lay a litter of dead leaves, cigarette cartons and glass crystals. These fragments of broken safety glass, brushed to one side by generations of ambulance attendants, lay in a small drift. I stared down at this dusty necklace, the debris of a thousand automobile accidents. Within fifty years, as more and more cars collided here, the glass fragments would form a sizable bar, within thirty years a beach of sharp crystal. A new race of beachcombers might appear, squatting on these heaps of fractured windshields, sifting them for cigarette butts, spent condoms and loose coins. Buried beneath this new geological layer laid down by the age of the automobile accident would be my own small death, as anonymous as a vitrified scar in a fossil tree.

A hundred yards behind us a dusty American car was parked on the verge. The driver watched me through his mud-spattered windshield, broad shoulders hunched against the door pillar. As I crossed the road he picked up a camera fitted with a zoom lens and peered at me through the eyepiece.

Renata looked back at him over her shoulder, surprised like myself by his aggressive pose. She opened my door for me.

'Can you drive? Who is he – a private detective?'

As we set off along Western Avenue the man's tall, leather-jacketed figure walked down the road to where we had parked. Curious to see his face, I made a circuit of the roundabout.

We passed within ten feet of him. He was sauntering in a loose, erratic walk among the tyre-marks on the road surface, as if miming some invisible trajectory within his mind. The sunlight picked at the scars on his forehead and mouth. As he looked up at me I recognized the young doctor I had last seen leaving Helen Remington's room at the Ashford casualty hospital.

6

DURING THE FOLLOWING days I hired a series of cars from the studio rental company, choosing every available variant of the automobile, from a heavy American convertible to a high-performance sports saloon and an Italian micro-car. What began as an ironic gesture intended to provoke Catherine and Renata – both women wanted me never to drive again – soon took on a different role. My first brief journey to the accident site had raised again the spectre of the dead man and, more important, the notion of my own death. In each of these cars I drove along the accident route, visualizing the possibility of a different death and victim, a different profile of wounds.

Despite the efforts made to clean these cars, the residues of the previous drivers clung to their interiors – the heelmarks on the rubber mats below the driving pedals; a dry cigarette stub, stained with an unfashionable lipstick shade, trapped by a piece of chewing gum in the roof of the ashtray; a complex of strange scratches, like the choreography of a frantic struggle, that covered a vinyl seat, as if two cripples had committed rape on each other. As I eased my feet on to the control pedals I was aware of all these drivers, of the volumes their bodies had occupied, their assignations, escapes, boredoms that preempted any response of my own. Aware of these overlays, I had to force myself to drive carefully, as I offered the possibilities of my own body to the projecting steering columns and windshield vizors.

At first I aimlessly followed the perimeter roads to the south of the airport, feeling out the unfamiliar controls among the water reservoirs of Stanwell. From here I moved around the eastern flank of the airport to the motorway interchanges at Harlington, where the rush-hour traffic leaving London swept me back in a huge tidal race of metal along the crowded lanes of Western Avenue. Invariably, at the hour of my accident, I found myself at the foot of the flyover, either wrenched past the collision site as the traffic jerked away towards the next traffic lights, or stalled in a massive jam ten insane feet from the precise impact point.

When I collected the American convertible, the rental company salesman remarked, 'We had a job cleaning it up, Mr Ballard. One of your TV companies was using it – camera clamps on the roof, all over the doors and bonnet.'

The notion that the car was still being used as part of an imaginary event occurred to me as I drove away from the garage in Shepperton. Like the other cars I had hired, this one was covered with scratches and heel-marks, cigarette burns and scuffings, translated through the glamorous dimension of Detroit design. On the pink vinyl seat was a deep tear large enough to take a flagstaff or, conceivably, a penis. Presumably these marks had been made within the context of imaginary dramas devised by the various companies using the car, by actors playing the roles of detectives and petty criminals, secret agents and absconding heiresses. The worn steering wheel carried in its cleats the grease of hundreds of hands held there in the positions dictated by the film director and the cameraman.

As I moved in the evening traffic along Western Avenue, I thought of being killed within this huge accumulation of fictions, finding my body marked with the imprint of a hundred television crime serials, the signatures of forgotten dramas which, years after being shelved in a network shake-up, would leave their last credit-lines in my skin.

Confused by these beckoning needs, I found myself in the wrong traffic lane at the junction with the motorway interchange. The heavy car, with its powerful engine and over-sensitive brakes, reminded me that I was being too ambitious in thinking that I could fit my own wounds and experience into its mastodonic contours. Deciding to hire a car of the same model as my own, I turned into the airport access road.

A massive traffic jam blocked the tunnel entrance, and I pulled across the oncoming lanes and drove into the airport plaza, a wide area of transit hotels and all-night supermarkets. As I drove out of the filling station nearest the tunnel slip-road I recognized the trio of airport whores strolling up and down a small traffic island.

Seeing my car, and presumably thinking that I was an American or German tourist, the eldest of the three women came across to me. They paced about on this traffic island in the evening, gazing at the speeding cars as if trying to pick up travellers waiting to cross the Styx. The three of them – a talkative brunette from Liverpool who had been everywhere and done everything under the sun; a timid and unintelligent blonde, whom Catherine clearly fancied from the way she often pointed her out to me; and an older, tired-faced woman with heavy breasts who had once worked as a filling-station attendant at a Western Avenue garage – seemed to form a basic sexual unit, able in one way or another to satisfy all comers.

I stopped by the traffic island. The older woman came forward as I nodded to her. She leaned against the off-side door, her strong right arm pressing against the chromium window pillar. As she stepped into the car she signalled with her hands to her two companions, whose eyes were flicking like windshield wipers across the light-impacted glass of the passing cars.

I followed the traffic stream through the airport tunnel. The woman's hard body beside me in the rented American car, unknown star of so many second-rate television serials, made me suddenly aware of my aching knees and thighs. Despite its servo-brakes and power steering, the American car was exhausting to drive.

'Where are we going?' she asked as I left the tunnel and headed towards the terminal buildings.

'The multi-storey car-parks – the top decks are empty in the evening.'

A loose hierarchy of prostitutes occupied the airport and

its suburbs – within the hotels, in discotheques where music was never played, conveniently sited near the bedrooms for the thousands of transit passengers who never left the airport; a second echelon working the terminal building concourses and restaurant mezzanines; and beyond these an army of freelances renting rooms on a daily basis in the apartment complexes along the motorway.

We reached the multi-storey car-park behind the air-freight building. I drove around the canted concrete floors of this oblique and ambiguous building and parked in an empty bay among the cars on the sloping roof. After tucking the banknotes away in her silver handbag, the woman lowered her preoccupied face across my lap, expertly releasing my zip with one hand. She began to work systematically at my penis with both mouth and hand, spreading her arms comfortably across my knees. I flinched from the pressure of her hard elbows.

'What's the matter with your legs – have you been in an accident?'

She made it sound like a sexual offence.

As she brought my penis to life I looked down at her strong back, at the junction between the contours of her shoulders demarked by the straps of her brassière and the elaborately decorated instrument panel of this American car, between her thick buttock in my left hand and the pastel-shaded binnacles of the clock and speedometer. Encouraged by these hooded dials, my left ring-finger moved towards her anus.

Horns sounded from the concourse below. A flashbulb flared over my shoulder, illuminating the startled face of this tired prostitute with her mouth around my penis, faded hair spilling through the chromium spokes of the steering wheel. Pushing her aside, I peered over the balcony. An airline coach had rammed the rear of a taxi parked outside the European Terminal. Two taxi-drivers and a man still carrying his plastic briefcase were lifting the injured driver from his cab. A huge traffic jam of buses and taxis blocked the concourse. Flashing its headlamps, a police car climbed on to the sidewalk and moved through the passengers and porters, knocking over a suitcase with its fender.

Distracted by a flicker of movement in the chromium windshield pillar, I looked to my right. Twenty feet away across the empty parking bays a man with a camera sat on the bonnet of a car parked against the concrete balcony. I recognized the tall man with the scarred forehead who had watched me near the accident site below the flyover, the doctor in the white coat at the hospital. He released the opaque bulb from the flashlight and kicked it away under the cars. As he pulled the film from the back of his polaroid camera he eyed me without any particular interest, as if well-used to seeing prostitutes and their customers on the roof of this multi-storey car-park.

'You can finish. That's all right.' The woman was now searching my groin again for an errant penis. I beckoned to her to sit up. When she had straightened her hair in the rear-view mirror she left the car without glancing at me and walked to the elevator shaft.

The tall man with the camera sauntered across the roof. I looked through the rear window of his car. The passenger seat was loaded with photographic equipment – cameras, a tripod, a carton packed with flashbulbs. A cine-camera was fastened to a dashboard clamp.

He walked back to his car, camera held like a weapon by its pistol grip. As he reached the balcony his face was lit by the headlamps of the police car. I realized that I had seen his pock-marked face many times before, projected from a dozen forgotten television programmes and news-magazine profiles – this was Vaughan, Dr Robert Vaughan, a one-time computer specialist. As one of the first of the new-style TV scientists, Vaughan had combined a high degree of personal glamour – heavy black hair over a scarred face, an American combat jacket – with an aggressive lecture-theatre manner and complete conviction in his subject matter, the application of computerized techniques to the control of all international traffic systems. In the first programmes of his series three years earlier Vaughan had projected a potent image, almost that of the scientist as hoodlum, driving about from laboratory to television centre on a high-powered motorcycle. Literate, ambitious and adept at self-publicity, he was saved from being no more than a pushy careerist with a Ph.D. by a strain of naive idealism, his strange vision of the automobile and its real role in our lives.

He stood by the balcony, looking down at the collision below. The headlamps illuminated the hard ridges of scar tissue above his eyebrows and mouth, the broken and re-set nose bridge. I remembered why Vaughan's career had come to an abrupt end – halfway through his television series he had been seriously injured in a motorcycle crash. All too clearly his face and personality still carried the memory of that impact, some terrifying collision on a motorway in the North when his legs had been broken by the rear wheels of a truck. His features looked as if they had been displaced laterally, reassembled after the crash from a collection of faded publicity photographs. The scars on his mouth and forehead, the self-cut hair and two missing upper canine gave him a neglected and hostile appearance. The bony knuckles of his wrists projected like manacles from the frayed cuffs of his leather jacket.

He stepped into his car. This was a ten-year-old model of a Lincoln Continental, the same make of vehicle as the open limousine in which President Kennedy had died. I remembered that one of Vaughan's obsessions had been Kennedy's assassination.

He reversed past me, the left fender of the Lincoln brushing against my knee. I crossed the roof as he swept away down the ramp. This first meeting with Vaughan remained vividly in my mind. I knew that his motives for following me had nothing to do with revenge or blackmail.

7

AFTER OUR MEETING on the roof of the airport car-park I was continually aware of Vaughan's presence. He no longer followed me, but seemed to hover like an invigilator in the margins of my life, for ever monitoring my head. Along the high-speed lanes of Western Avenue I watched the rear-view mirror, and scanned the parapets of overpasses and multi-storey car-parks.

In a sense I had already enlisted Vaughan in my confused hunt. I sat in the crowded traffic lanes of the flyover, the aluminium walls of the airline coaches shutting off the sky. As I watched the packed concrete decks of the motorway from our veranda while Catherine prepared our first evening drinks, I was convinced that the key to this immense metallized landscape lay somewhere within these constant and unchanging traffic patterns.

Luckily, my messianic obsessions soon made themselves evident to Paul Waring, my partner. He arranged with Catherine to restrict my visits to the studio offices to an hour a day. Easily tired and excited, I had an absurd row with Waring's secretary. But all this seemed trivial and unreal. Far more important was the delivery of my new car from the local distributors.

Catherine regarded with profound suspicion my choice of the same make and model as the car in which I had crashed. I had even selected the same make of wing mirror and mudguard spat. She and her secretary watched me critically from the forecourt of the airfreight offices. Karen stood behind Catherine, a cocked elbow almost touching her shoulder blade, like a young and ambitious madame keeping a protective eye on her latest discovery.

'Why did you ask us here?' Catherine said. 'I don't think either of us ever wants to look at a car again.'

'Certainly not this one, Mrs Ballard.'

'Is Vaughan following you?' I asked Catherine. 'You spoke to him at the hospital.'

'He said he was a police photographer. What does he want?'

Karen's eyes gazed at my scarred scalp. 'It's hard to believe he was ever on television.'

I outstared Karen with an effort. She watched me like a predatory animal behind the silver bars of her mouth.

'Did anyone see him at the accident?'

'I've no idea. Are you planning to have another crash for him?' Catherine sauntered around the car. She settled herself in the front passenger seat, savouring the sharp tang of salesroom vinyl.

'I'm not thinking about the crash at all.'

'You're getting involved with this man, Vaughan – you're talking about him all the time.' Catherine stared through the immaculate windshield, her thighs held open in a formalized posture.

I was thinking, in fact, about the contrast between this generous pose and the glass curtain-walling of the airport buildings, the showroom glitter of the new car. Sitting here in the exact replica of the vehicle in which I had nearly killed myself, I visualized the crushed fenders and radiator grille, the precise deformation of the hood trim, the angular displacement of the windshield pillars. The triangle of Catherine's pubis reminded me that the first sexual act within the car had yet to take place.

At the Northolt police pound I showed my pass to the guard, custodian of this museum of wrecks. I hesitated there, like a husband collecting his wife from the depot of a strange and perverse dream. Some twenty or so crashed vehicles were parked in the sunlight against the rear wall of an abandoned cinema. At the far end of the asphalt yard was a truck whose entire driving cabin had been crushed, as if the dimensions of space had abruptly contracted around the body of the driver.

Unnerved by these deformations, I moved from one car to the next. The first vehicle, a blue taxi, had been struck at the point of its near-side headlamp – on one side the bodywork was intact, on the other the front wheel had been forced back into the passenger compartment. Next to it was a white saloon which had been run over by an enormous vehicle. The marks of giant tyres ran across its crushed roof, forcing it down to the transmission hump between the seats.

I recognized my own car. The remains of towing tackle were attached to the front bumper, and the body panels were splashed with oil and dirt. I peered through the windows into the cabin, running my hand over the mud-stained glass. Without thinking, I knelt in front of the car and stared at the crushed fenders and radiator grille.

For several minutes I gazed at this wrecked car, reassembling its identity. Terrifying events rolled through my mind on its flattened wheels. What most surprised me was the extent of the damage. During the accident the hood had climbed over the engine compartment, hiding from me the real extent of the collision. Both front wheels and the engine had been driven back into the driver's section, bowing the floor. Blood still marked the bonnet, streamers of black lace running towards the windshield wiper gutters. Minute flecks were spattered across the seat and steering wheel. I thought of the dead man lying on the hood of the car. The blood rilling across the bruised cellulose was a more potent fluid than the semen cooling in his testicles.

Two policemen crossed the yard with a black Alsatian dog. They watched me hovering around my car as if they vaguely resented my touching it. When they had gone I unlatched the driver's door, and with an effort pulled it open.

I eased myself on to the dusty vinyl seat, tipped back by the bowing of the floor. The steering column had reared forward six inches towards my chest. I lifted my nervous legs into the car and placed my feet on the rubber cleats of the pedals, which had been forced out of the engine compartment so that my knees were pressed against my chest. In front of me the instrument panel had been buckled inwards, cracking the clock and speedometer dials. Sitting here in this deformed cabin, filled with dust and damp carpeting, I tried to visualize myself at the moment of collision, the failure of the technical relationship between my own body, the assumptions of the skin, and the engineering structure which supported it. I remembered visiting the Imperial War Museum with a close friend, and the pathos that surrounded the cockpit segment of a World War II Japanese Zero fighter aircraft. The clutter of electrical wiring and torn canvas webbing on the floor expressed all the isolation of war. The blurring perspex of the cockpit canopy contained a small segment of the Pacific sky, the roar of aircraft warming up on a carrier deck thirty years before.

I watched the two policemen exercising their dog across the yard. I opened the dashboard locker and forced the shelf downwards. Inside, covered with dirt and flaked plastic, were several items Catherine had been unable to reclaim: a set of route maps, a mild pornographic novel which Renata had lent me as a brave joke, a polaroid photograph I had taken of her sitting in the car near the water reservoirs with her left breast exposed.

I pulled back the ashtray. The metal tray jumped on to my lap, releasing a dozen lipstick-smeared butts. Each of these cigarettes, smoked by Renata as we drove from the office to her flat, reminded me of one of the sexual acts that had taken place between us. Looking down at this small museum of excitement and possibility, I realized that the crushed cabin of my car, like some bizarre vehicle modified for an extreme cripple, was the perfect module for all the quickening futures of my life.

Someone passed in front of the car. A policeman's voice called from the gatehouse. Through the windshield I saw a woman in a white raincoat walking along the line of wrecked cars. The appearance in this drab yard of an attractive woman, moving from one car to the next like an intelligent gallery visitor, roused me from this reverie upon twelve cigarette ends. The woman approached the car next to mine, a crushed convertible involved in a massive rear-end collision. Her intelligent face, that of an overworked doctor, broad forehead disguised by a lowered hairline, gazed down at the vanished passenger compartment.

Without thinking, I started to climb from my car, then sat quietly behind the steering wheel. Helen Remington turned from the crashed convertible. She glanced at the bonnet of my car, clearly not recognizing the vehicle which had killed her husband. As she raised her head she saw me through the empty windshield, sitting behind the deformed steering wheel among the dried bloodstains of her husband. Her strong eyes barely changed their focus, but one hand rose involuntarily to her cheek. She took in the damage to my car, her attention moving from the impacted radiator grille to the high-rising steering wheel in my hands. Then she began a brief scrutiny of myself, inspecting me with a tolerant eye like a doctor faced with a difficult patient suffering from a set of largely self-indulgent symptoms.

She moved away towards the damaged truck. What struck me again was her unusual leg-stance, the inner surface of her thighs, set in a broad pelvis, turned outwards as if exposed to the line of crashed vehicles. Had she been waiting for me to visit the police pound? I knew that some kind of confrontation between us was inevitable, but in my mind this was already overlaid by other feelings – pity, eroticism, even a strange jealousy of the dead man, whom she but not I had known.

She came back as I waited on the oil-stained asphalt in front of my car.

She pointed to the damaged vehicles. 'After this sort of thing, how do people manage to look at a car, let alone drive one?' When I made no reply she said flatly, 'I'm trying to find Charles's car.'

'It's not here. Perhaps the police are still holding it. Their forensic people . . .'

'They said it was here. They told me this morning.' She peered critically at my car, as if puzzled by its distorted geometry, and then finding this confirmed in my own bent of character. 'This is your car?'

She reached out a gloved hand and touched the radiator grille, feeling a torn chrome pillar from the accordion, as if searching for some trace of her husband's presence among the blood-spattered paintwork. I had never spoken to this tired woman, and felt that I should launch into a formal apology for her husband's death and the appalling act of violence which had involved us. At the same time, her gloved hand on the scarred chrome aroused a feeling of sharp sexual excitement.

'You'll tear your gloves.' I moved her hand away from the grille. 'I don't think we should have come here – I'm surprised the police don't make it more difficult.'

Her strong wrist pressed back against my fingers, out of a kind of wayward irritation, as if she were rehearsing her physical revenge against me. Her eyes lingered on the black confetti scattered across the bonnet and seats.

'Were you badly hurt?' she asked. 'I think we saw each other at the hospital.'

I found it impossible to say anything to her, aware of the almost obsessive way in which she brushed her hair across her cheek. Her strong body, with its nervous sexuality, formed a powerful junction with the dented and mud-stained car.

'I don't want the car,' she said. 'In fact, I was appalled to find that I have to pay a small fee to have it scrapped.'

She hung around the car, watching me with a mixture of hostility and interest, as if admitting that her motives for coming to the pound were as ambiguous as my own. I sensed that in her refined and matter-of-fact way she was already trying out the possibilities I had opened for her, examining this instrument of a perverse technology which had killed her husband and closed the principal avenue of her life.

I offered her a lift to her surgery.

'Thanks.' She walked ahead of me. 'To the airport, if you could.'

'The airport?' I had an odd feeling of loss. 'Why – are you leaving?'

'Not yet – though not soon enough for some people, I've already found.' She took off her sunglasses and gave me a bleak smile. 'A death in the doctor's family makes the patients doubly uneasy.'

'I take it you're not wearing white to reassure them?'

'I'll wear a bloody kimono if I want to.'

We took our seats in my car. She told me that she worked in the immigration department at London Airport. Holding herself well away from me, she leaned back against the door pillar, surveying the interior of the car with a critical eye, this apparent resurrection of smooth vinyl and polished glass. She followed my hands as they moved across the controls. The pressure of her thighs against the hot plastic formed a module of intense excitement. Already I guessed that she was well aware of this. By a terrifying paradox, a sexual act between us would be a way of taking her revenge on me.

Heavy traffic jammed the northbound motorway from Ashford to London Airport. The sunlight burned on the overheated cellulose. Tired drivers leaned through open windows around us, listening to the endless newscasts on their radios. Sealed inside their airline coaches, would-be passengers watched the jetliners lifting from the distant runways of the airport. To the north of the terminal buildings I could see the high deck of the flyover straddling the airport entrance tunnel, clogged with traffic that seemed about to re-enact a slow-motion dramatization of our crash.

Helen Remington pulled a cigarette packet from the pocket of her raincoat. She searched the instrument panel for the lighter, right hand moving above my knees like a nervous bird.

'Do you want a cigarette?' Her strong fingers tore away the cellophane. 'I started to smoke at Ashford – it's rather stupid of me.'

'Look at all this traffic – I need every sedative I can lay my hands on.'

'It's much worse now – you noticed that, did you? The day I left Ashford I had the extraordinary feeling that all these cars were gathering for some special reason I didn't understand. There seemed to be ten times as much traffic.'

'Are we imagining it?'

She pointed to the interior of the car with her cigarette. 'You've bought yourself exactly the same car again. It's the same shape and colour.'

She turned her face towards me, making no effort now to hide the scar-line on her face. I was well aware of the strong undertow of hostility moving towards me. The traffic stream reached the Stanwell intersection. I followed the queue of cars, already thinking of how she would behave during sexual intercourse. I tried to visualize her broad mouth around her husband's penis, sharp fingers between his buttocks searching out his prostate. She touched the yellow hull of a fuel tanker beside us, its massive rear wheels only six inches from her elbow. As she read the fire instructions on the tank I stared at her firm calves and thighs. Had she any notion of the man, or woman, with whom her next sex act would take place? I felt my penis stirring as the lights changed. I moved from the fast into the slow lane, taking up my position in front of the fuel tanker.

The arch of the flyover rose against the skyline, its northern ramp shielded by the white rectangle of a plastics factory. The untouched, rectilinear volumes of this building fused in my mind with the contours of her calves and thighs pressed against the vinyl seating. Clearly unaware that we were moving towards our original meeting ground, Helen Remington crossed and uncrossed her legs, shifting these white volumes as the front elevations of the plastics factory moved past.

The pavement fell away below us. We sped towards the junction with the Drayton Park motorway spur. She steadied herself against the chromium pillar of the quarter-window, almost dropping her cigarette on to her lap. Trying to control the car, I pressed the head of my penis against the lower rim of the steering wheel. The car swept towards its first impact point with the central reservation. Marker lines unravelled diagonally below us, and a car's horn blared faintly from behind my shoulder. The drifts of broken windshield glass flashed like morse lamps in the sunlight.

Semen jolted through my penis. As I lost control of the

car the front wheel struck the kerb of the central reservation, throwing a tornado of dust and cigarette packs on to the windshield. The car swerved from the fast lane and veered towards an airline coach coming out of the roundabout. As the semen oozed from my penis I pulled the car behind the coach. The last tremor of this small orgasm faded.

I felt Helen Remington's hand on my arm. She had moved into the centre of the seat, strong shoulder pressed against mine, her hand on the wheel over my own. She watched the cars that swerved past on both sides of us, horns sounding.

'Turn off here – you can drive quietly for a while.'

I wheeled the car on to the slip road that led into the deserted concrete boulevards of a bungalow estate. For an hour we drove through the empty streets. Children's bicycles and painted carts stood by the gates of the bungalows. Helen Remington held my shoulder, her eyes hidden behind her glasses. She talked to me of her work in the immigration department of the airport, and of her difficulties over the probate of her husband's will. Was she aware of what had taken place within my car, of the route I had rehearsed so many times in so many different vehicles, and that I had celebrated in her husband's death the unity of our injuries and my orgasm?

8

THE TRAFFIC MULTIPLIED, concrete lanes moving laterally across the landscape. As Catherine and I drove from the coroner's inquest the flyovers overlaid one another like copulating giants, immense legs straddling each other's backs. A verdict of accidental death had been returned, without any show of interest or ceremony; no charges of manslaughter or negligent driving were brought against me by the police. After the inquest I let Catherine drive me to the airport. For half an hour I sat by the window in her office, looking down at the hundreds of cars in the parking lot. Their roofs formed a lake of metal. Catherine's secretary stood behind her shoulder, waiting for me to leave. As she handed Catherine's glasses to her I saw that she was wearing a white lipstick, presumably an ironic concession to this day of death.

Catherine walked me to the lobby. 'James, you must go to the office – believe me, love, I'm trying to be helpful.' She touched my right shoulder with a curious hand, as if searching for some new wound which had flowered there. During the inquest she had held my arm in a peculiar grip, frightened that I might be swept sideways out of the window.

Unwilling to haggle with the surly and baronial taxidrivers only interested in taking London fares, I walked through the car-park opposite the air-freight building. Overhead, across the metallized air, a jet-liner screamed. When the aircraft had passed I raised my head and saw Dr Helen Remington moving among the cars a hundred yards to my right.

At the inquest I had been unable to take my eyes away

from the scar on her face. I watched her walk calmly through the lines of cars towards the entrance of the immigration department. Her strong jaw was held at a jaunty angle, her face turned away from me as if she were ostentatiously blotting out all traces of my existence. At the same time I had the strong impression that she was completely lost.

A week after the inquest she was waiting at the taxi rank of the Oceanic Terminal as I drove away from Catherine's office. I called to her and stopped behind an airline bus, beckoning her into the passenger seat. Swinging her handbag from a strong wrist, she came across to my car, recognizing me with a grimace.

As we headed towards Western Avenue she surveyed the traffic with frank interest. She had brushed her hair back from her face, openly wearing the fading scar-line.

'Where can I take you?'

'Can we drive a little?' she asked. 'There's all this traffic – I like to look at it.'

Was she trying to taunt me? I guessed that in her matter-of-fact way she was already assessing the possibilities I had revealed to her. From the concrete aprons of the parking lots and the roofs of the multi-storey car-parks she was now inspecting with a clear and unsentimental eye the technology which had brought about the death of her husband.

She began to chatter with contrived animation. 'Yesterday I hired a taxi-driver to drive me around for an hour. "Anywhere," I said. We sat in a massive traffic jam near the underpass. I don't think we moved more than fifty yards. He wasn't in the least put out.'

We drove along Western Avenue, the service buildings and perimeter fence of the airport on our left. I kept the car in the slow lane as the high deck of the flyover receded in the rear-view mirror. Helen talked about the second life she was already planning for herself.

'The Road Research Laboratory need a medical officer – the salary is larger, something I've got to think about now. There's a certain moral virtue in being materialistic.'

'The Road Research Laboratory . . .' I repeated. The newsreels of simulated car-crashes were often shown in television documentaries; these mutilated machines were haunted by a strange pathos. 'Isn't that rather too close . . . ?'

'That's the point. Besides, I know I can give something now that I wasn't remotely aware of before. It's not a matter of duty so much as of commitment.'

Fifteen minutes later, as we moved back towards the flyover, she came and sat beside me, watching my hands on the controls as we once again entered the collision course.

The same calm but curious gaze, as if she were still undecided how to make use of me, was fixed on my face shortly afterwards as I stopped the car on a deserted service road among the reservoirs to the west of the airport. When I put my arm around her shoulders she smiled briefly to herself, a nervous rictus of the upper lip which exposed her gold-tipped right incisor. I touched her mouth with my own, denting the waxy carapace of pastel lipcoat, watching her hand reach out to the chromium pillar of the quarter window. I pressed my lips against the bared and unmarked dentine of her upper teeth, fascinated by the movement of her fingers across the smooth chrome of the window pillar. Its surface was marked along its forward edge by a smear of blue paint left by some disaffected production-line worker. The nail of her forefinger scratched at this fretline, which rose diagonally from the window-sill at the same angle as the concrete ledge of the irrigation ditch ten feet from the car. In my eyes this parallax fused with the image of an abandoned car lying in the rust-stained grass on the lower slopes of the reservoir embankment. The brief avalanche of dissolving talc that fell across her eyes as I moved my lips across their lids contained all the melancholy of this derelict vehicle, its leaking engine oil and radiator coolant.

Six hundred yards behind us the traffic waited on the raised deck of the motorway, the afternoon sunlight crossing the windows of the airline buses and cars. My hand moved around the outer curvature of Helen's thighs, feeling the open zip of her dress. As these razor-like links cut my knuckles I felt her teeth across my ear. The sharpness of these pains reminded me of the bite of the windshield glass during my crash. She opened her legs and I began to stroke the nylon mesh that covered her pubis, a glamorous veil for the loins of this serious-minded woman doctor. Looking into her face, with its urgent mouth gasping as if trying to devour itself, I moved her hand around her breasts. She was now talking to herself, rambling away like some demented accident casualty. She lifted her right breast from her brassière, pressing my fingers against the hot nipple. I kissed each breast in turn, running my teeth across the erect nipples.

Seizing me with her body in this arbour of glass, metal and vinyl, Helen moved her hand inside my shirt, feeling for my nipples. I took her fingers and placed them around my penis. Through the rear-view mirror I saw a water-board maintenance truck approaching. It moved past in a roar of dust and diesel exhaust that drummed against the doors of my car. This surge of excitement drew the first semen to my penis. Ten minutes later, when the truck returned, the vibrating windows brought on my orgasm. Helen knelt across me, elbows pressed into the seat on either side of my head. I lay back, feeling the hot, scented vinyl. My hands pushed her skirt around her waist so that I could see the curve of her hips. I moved her slowly against me, pressing the shaft of my penis against her clitoris. Elements of her body, her square kneecaps below my elbows, her right breast jacked out of its brassière cup, the small ulcer that marked the lower arc of her nipple, were framed within the cabin of the car. As I pressed the head of my penis against the neck of her uterus, in which I could feel a dead machine, her cap, I looked at the cabin around me. This small space was crowded with angular control surfaces and rounded sections of human bodies interacting in unfamiliar junctions, like the first act of homosexual intercourse inside an Apollo capsule. The volumes of Helen's thighs pressing against my hips, her left fist buried in my shoulder, her mouth grasping at my own, the shape and moisture of her anus as I stroked it with my ring finger, were each overlaid by the inventories of a benevolent technology – the moulded binnacle of the instrument dials, the jutting carapace of the steering column shroud, the extravagant pistol grip of the handbrake. I felt the warm vinyl of the seat beside me, and then stroked the damp aisle of Helen's perineum. Her hand pressed against my right testicle. The plastic laminates around me, the colour of washed anthracite, were the same tones as her pubic hairs parted at the vestibule of her vulva. The passenger compartment enclosed us like a machine generating from our sexual act an homunculus of blood, semen and engine coolant. My finger moved into Helen's rectum, feeling the shaft of my penis within her vagina. These slender membranes, like the mucous septum of her nose which I touched with my tongue, were reflected in the glass dials of the instrument panel, the unbroken curve of the windshield.

Her mouth bit my left shoulder, blood marking my shirt like the imprint of a mouth. Without thinking, I struck the side of her head with the palm of my hand.

'I'm sorry!' she gasped into my face. 'Please, don't move!' She steered my penis back into her vagina. Holding her buttocks with both hands, I moved rapidly towards my orgasm. Above me, Helen Remington's serious faced gazed down at me as if she were resuscitating a patient. The sheen of moisture on the skin around her mouth was like the bloom on a morning windshield. She pumped her buttocks rapidly, forcing her pubic bone against mine, then leaned back against the dashboard as a Land-Rover thudded past along the track, sending a cloud of dust against the windows.

She lifted herself off my penis when it had gone, letting the semen fall on to my crotch. She sat herself behind the steering wheel, holding the wet glans in her hand. She looked around the compartment of the car, as if speculating on any other uses to which she could put our sexual act. Lit by the afternoon sun, the fading scar on her face marked off these concealed motives like the secret frontier of an annexed territory. Thinking that I might reassure her in some way, I took her left breast from the brassière and began to stroke it. Stirred happily by its familiar geometry, I gazed at the jewelled grotto of the instrument panel, at the jutting shroud of the steering assembly and the chromium heads of the control switches.

A police car appeared on the service road behind us, its white hull rolling heavily through the dips and ruts. Helen sat up and put away her breast with a deft hand. She dressed quickly, and began to remake her face in the mirror of her compact. As abruptly as we had begun, she was now distanced from her own eager sexuality.

However, Helen Remington clearly felt no concern herself at these out-of-character actions, these sexual acts in the cramped compartment of my motor-car parked in various deserted service roads, culs-de-sac and midnight parkways. When I collected her during the following weeks from the house she had rented in Northolt, or waited for her in the reception lounge outside the airport immigration offices, it seemed incredible to me that I had any kind of sexual involvement with this sensitive woman doctor in her white coat, listening indulgently to the self-defeating arguments of some tubercular Pakistani.

Strangely, our sexual acts took place only within my automobile. In the large bedroom of her rented house I was unable even to mount an erection, and Helen herself would become argumentative and remote, talking endlessly about the more boring aspects of her work. Once together in my car, with the crowded traffic lanes through which we had moved forming an unseen and unseeing audience, we were able to arouse each other. Each time she revealed a growing tenderness towards myself and my body, even trying to allay my concern for her. In each sexual act together we recapitulated her husband's death, re-seeding the image of his body in her vagina in terms of the hundred perspectives of our mouths and thighs, nipples and tongues within the metal and vinyl compartment of the car.

I waited for Catherine to discover my frequent meetings with this lonely woman doctor, but to my surprise she showed only a cursory interest in Helen Remington. Catherine had rededicated herself to her marriage. Before my accident our sexual relationship was almost totally abstracted, maintained by a series of imaginary games and perversities. When she stepped out of bed in the mornings she seemed like some efficient mechanic servicing herself: a perfunctory shower; the night's urine discharged into the lavatory pan; her cap extracted, regreased and once again inserted (how and where did she make love during her lunch-hour, and with which of the pilots and airline executives?); the news programme played while she percolated the coffee . . .

All this had now passed, replaced by a small but growing repertory of tendernesses and affections. As she lay beside me, willingly late for her office, I could bring myself to orgasm simply by thinking of the car in which Dr Helen Remington and I performed our sexual acts.

9

THIS PLEASANT DOMESTIC idyll, with its delightful promiscuities, was brought to an end by the reappearance of Robert Vaughan, nightmare angel of the expressways.

Catherine was away for three days, attending an airline conference in Paris, and out of curiosity I took Helen to the stock-car races in the stadium at Northolt. Several of the stunt drivers working on the Elizabeth Taylor feature at Shepperton Studios put on displays of 'hell-driving'. Unwanted tickets circulated around the studios and our own offices. Disapproving of my affair with the widow of the man I had killed, Renata gave me a pair of tickets, presumably as an ironic gesture.

Helen and I sat together in the half-empty stand, waiting as a succession of stripped-down saloon cars circled the cinder track. A bored crowd watched from the perimeter of the converted football ground. The announcer's voice boomed away over our heads. At the conclusion of each heat the drivers' wives cheered half-heartedly.

Helen sat close to me, arm around my waist, face touching my shoulder. Her face was deadened by the continuous roar of defective silencer units.

'It's strange – I thought all this would be far more popular.'

'The real thing is available free of charge.' I pointed to the yellow programme sheet. 'This should be more interesting – "The Recreation of a Spectacular Road Accident".'

The track was cleared and lines of white bollards were arranged to form the outline of a road intersection. Below us, in the pits, the huge, oil-smeared body of a man in a silver-studded jacket was being strapped into the driver's seat of a doorless car. His shoulder-length dyed-blond hair was tied behind his head with a scarlet rag. His hard face had the pallid and hungry look of an out-of-work circus hand. I recognized him as one of the stuntmen at the studios, a former racing driver named Seagrave.

Five cars were to take part in the re-enactment of the accident – a multiple pile-up in which seven people had died on the North Circular Road during the previous summer. As they were driven to their positions in the field the announcer began to work up the audience's interest. The amplified fragments of his commentary reverberated around the empty stands as if trying to escape.

I pointed to a tall cameraman in a combat jacket who was hovering around Seagrave's car, shouting instructions to him over the engine roar through the missing windshield.

'Vaughan again. He talked to you at the hospital.'

'Is he a photographer?'

'Of a special kind.'

'I thought he was doing some sort of accident research. He wanted every conceivable detail about the crash.'

Vaughan's present role in the stadium seemed that of a film director. As if Seagrave were his star, an unknown who would make Vaughan's reputation, he leaned intently against the windshield pillar, outlining with aggressive gestures some new choreography of violence and collision. Seagrave lolled back, smoking away at a loosely wrapped hash cigarette which Vaughan held for him as he adjusted his straps and the rake of the steering column. His dyed blond hair provided the chief focus of interest in the stadium. From the announcer we learned that Seagrave would drive the target car, which would be cannonaded by a skidding truck into the path of four oncoming vehicles.

At one point Vaughan left him and ran up the stand to the commentator's box behind us. A brief silence followed, after which we were told in tones of some triumph that Seagrave had asked for his closest friend to drive the skidding truck. This last dramatic addition failed to rouse the crowd, but Vaughan seemed satisfied. His hard mouth, with its scarred lips, was parted in a droll smile as he came down the gangway.

Seeing Helen Remington and me together, he waved to us as if we were long-standing aficionados of these morbid spectacles in the arena.

Twenty minutes later, I sat in my car behind Vaughan's Lincoln as a concussed Seagrave was helped across the parking-lot. The accident re-enactment had been a fiasco – struck by the skidding truck, Seagrave's car had been locked on to the raw fenders like a myopic bullfighter running straight on to the bull's horns. The truck carried him fifty yards before ramming him into one of the oncoming saloon cars. The hard, unshielded collision had brought the entire crowd, Helen and myself to our feet.

Vaughan alone was unmoved. As the stunned drivers clambered from their cars and eased Seagrave from behind his driving wheel Vaughan walked swiftly across the arena, beckoning in a peremptory way to Helen Remington. I followed her across the cinders, but Vaughan ignored me, steering Helen through the crowd of mechanics and hangers-on.

Although Seagrave was able to walk, wiping his greasy hands on his silver overall trousers and groping blankly at the air a few feet in front of him, Vaughan persuaded Helen to accompany them to Northolt General Hospital. Once we had set off I found myself hard pressed to keep up with Vaughan's car, the dusty Lincoln with a rear-mounted spotlight. As Seagrave slumped beside Helen in the back seat, Vaughan drove at speed through the night air, one elbow on the door sill, tapping the roof with his hand. I guessed that in his off-hand way he was testing me to see if he could throw me off; at the traffic lights he watched me in the rear-view mirror as I hauled up behind him, then surged away powerfully across the amber. On the Northolt overpass he moved along at well above the speed limit, casually overtaking a cruising police car on the wrong side. The driver flashed his headlamps, hesitating only when he saw the scarlet rag like a bloodstain across Seagrave's hair and my urgent headlamps behind.

We left the overpass and moved down a concrete road

through west Northolt, a residential suburb of the airport. Single-storey houses stood in small gardens separated by wire fences. The area was inhabited by junior airline personnel, car-park attendants, waitresses and ex-stewardesses. Many of them were shift-workers, sleeping through the afternoon and evening, and the windows were curtained as we wheeled through the empty streets.

We turned into the hospital entrance. Ignoring the visitor's car-park, Vaughan pressed on past the casualty department entrance and slammed to a halt in the parking-lot reserved for consultant physicians. He leapt from the driver's seat and beckoned Helen out of the car. Smoothing back his blond hair, Seagrave climbed reluctantly from the rear compartment. He had still not recovered his sense of balance, and rested his huge body against the windshield pillar. Looking at his unfocused eyes and bruised head, I was sure that this was only the latest in a long series of previous concussions. He spat on his oil-stained hands as Vaughan held his head, took Vaughan's arm and lurched after Helen towards the casualty department.

We waited for them to return. Vaughan sat on the hood of his car in the darkness, one thigh cutting off the beam of his nearside headlamp. He stood up restlessly and prowled around the car, head raised above the stares of the evening visitors walking to their wards. Watching him from my car, parked alongside his own, I could see that even now Vaughan was dramatizing himself for the benefit of these anonymous passers-by, holding his position in the spotlight as if waiting for invisible television cameras to frame him. The frustrated actor was evident in all his impulsive movements, and in an irritating way pre-empted my responses to him. Springing on his scuffed white tennis shoes, he moved to the rear of the car and unlatched the trunk.

Disturbed by the reflection of his headlamps in the glass doors of the nearby physiotherapy department, I stepped from my car and watched Vaughan searching through the cameras and flash equipment in the trunk. Selecting a pistol-grip cine-camera, he closed the trunk and sat behind his steering wheel, one leg placed in a glamorous pose on the black asphalt.

He opened the passenger door. 'Come in here, Ballard – they'll be longer than the Remington girl imagines.'

I sat beside him in the front seat of the Lincoln. He peered through the view-finder of the camera, tracking across the entrance of the casualty department. A clutter of photographs of crashed vehicles lay in the dirt on the floor. What most disturbed me about Vaughan was the strange stance of his thighs and hips, almost as if he were trying to force his genitals through the instrument panel of the car. I watched his thighs contracting as he gazed through the camera, buttocks forcing themselves together. Without thinking, I was suddenly tempted to reach forward and take his penis in my hands, steer its head to the luminescent dials. I visualized Vaughan's strong leg flooring the accelerator. The globes of his semen would blot out the stylized intervals on the speedometer counter as the sweep of its arm rose with us while we sped along the swerving concrete.

I was to know Vaughan from this first evening until his death a year later, but the entire course of our relationship was fixed within those few minutes as we waited in the physicians' car-park for Seagrave and Helen Remington. Sitting beside him, I felt my hostility giving way to a certain deference; even, perhaps, subservience. The way Vaughan handled the car set the tone for all his behaviour – by turns aggressive, distracted, sensitive, clumsy, absorbed and brutal. The Lincoln had lost the second gear of its automatic drive – ripped out, as Vaughan explained later, during a road-race with Seagrave. At times, along Western Avenue, we would sit holding up the traffic in the fast lane, dragging along at ten miles an hour as we waited for the injured transmission to build up speed. Vaughan could behave like some kind of paraplegic, fumbling bluntly with the wheel as if expecting the car to be fitted with invalid controls, feet hanging helplessly as we moved rapidly towards the rear of a taxi waiting at a stoplight. At the last moment he would jerk the car to a halt, mocking his whole role as a driver.

His behaviour with all the women he knew was governed by the same obsessive games. To Helen Remington he usually spoke in an off-hand and ironic way, but at other times he became polite and deferential, confiding to me endlessly in the latrines of airport hotels, inquiring whether she would treat Seagrave's wife and small son or, possibly, himself. Then, distracted by something else, he would dismiss her work and medical qualifications altogether. Even after their affair Vaughan's moods would swing from affection to protracted spells of boredom. He would sit behind the wheel of his car as she walked towards us from the immigration offices, his eyes set in a cold appraisal of hoped-for wound areas.

Vaughan propped the cine-camera against the rim of the steering wheel. He lounged back, legs apart, one hand adjusting his heavy groin. The whiteness of his arms and chest, and the scars that marked his skin like my own, gave his body an unhealthy and metallic sheen, like the worn vinyl of the car interior. These apparently meaningless notches on his skin, like the gouges of a chisel, marked the sharp embrace of a collapsing passenger compartment, a cuneiform of the flesh formed by shattering instrument dials, fractured gear levers and parking-light switches. Together they described an exact language of pain and sensation, eroticism and desire. The reflected light of Vaughan's headlamps picked out a semi-circle of five scars that surrounded his right nipple, an outline prepared for a hand that would hold his breast.

In the lavatory of the casualty department I stood beside Vaughan at the urinal stalls. I looked down at his penis, wondering if this too was scarred. The glans, propped between his index and centre fingers, carried a sharp notch, like a canal for surplus semen or vaginal mucus. What part of some crashing car had marked this penis, and in what marriage of his orgasm and a chromium instrument head?

The terrifying excitements of this scar filled my mind as I followed Vaughan back to his car through the dispersing hospital visitors. Its slight lateral deflection, like the rake of the Lincoln's windshield pillars, expressed all Vaughan's oblique and obsessive passage through the open spaces of my mind.

10

ABOVE US, ALONG the motorway embankment, the headlamps of the waiting traffic illuminated the evening sky like lanterns hung on the horizon. An airliner rose from the runway four hundred yards to our left, wired by its nervous engines to the dark air. Beyond the perimeter fence long lines of metal poles stood in the untended grass. The tracts of landing lights formed electric fields like the sections of an overlit metropolis. I followed Vaughan's car along the deserted slip road. We were moving through a development zone on the southern fringes of the airport, an unlit area of three-storey apartment buildings for airline personnel, half-constructed hotels and filling stations. We passed an empty supermarket standing in a sea of mud. Along the verge of the road white dunes of builder's shingle rose in Vaughan's headlamps.

A line of street-lamps appeared in the distance, marking the perimeter of this transit and leisure complex. Immediately beyond its margins, in the western approaches to Stanwell, was an area of breakers' yards and vehicle dumps, small auto-repair shops and panel beaters. We passed a parked two-tier trailer loaded with wrecked cars. Seagrave sat up in the rear seat of Vaughan's car, some familiar stimulus reaching his exhausted brain. During the drive from the hospital he lay back against the rear window-sill, his dyed blond hair lit like a nylon fleece by my headlamps. Helen Remington sat beside him, now and then looking back at me. She had insisted that we accompany Seagrave to his home, apparently distrusting Vaughan's motives.

We turned into the forecourt of Seagrave's garage and

salesroom. His business, which had clearly seen better times during his brief heyday as a racing driver, specialized in hot-rod and customized cars. Behind the unwashed glass of the show-room was a fibreglass replica of a 1930s Brooklands racer, faded bunting stuffed into the seat.

Waiting until we could leave, I watched Helen Remington and Vaughan steer Seagrave into the living-room. The stunt-driver gazed unclearly at the cheap leatherette furniture, for a moment failing to recognize his own house. He lay back on the sofa as his wife remonstrated with Helen, as if she, the doctor, were responsible for her patient's symptoms. For some reason, Vera Seagrave absolved Vaughan of any responsibility, although – as I realized later and she must have known already – Vaughan was clearly using her husband as an experimental subject. A handsome, restless woman of about thirty, she wore her hair in a simulated Afro wig. A small child watched us all from between her legs, its blunt fingers straying to the two long scars on the mother's thighs exposed by her mini-skirt.

Briefly holding Vera Seagrave's waist as she questioned Helen Remington, Vaughan stepped past to the trio sitting on the twin sofa opposite. The man, a television producer who had made Vaughan's first programmes, nodded encouragingly as Vaughan described Seagrave's accident, but was too glazed by the hash he had been smoking – the body-sweet smoke hung in a diagonal drift across the room – to focus his mind on the possibilities of a programme. Beside him on the sofa a sharp-faced young woman was preparing another joint; as she rolled a small piece of resin in a twist of silver foil Vaughan brought a brass lighter out of his hip pocket. She cooked the resin, and shook the powder into the open cigarette waiting in the roller machine on her lap. A social worker in the Stanwell child-welfare department, she was a long-standing friend of Vera Seagrave.

On her legs were traces of what seemed to be gas bacillus scars, faint circular depressions on the kneecaps. She noticed me staring at the scars, but made no effort to close her legs. On the sofa beside her was a chromium metal cane. As she moved I saw that the instep of each leg was held in the steel clamp of a surgical support. From the over-rigid posture of her waist I guessed that she was also wearing a back-brace of some kind. She rolled the cigarette out of the machine, glancing at me with evident suspicion. I guessed that this reflex of hostility was prompted by her assumption that I had not been injured in an automobile crash, unlike Vaughan, herself and the Seagraves.

Helen Remington touched my arm. 'Seagrave – ' She pointed to the sprawling figures of the blond-haired driver. He had revived and was now playfully tripping up his infant son. 'Apparently there's some stunt-driving at the studios tomorrow. Can you stop him?'

'Ask his wife. Or Vaughan – he seems to call the tune.'

'I don't think we should.'

The television producer called out, 'Seagrave is doubling now for all the actresses. It's that beautiful blond hair. What do you do for a brunette, Seagrave?'

Seagrave flicked at his son's minuscule penis. 'Shove it up her arse. Hash first, make a tight little suppository, then ramrod it home. Two trips for the price of one.' He peered reflectively at his grimy hands. 'I'd like to get them all in those cars we have to drive. What do you think of that, Vaughan?'

'We will, one day.' There was a surprising hint of deference in Vaughan's voice as he looked down at the stunt-driver. 'We'll do that.'

'With those cheap bloody harnesses we have to wear.' Seagrave drew on the loosely packed cigarette Vaughan passed to him. He held the smoke in his lungs as he stared at the mountain of derelict cars at the bottom of his garden. 'Can you see them, Vaughan, in one of those high-speed pile-ups? Doing a really groovy roll-over. Or a hard head-on job. I dream about that. It's your whole thing, Vaughan.'

Vaughan smiled reassuringly, a metallic grimace. 'You're right, of course. Who do we start with?'

Seagrave smiled through the smoke. He ignored his wife, who was trying to calm him, and stared with level eyes at Vaughan. 'I know who I'd start with . . .'

'Maybe.'

'. . . I can see those big tits cut up on the dash.'

Vaughan turned away abruptly, almost as if he were afraid

of Seagrave stealing a march on him. The scars on his mouth and forehead carried his face beyond ordinary feeling. He glanced at the other sofa, where his television producer and the crippled young woman, Gabrielle, were passing a cigarette to and fro.

I turned to go, deciding to wait for Helen in my car. Vaughan followed me through the door. He held my arm in a strong grip.

'Don't leave yet, Ballard, I want you to help me.'

As he surveyed the scene I had the sense that Vaughan was controlling us all, giving each of us what we most wanted and most feared.

I followed him down the corridor into a photographic workshop. He beckoned me into the centre of the room, closing the door.

'This is the new project, Ballard.' He waved confidently around the room. 'I'm doing a special television series as part of the spin-off.'

'You've left the N.C.L.?'

'Of course – the project is too important.' He shook his head, ridding himself of the association. 'A large government laboratory isn't equipped to handle something like this, psychologically or otherwise.'

Pinned to the walls and lying on the benches among the enamel pails were hundreds of photographs. The floor around the enlarger was littered with half-plate prints, developed and cast aside once they had yielded their images. As Vaughan hunted around the central table, turning the pages of a leatherbound album, I looked down at the discarded prints below my feet. Most of them were crude frontal pictures of motor-cars and heavy vehicles involved in highway collisions, surrounded by spectators and police, and close-ups of impacted radiator grilles and windshields. Many had been taken by an unsteady hand from a moving car, showing the blurred outlines of angry police and ambulance attendants, remonstrating with the cameraman as he swerved past them.

At a first glance no recognizable human figures appeared in these photographs, but on the wall above the metal sink beside the window were the enlarged prints of six middle-aged women. I was struck by their marked resemblance to Vera Seagrave, as she might appear in twenty years' time. They varied from what I guessed was the well-preserved wife of a successful businessman, fox fur around her shoulders, to a menopausal supermarket cashier and an overweight usherette in a braided gaberdine uniform. Unlike the remainder of the photographs, these six pictures had been taken with elaborate care, using a zoom lens trained through windshields and revolving doors.

Vaughan opened the album at random and handed it to me. Leaning back against the door, he watched me as I adjusted the desk lamp.

The first thirty pages recorded the crash, hospitalization and post-recuperative romance of the young social worker, Gabrielle, who was at that moment sitting on the sofa in Seagrave's sitting-room and rolling the cigarettes which they were smoking. By coincidence, her small sports car had collided with an airline bus at the entry to the airport underpass not far from the site of my own accident. Her sharp-jawed face, its skin beginning to sag like the first slide of an avalanche, lay back against the oil-smeared seat. Around the crushed car was a group of police, ambulance attendants and spectators. In the foreground of the first photographs a fireman with cutting equipment was severing the right-hand windshield pillar. The young woman's injuries were not yet apparent. Her expressionless face looked up at the fireman as he held his torch, almost as if waiting for some bizarre sexual assault. In the later photographs the bruises that were to mask her face began to appear, like the outlines of a second personality, a preview of the hidden faces of her psyche which would have emerged only in late middle age. I was struck by the prim lines these bruises formed around her broad mouth. These morbid depressions were like those of a self-centred spinster with a history of unhappy affairs. Later, even more bruises appeared on her arms and shoulders, the marks of the steering column and instrument panel, as if these lovers had beaten her out of an increasingly abstracted despair with a series of grotesque implements.

Behind me, Vaughan still leaned against the door. For the first time since I had met him his body was completely at rest, its manic movements in some way calmed by my immersion in his album. I turned the next pages. Vaughan had compiled an elaborate photographic dossier on the young woman. I guessed that he had chanced upon her accident a few minutes after she had skidded into the rear of the airline bus. The alarmed faces of several Varig passengers peered through the rear window at the crushed sports car which this injured young woman had delivered like a tableau sculpture to the unprotected overhang below their seats.

The next pictures showed her being lifted from the car, her white skirt heavy with blood. Her face leaned emptily against the arm of a fireman raising her from the bloody basin of the driving seat like some insane cultist in the American South baptized in a font of lamb's blood. A hatless police driver held one handle of the stretcher, his square jaw pushed to one side by her left thigh. Between these two was the darkening triangle of her crotch.

Several pages followed, showing the crashed sports car in the breaker's yard, close-ups of the dried bloodstains on the driving and passenger seats. Vaughan himself appeared in one of these photographs, staring down at the car in a Byronic pose, his heavy penis visible in the tight crotch of his jeans.

The last group of photographs showed the young woman in a chromium wheelchair, guided by a friend across the rhododendron-screened lawn of a convalescent institution, propelling her shiny vehicle herself at an archery meeting, and finally taking her first lessons at the wheel of an invalid car. As she pondered the complex, treadle-operated brakes and gear changes I realized the extent to which this tragically injured young woman had been transformed during her recovery from the accident. The first photographs of her lying in the crashed car showed a conventional young woman whose symmetrical face and unstretched skin spelled out the whole economy of a cozy and passive life, of minor flirtations in the backs of cheap cars enjoyed without any sense of the real possibilities of her body. I could imagine her sitting in the car of some middle-aged welfare officer, unaware of the conjunction formed by their own genitalia and the stylized instrument panel, a euclid of eroticism and fantasy that would be revealed for the first time within the car-crash, a fierce marriage pivoting on the fleshy points of her knees and pubis. This agreeable young woman, with her pleasant sexual dreams, had been reborn within the breaking contours of her crushed sports car. Three months later, sitting beside her physiotherapy instructor in her new invalid car, she held the chromium treadles in her strong fingers as if they were extensions of her clitoris. Her knowing eyes seemed well aware that the space between her crippled legs was constantly within the gaze of this muscled young man. His eyes roved among the damp moor of her pubis as she moved the gear lever through its cage. The crushed body of the sports car had turned her into a creature of free and perverse sexuality, releasing within its twisted bulkheads and leaking engine coolant all the deviant possibilities of her sex. Her crippled thighs and wasted calf muscles were models for fascinating perversities. As she peered through the window at Vaughan's camera her canny eyes were clearly aware of his real interest in her. The posture of her hands on the steering wheel and accelerator treadle, the unhealthy fingers pointing back towards her breasts, were elements in some stylized masturbatory rite. Her strong face with its unmatching planes seemed to mimic the deformed panels of the car, almost as if she consciously realized that these twisted instrument binnacles provided a readily accessible anthology of depraved acts, the keys to an alternative sexuality. I stared at the photographs in the harsh light. Without thinking, I visualized a series of imaginary pictures I might take of her: in various sexual acts, her legs supported by sections of complex machine tools, pulleys and trestles; with her physical education instructor, coaxing this conventional young man into the new parameters of her body, developing a sexual expertise that would be an exact analogue of the other skills created by the multiplying technologies of the twentieth century. Thinking of the extensor rictus of her spine during orgasm, the erect hairs on her undermuscled thighs, I stared at the stylized manufacturer's medallion visible in the photographs, the contoured flanks of the window pillars.

Vaughan leaned silently against the door. I turned the pages. The remainder of the album, as I anticipated, described the course of my own accident and recovery. From the first photograph, which showed me being carried into the hospital casualty unit at Ashford, I knew that Vaughan had been there when I arrived – later I learned that he listened to the ambulance broadcasts on the VHF band of his car radio.

The sequence of pictures formed a record of Vaughan rather than myself, far more of the landscape and preoccupations of the photographer than of his subject. Apart from those photographs of myself in hospital, taken with a zoom lens through the open window as I lay in bed, swathed in more bandages than I realized at the time, the background to all the pictures was the same – the automobile, moving along the highways around the airport, in the traffic jams on the flyover, parked in culs-de-sac and lovers lanes. Vaughan had followed me from the police pound to the airport reception area, from the multi-storey car-park to Helen Remington's house. From these coarse prints it seemed that my whole life was spent in or near the motor-car. Vaughan's interest in myself was clearly minimal; what concerned him was not the behaviour of a 40-year-old producer of television commercials but the interaction between an anonymous individual and his car, the transits of his body across the polished cellulose panels and vinyl seating, his face silhouetted against the instrument dials.

The leitmotiv of this photographic record emerged as I recovered from my injuries: my relationships, mediated by the automobile and its technological landscape, with my wife, Renata and Dr Helen Remington. In these crude photographs, Vaughan had frozen my uncertain embraces as I edged my wounded body into its first sexual encounters since the accident. He had caught my hand stretching across the transmission tunnel of my wife's sports car, the inner surface of my forearm dented by the chromium gear lever, my bruised wrist pressing against the white flank of her thigh; my still-numb mouth against Renata's left nipple, lifting her breast from her blouse as my hair fell across the window-sill; Helen Remington sitting astride me in the passenger seat of her black saloon, skirt hitched around her waist, scarred knees pressing against the vinyl seat as my penis entered her vulva, the oblique angle of the instrument panel forming a series of blurred ellipses like globes ascending from our happy loins.

Vaughan stood at my shoulder, like an instructor ready to help a promising pupil. As I stared down at the photograph of myself at Renata's breast, Vaughan leaned across me, his real attention elsewhere. With a broken thumbnail, its rim caked with engine oil, he pointed to the chromium window-sill and its junction with the over-stretched strap of the young woman's brassière. By some freak of photography these two formed a sling of metal and nylon from which the distorted nipple seemed to extrude itself into my mouth.

Vaughan's face was without expression. Childhood boils had left an archipelago of pockmarks across his neck. A sharp but not unpleasant smell rose from his white jeans, a blend of semen and engine coolant. He turned through the photographs, now and then tilting the album to emphasize an unusual camera angle for me.

I watched Vaughan close the album, wondering why I was unable to rouse myself into at least a parade of anger, remonstrate with him for this intrusion into my life. But Vaughan's detachment from any emotion or concern had already had its effect. Perhaps some latent homo-erotic element had been brought to the surface of my mind by his photographs of violence and sexuality. The deformed body of the crippled young woman, like the deformed bodies of the crashed automobiles, revealed the possibilities of an entirely new sexuality. Vaughan had articulated my needs for some positive response to my crash.

I looked down at Vaughan's long thighs and hard buttocks. However carnal an act of sodomy with Vaughan would have seemed, the erotic dimension was absent. Yet this absence made a sexual act with Vaughan entirely possible. The placing of my penis in his rectum as we lay together in the rear seat of his car would be an event as stylized and abstracted as those recorded in Vaughan's photographs.

The television director came hazily to the door, a wet cigarette unravelling between his fingers.

'V. – can you fix this? Seagrave messed it up.' He drew emptily on a crack on the side of the cigarette, and nodded to me. 'The nerve centre, eh? Vaughan makes everything look like a crime.'

Vaughan put down the camera tripod he was oiling and expertly tucked the tobacco into the cigarette, pouring back the grains of hash that landed on his palm. He licked the paper with a sharp tongue that darted from his scarred mouth like a reptile's. His nostrils sucked at the smoke.

I looked through a batch of freshly developed prints on the table below the window. They showed the familiar face of the film actress, photographed as she was stepping from her limousine outside a London hotel.

'Elizabeth Taylor – are you following her?'

'Not yet. I need to meet her, Ballard.'

'As part of your project? I doubt if she'll be able to help you.'

Vaughan sauntered around the room on his uneven legs.

'She's working at Shepperton now. Aren't you using her in a Ford commercial?'

Vaughan waited for me to speak. I knew that he would act on any evasion. Thinking of Seagrave's grim concussion-fantasy – the film stars forced to crash their own stunt-cars – I decided not to answer.

Seeing all this cross my face, Vaughan turned to the door. 'I'll call Dr Remington for you – we'll talk about this again, Ballard.'

He handed to me, presumably as a pacifier, a bundle of well-thumbed Danish sex magazines. 'Have a look at these – they're more professionally done. You and Dr Remington might enjoy them together.'

Gabrielle, Vera Seagrave and Helen were in the garden, their voices drowned by the blare of aircraft taking off from the airport. Gabrielle walked in the centre, her shackled legs in a parody of a finishing-school carriage. Her pallid skin reflected the amber street-lights. Helen held her left elbow, steering her gently through the knee-high grass. It suddenly occurred to me that during all the time I had spent with Helen Remington I had never discussed her dead husband with her.

I looked through the colour photographs in the magazines; in all of them the motor-car in one style or another figured as the centrepiece – pleasant images of young couples in group intercourse around an American convertible parked in a placid meadow; a middle-aged businessman naked with his secretary in the rear seat of his Mercedes; homosexuals undressing each other at a roadside picnic; teenagers in an orgy of motorized sex on a two-tier vehicle transporter, moving in and out of the lashed-down cars; and throughout these pages the gleam of instrument panels and window louvres, the sheen on over-polished vinyl reflecting the soft belly of a stomach or a thigh, the forests of pubic hair that grew from every corner of these motor-car compartments.

Vaughan watched me from the yellow armchair as Seagrave played with his small son. I remember his face, detached but serious, as Seagrave unbuttoned his shirt and placed the child's mouth on his nipple, squeezing the hard skin into the parody of a breast.

11

MY MEETING WITH Vaughan, and the album of photographs documenting my accident, had quickened all my memories of that trauma of dreams. Going down to the basement garage a week later, I found myself unable to point the car in the direction of the studios at Shepperton, almost as if the vehicle had been transformed during the night into a Japanese uni-directional toy, or fitted like my own head with a powerful gyroscope that pointed only towards the foot of the airport flyover.

Waiting for Catherine to leave for her flying lesson, I drove my car towards the motorway, and within a few minutes had trapped myself in a traffic jam. The lines of stalled vehicles reached to the horizon, where they joined the clogged causeways of the motor routes to the west and south of London. As I edged forward, my own apartment house came into sight. Above the rails of the sitting-room balcony I could actually see Catherine moving about on some complex errand, making two or three telephone calls and scribbling away on a pad. In an unexpected way she seemed to be playing at being myself – already I knew that I would be back in the apartment the moment she left, taking up my convalescent position on that exposed balcony. For the first time I realized that sitting there, halfway up that empty apartment face, I had been visible to tens of thousands of waiting motorists, many of whom must have speculated about the identity of this bandaged figure. In their eyes I must have appeared like some kind of nightmarish totem, a domestic idiot suffering from the irreversible brain damage of a motorway accident and now put out each morning to view the scene of his own cerebral death.

The traffic stirred slowly towards the Western Avenue interchange. I lost sight of Catherine as the glass curtain-walling of the high-rise apartment blocks moved between us. Around me the morning traffic lay in the fly-infested sunlight. Strangely, I felt almost no sense of anxiety. That profound feeling of foreboding, which had hung like the overhead traffic lights over my previous excursions along the motorways, had now faded. Vaughan's presence, somewhere around me on these crowded causeways, convinced me that some kind of key could be found to this coming autogeddon. His photographs of sexual acts, of sections of automobile radiator grilles and instrument panels, conjunctions between elbow and chromium window-sill, vulva and instrument binnacle, summed up the possibilities of a new logic created by these multiplying artefacts, the codes of a new marriage of sensation and possibility.

Vaughan had frightened me. The callous way in which he had exploited Seagrave, playing on the violent fantasies of this punch-drunk stunt-driver, warned me that he would probably go to any lengths to take advantage of the immediate situation around him.

I accelerated as the traffic reached the Western Avenue interchange, then moved northwards at the first right-hand junction towards Drayton Park. Like an up-ended glass coffin, the apartment block lifted into the sky over my head as I drove back into the basement garage.

In the apartment I wandered about restlessly, searching for the dictation pad on which Catherine recorded her telephone calls. I wanted to intercept any messages from her lovers, not out of sexual jealousy, but because these affairs would cut irrelevantly across whatever Vaughan was planning for us all.

Catherine had been untiringly generous and affectionate to me. She continued to urge me to see Helen Remington, so much so that at times I thought she was laying the ground for a free consultation, marked by strong lesbian overtones, about some obscure gynaecological complaint – the intercontinental pilots with whom she fraternized probably carried more diseases than all the terrified immigrants herded through Helen Remington's bureaux.

Searching for Vaughan, I spent the morning haunting the approach roads to the airport. From the parking aprons of the filling stations along Western Avenue I watched the oncoming traffic. I hung about the observation platform of the Oceanic Terminal, hoping to see Vaughan trail a visiting pop star or politician.

In the distance the traffic moved sluggishly along the exposed deck of the flyover. For some reason I remembered Catherine saying once that she would never be satisfied until every conceivable act of copulation in the world had at last taken place. Somewhere in this nexus of concrete and structural steel, this elaborately signalled landscape of traffic indicators and feeder roads, status and consumer goods, Vaughan moved like a messenger in his car, his scarred elbow resting on the chromium window-sill, cruising the highways in a dream of violence and sexuality behind an unwashed windshield.

Giving up my attempt to find Vaughan, I drove to the studios at Shepperton. A large breakdown truck blocked the gates. The driver hung from his cab, shouting at the two commissionaires. On the back of the truck lay a black Citroën Pallas saloon car, its long bonnet crushed by a head-on collision.

'That terrible machine.' Renata joined me in the sunlight as I parked my car. 'Did you order it, James?'

'It's needed for the Taylor film – there's a crash sequence being taken this afternoon.'

'She'll drive that car? Don't tell me.'

'She'll drive another car – this one is used for the post-crash sequences.'

Later that afternoon I thought of Gabrielle's crippled body as I looked down over the make-up woman's shoulder at the infinitely more glamorous and guarded figure of the screen actress sitting behind the wheel of the crashed Citroën.

At a discreet distance the sound and lighting men watched her like spectators at a real accident. The make-up woman, a refined girl with a reassuring sense of humour – so unlike those casualty ward nurses whose opposite number, in a sense, she was – had worked for more than hour on the simulated wounds.

The actress sat motionlessly in the driving seat as the last brushstrokes completed the elaborate lacework of blood that fell from her forehead like a red mantilla. Her small hands and forearms were streaked with the blue shadows of simulated bruises. Already she was assuming the postures of a crash victim, her fingers weakly touching the streaks of carmine resin on her knees, thighs delicately raised from the plastic seat cover as if flinching from some raw mucous membrane. I watched her touch the steering wheel, barely recognizing the structure.

In the dashboard locker below the buckled instrument panel lay a woman's dusty suède glove. Did the actress sitting in the car under her death-paint visualize the real victim injured in the accident that had crushed this vehicle – some Francophile suburban housewife, perhaps, or Air France stewardess? Did she instinctively mimic the postures of this injured woman, transforming in her own magnificent person the injuries of a commonplace accident, the soon-forgotten bloodstains and sutures? She sat in the damaged car like a deity occupying a shrine readied for her in the blood of a minor member of her congregation. Although I was twenty feet from the car, standing beside a sound engineer, the unique contours of her body and personality seemed to transform the crushed vehicle. Her left leg rested on the ground, the door pillar realigning both itself and the dashboard mounting to avoid her knee, almost as if the entire car had deformed itself around her figure in a gesture of homage.

The sound engineer turned on his heel, jarring my elbow with his boom microphone. As he apologized a uniformed commissionaire jostled past me. An altercation had broken out on the opposite corner of the highway junction which had been built on this outdoor set. The young American assistant producer was remonstrating with a dark-haired man in a leather jacket, trying to take a camera away from him. As the sunlight glanced off the zoom lens I recognized Vaughan. He was leaning against the roof of a second Citroën, staring at the producer and now and then fending him off with a scarred hand. Beside him, Seagrave was sitting on the bonnet of the car. His blond hair was tied in a knot on the top of his head, and over his jeans he wore a woman's fawn suède driving coat. Beneath his red polo-necked jumper a well-stuffed brassière formed the contours of two large breasts.

Seagrave's face had already been made up to resemble the screen actress's, mascara and pancake darkening his pale skin. This immaculate mask of a woman's face resembled a nightmare parody of the actress, far more sinister than the cosmetic wounds at that moment being applied to her. I assumed that Seagrave, wearing a wig over his blond hair and the same clothes as the actress, would drive this intact Citroën into a collision with the third vehicle containing a mannequin of her lover.

Already, as he watched Vaughan from behind his grotesque mask, Seagrave looked as if he had been obscurely injured in this collision. With his woman's mouth and over-bright eyes, his dyed blond hair fastened into a bun on top of his head, he resembled an elderly transvestite caught drunk in his boudoir. He watched Vaughan with some resentment, as if Vaughan had forced him to dress up each day in this parody of the actress.

Vaughan had pacified the assistant producer and the commissionaire, without having to surrender his camera. He gave Seagrave a cryptic signal, his scarred mouth breaking into a smile, and sidestepped towards the production offices. As I approached, he beckoned me forwards, incorporating me into an instant entourage.

Behind him, forgotten now by Vaughan, Seagrave sat alone in the Citroën like a distraught witch.

'Is he all right? You should have photographed Seagrave.'

'I did – of course.' Vaughan slung the camera on to his

right hip. Wearing the white leather jacket he resembled a handsome actor more than a renegade scientist.

'Can he still drive a car?'

'As long as it moves in a straight line for him.'

'Vaughan, get him to a doctor.'

'That would spoil everything. Besides, I can't spare the time. Helen Remington has seen him.' Vaughan turned his back on the set. 'She's joining the Road Research Laboratory. There's an Open Day in a week's time – we'll all go together.'

'That's the sort of frolic I can well do without.'

'No, Ballard – you'll find it reassuring. It's a vital section in the television series.'

He strode away to the car-park.

These potent confusions of fiction and reality, summed up in the pathetic but sinister figure of Seagrave disguised as the screen actress, remained in my mind all afternoon, even overlaying my response to Catherine when she came to collect me.

She chattered pleasantly to Renata, but was soon distracted by the coloured photographs on the walls, sections of custom-built sports cars and de luxe saloons which appeared in a dealer commercial we were making. These emblematic portraits of tail-fin and radiator grille, body panel and windshield hood, air-brushed in vivid pastel and acrylic colours, seemed to fascinate her. Her good-humoured tolerance of Renata surprised me. I led her into the cutting room, where two young editors were working on the rough cut. Presumably Catherine was convinced that within this visual context some kind of erotic junction between Renata and myself was inevitable, and that if she herself were left in this office, working among the contour photographs and layouts of fender assemblies, she too would have formed a sexual liaison, not only with the two young editors, but with Renata as well.

She had spent the day in London. In the car outside, her wrists were keyboards of perfumes. What had first struck me about Catherine was her immaculate cleanliness, as if she had individually reamed out every square centimetre of her elegant body, separately ventilated every pore. At times the porcelain appearance of her face, an over-elaborate make-up like some demonstration model of a beautiful woman's face, had made me suspect that her whole identity was a charade. I tried to visualize the childhood that had created this beautiful young woman, the perfect forgery of an Ingres.

This passivity, her total acceptance of any situation, was what had attracted me to Catherine. During our first sex acts, in the anonymous bedrooms of the airport hotels, I would deliberately inspect every orifice I could find, running my fingers around her gums in the hope of seeing even one small knot of trapped veal, forcing my tongue into her ear in the hope of finding a trace of the taste of wax, inspecting her nostrils and navel, and lastly her vulva and anus. I would have to run my forefinger to its root before I could extract even a faint scent of faecal matter, a thin brown rim under my fingernail.

We set off for home in our separate cars. At the traffic lights on the access road to the northbound lanes of the motorway I watched Catherine resting her hands on the steering wheel. Her right index finger picked at an old adhesive label on the windshield. Waiting beside her, I watched her thighs move against each other as she pressed the foot-brake.

As we drove along Western Avenue I wanted her body to embrace the compartment of the car. In my mind I pressed her moist vulva against every exposed panel and fascia, I crushed her breasts gently against the door pillars and quarter windows, moved her anus in a slow spiral against the vinyl seat covers, placed her small hands against the instrument dials and window-sills. The junction of her mucous membranes and the vehicle, my own metal body, was celebrated by the cars speeding past us. The complex of an immensely perverse act waited upon her like a coronation.

Almost mesmerized by this reverie, I was abruptly aware of the dented fender of Vaughan's Lincoln only a few feet behind Catherine's sports car. Vaughan surged past me, crowding along the roadway as if waiting for her to make a mistake. Startled, Catherine took refuge in front of an airline bus in the nearside lane. Vaughan drove alongside the bus, using his horn and spotlights to force the driver back, and again cut in behind Catherine. I moved ahead along the centre lane, shouting to Vaughan as I passed him, but he was signalling to Catherine, pumping his headlamps at her rear fender. Without thinking, Catherine pulled her small car into the courtyard of a filling station, forcing Vaughan into a heavy U-turn. Tyres screaming, he swung around the ornamental flower-bed with its glazed pottery plants, but I blocked his way with my own car.

Excited by all this, Catherine sat among the scarlet fuel pumps, her eyes flashing at Vaughan. The wounds on my legs and chest ached from the effort of keeping up with them. I stepped from my car and walked across to Vaughan. He watched me approach as if he had never seen me before, scarred mouth working on a piece of gum as he gazed at the airliners lifting from the airport.

'Vaughan, you're not on a bloody stunt track now.'

Vaughan made a brief pacifying gesture with one hand. He hooked the gear lever into reverse. 'She enjoyed it, Ballard. It's a form of compliment. Ask her.'

He reversed in a wide circle, almost running down a passing pump attendant, and set off across the early afternoon traffic.

12

VAUGHAN WAS RIGHT. Catherine's sexual fantasies began more and more to involve him. At night, as we lay together in our bedroom, we approached Vaughan through the pantheon of our familiar partners like Vaughan himself tracking us through the lobbies of the terminal buildings.

'We must get some more hash.' Catherine looked up at the traffic lights sweeping across the windows. 'Why is Seagrave so obsessed with these film actresses? You say he wants to crash into them?'

'Vaughan put the idea into his head. He's using Seagrave in some experiment.'

'What about the wife?'

'She's under Vaughan's thumb.'

'And you?'

Catherine lay with her back to me, buttocks pressed into my groin. As I moved my penis I looked past my scarred navel at the cleft between her buttocks, as immaculate as a doll's. I held her breasts in my hands, her rib cage crushing my wristwatch into my forearm. Catherine's passive stance was deceptive; from long practice I knew that this was the prelude to an erotic fantasy, a slow and circular inspection of some fresh sexual quarry.

'Am I under his thumb? No. But it's difficult to know where the centre of his personality is.'

'You don't resent him taking all those photographs? It sounds as if he's using you.'

I began to play with Catherine's right nipple. Not yet ready for this, she took my hand and placed it around her breast.

'Vaughan annexes people to him. There's still a strong element of the TV personality about his whole style.'

'Poor man. These girls he picks up – some of them are just children.'

'You keep coming back to them. It isn't sex that Vaughan is interested in, but technology.'

Catherine pressed her head into the pillow, a familiar gesture of concentration.

'Do you like Vaughan?'

I moved my fingers to her nipple again and began to erect it. Her buttocks moved on to my penis. Her voice was pitched on a low, thick note.

'In what way?' I asked.

'He fascinates you, doesn't he?'

'There is something about him. About his obsessions.'

'His flashy car, the way he drives, his loneliness. All the women he's fucked there. It must smell of semen . . .'

'It does.'

'Do you find him attractive?'

I drew my penis from her vagina and placed the head against her anus, but she pressed it back into her vulva with a quick hand.

'He's very pale, covered with scars.'

'Would you like to fuck him, though? In that car?'

I paused, trying to delay the orgasm rushing like a tidal race up the shaft of my penis.

'No. But there is something about him, particularly as he drives.'

'It's sex – sex and that car. Have you seen his penis?'

As I described Vaughan to her I listened to my voice rising slightly above the sounds of our bodies. I itemized the elements that constituted Vaughan's image in my mind: his hard buttocks held within the worn jeans as he rolled himself on to one hip to leave the car; the sallow skin of his abdomen, almost exposing the triangle of his pubis as he lounged behind the steering wheel; the horn of his half-erect penis pressing against the lower rim through the damp crotch of his trousers; the minute nodes of dirt he picked from his sharp nose and wiped on the indented vinyl of the door panel; the ulcer on his left index finger as he handed me the cigarette lighter; his hard nipples through the frayed blue shirt brushing against the horn boss; his broken thumbnail scratching at the semen stains on the seat between us.

'Is he circumcised?' Catherine asked. 'Can you imagine what his anus is like? Describe it to me.'

My description of Vaughan continued, more for Catherine's benefit than for my own. She pressed her head deep into the pillow, right hand in a fierce dance as she forced my fingers to manipulate her nipple. Although stirred by the idea of intercourse with Vaughan, it seemed to me that I was describing a sex act involving someone other than myself. Vaughan excited some latent homosexual impulse only within the cabin of his car or driving along the highway. His attraction lay not so much in a complex of familiar anatomical triggers – a curve of exposed breast, the soft cushion of a buttock, the hair-lined arch of a damp perineum – but in the stylization of posture achieved between Vaughan and the car. Detached from his automobile, particularly his own emblem-filled highway cruiser, Vaughan ceased to hold any interest.

'Would you like to sodomize him? Would you like to put your penis right into his anus, thrust it up his anus? Tell me, describe it to me. Tell me what you'd do. How would you kiss him in that car? Describe how you'd reach over and unzip his trousers, then take out his penis. Would you kiss it or suck it straightaway? Which hand would you hold it in? Have you ever sucked a penis?'

Catherine had taken over the fantasy. Whom did she see lying beside Vaughan, herself or me?

'. . . do you know what semen tastes like? Have you ever tasted semen? Some semen is saltier than others. Vaughan's semen must be very salty . . .'

I looked down at her blonde hair that covered her face, at her hips kicking as she carried herself towards her orgasm. This was one of the first times that she had envisaged me in a homosexual act, and the intensity of the fantasy surprised me. She shuddered through her orgasm, her body in a rigor of pleasure. Before I could reach out to embrace her she turned over, lying face downwards to let my semen run from her vagina, then pulled herself from the bed and stepped briskly into the bathroom.

During the next week, Catherine drifted through the departure lounges of the airport like a queen in rut. Watching her from my car as Vaughan kept her within his aberrant gaze, I felt my loins surging, my penis pressing against the steering wheel.

13

'HAVE YOU COME?'

Helen Remington touched my shoulder with an uncertain hand, as if I were a patient she had worked hard to revive. As I lay against the rear seat of the car she dressed herself with abrupt movements, straightening her skirt around her hips like a department-store window-dresser jerking a garment on to a mannequin.

On our way to the Road Research Laboratory I had suggested that we park among the reservoirs to the west of the airport. During the previous week Helen had shifted her field of interest away from me, as if allocating myself and the accident to a past life whose reality she no longer recognized. I knew that she was about to enter that period of unthinking promiscuity through which most people pass after a bereavement. The collision of our two cars, and the death of her husband, had become the key to a new sexuality. During the first months after his death she moved through a series of rapidly consumed affairs, as if taking the genitalia of all these men into her hands and her vagina would in some way bring her husband back to life, and that all this semen mixed within her womb would quicken the fading image of the dead man within her mind.

The day after her first sexual act with me, she had taken another lover, the junior pathologist at Ashford Hospital. From him she moved through a succession of men: the husband of a fellow woman doctor, a trainee radiologist, the service manager at her garage. What I noticed about these affairs, which she described in an unembarrassed voice, was the presence in each one of the automobile. All had taken place within a motor-car, either in the multi-storey car-park at the airport, in the lubrication bay of her local garage at night, or in the laybys near the northern circular motorway, as if the presence of the car mediated an element which alone made sense of the sexual act. In some way, I assumed, the car re-created its role in the death of her husband within the new possibilities of her body. Only in the car could she reach her orgasm. Yet one evening, as I lay in my car with her on the roof of the multi-storey car-park at Northolt, I felt her body stiffen in a rictus of hostility and frustration. I placed my hand on the dark triangle of her pubis, the moisture turning it silver in the darkness. She pulled her arms away from me and stared at the cabin of the car, as if about to tear her exposed breasts on this trap of glass and metal knives.

The deserted reservoirs lay around us in the sunlight, an invisible marine world. Helen wound up her window, shutting out the noise of a climbing airliner.

'We won't come here again – you'll have to find somewhere else.'

I had felt the same fall in excitement. Without Vaughan watching us, recording our postures and skin areas with his camera, my orgasm had seemed empty and sterile, a jerking away of waste tissue.

In my mind I visualized the cabin of Helen's car, its hard chrome and vinyl, brought to life by my semen, transformed into a bower of exotic flowers, with creepers entwined across the roof light, the floor and seats lush with moist grass.

Looking across at Helen, as she accelerated along the open deck of the motorway, I suddenly wondered how I could hurt her. I thought of taking her again along the route of her husband's death – perhaps this would re-engage her sexual need for me, rekindle whatever erotic hostility she felt for me and the dead man.

As we were guided through the gates of the Laboratory Helen sat forward over the steering wheel, her slim arms holding it in a strange grip. Her body formed an awkward geometry with the windshield pillars and the angle of the steering column, almost as if she were consciously mimicking the postures of the crippled young woman, Gabrielle.

We walked from the crowded car-park to the test sites. With the research scientist who had greeted us Helen discussed projected Ministry legislation on anti-roll bars. Two lines of damaged cars had been drawn up on the concrete. The bodies of plastic mannequins sat in the crumpled hulls, their faces and chests splintered by the collisions, wound areas marked in coloured panels on their skulls and abdomens. Helen stared at them through the empty windshields, almost as if they were patients whom she hoped to treat. As we strolled through the gathering visitors in their smart suits and flowered hats Helen reached through the starred windows and caressed the plastic arms and heads.

This dreamlike logic hung over the entire afternoon. In the bright afternoon light the several hundred visitors took on the appearance of mannequins, no more real than the plastic figures which would play the roles of driver and passengers in a front-end collision between a saloon car and a motorcycle.

This sense of disembodiment, of the unreality of my own muscles and bones, increased when Vaughan appeared. In front of me, the engineers were shackling the motorcycle to the cradle which would be propelled along its steel rails towards the saloon car seventy yards away. Metering coils led from both vehicles to the recording devices set up on a line of trestle tables. Two cine-cameras were in position, the first mounted alongside the track, lens aimed at the point of impact, the second pointing downwards from an overhead gantry. A video-tape device was already playing back on to a small screen a picture of the engineers adjusting the sensors in the car's engine compartment. A family of four mannequins sat in the car – a husband, wife and two children – coils attached to their heads, chests and legs. Already the anticipated injuries they would suffer had been marked on their bodies; complex geometric shapes in carmine and violet zoned across their faces and thoraxes. An engineer settled the driver for the last time behind his steering wheel, arranging his hands in the correct ten-to-two position. Over the loudspeaker system the commentator, a senior principal scientific officer, welcomed the guests to this experimental crash and jocularly introduced the occupants of the car – 'Charlie and Greta, imagine them out for a drive with the kids, Sean and Brigitte . . .'

At the far end of the track, a smaller group of technicians prepared the motorcycle, securing the boom camera attached to the cradle which would travel down the rails. The visitors – Ministry officials, road safety engineers, traffic specialists and their wives – had gathered around the point of impact, like a crowd at a race track.

As Vaughan arrived, striding on his long, uneven legs from the car-park, everyone looked round, watching this black-jacketed figure advance towards the motorcycle. I myself half expected him to mount the machine and drive it down the rails at us. The scars on his mouth and forehead caught the air like sabre wounds. He hesitated, watching the technicians lift the plastic motorcyclist – 'Elvis' – on to his machine, and then strode on towards us, beckoning to Helen Remington and myself. He scanned the visitors with a somehow offensive gaze. Once again he struck me as being a strange mixture of personal hauntedness, complete confinement in his own panicky universe, and yet at the same time open to all kinds of experiences from the outer world.

Vaughan pushed his way through the visitors. In his right hand he carried a bundle of publicity folders and R.R.L. handouts. He bent over Helen Remington's shoulder as she looked up at him from her chair in the front row.

'Have you seen Seagrave?'

'Was he supposed to come?'

'Vera telephoned me about him this morning.' He turned his attention to me, tapping the bundle of handouts in his grip. 'Get all the paper you can, Ballard. Some of the stuff they give away – "Mechanisms of Occupant Ejection", "Tolerances of the Human Face in Crash Impacts" . . .' As the last of the engineers stood back from the test car Vaughan nodded appreciatively, and commented *sotto voce*, 'The technology of accident simulation at the R.R.L. is remarkably advanced. Using this set-up they could duplicate the Mansfield and Camus crashes – even Kennedy's – indefinitely.'

'They're trying to reduce the number of accidents here, not increase it.'

'I suppose that's a point of view.'

The commentator had called the crowd to order. The test crash was about to take place. Vaughan had forgotten me, starting forward like a patient suburban voyeur half asleep over his binoculars. His right hand, shielded by the publicity folders, was manipulating his penis through the fabric of his trousers. He squeezed the distal end, almost forcing the glans through the threadbare cloth, index finger rolling back the foreskin. All the while his eyes moved up and down the collision course, taking in every detail.

The electric winches which propelled the catapult began to drum at the rails, the cables tautening. Vaughan's hand worked away at his groin. The engineer in charge stepped back from the motorcycle and signalled to his assistant by the catapult. Vaughan switched his attention to the car in front of us, its four plastic occupants sitting up stiffly as if *en route* to a chapel meeting. Vaughan glanced at me over his shoulder, his face hard and flushed, as if making sure that I was involved.

With a loud jerk, the motorcycle sped down the track, its cables clanking between the metal rails. The mannequin rider sat well back, the onrushing air lifting his chin. His hands were shackled to the handlebars like a kamikaze pilot's. His long thorax was plastered with metering devices. In front of him, their expressions equally vacant, the family of four mannequins sat in their vehicle. Their faces were marked with cryptic symbols.

A harsh whipping noise came towards us, the sound of the metering coils skating along the grass beside the rail. There was a violent metallic explosion as the motorcycle struck the front of the saloon car. The two vehicles veered sideways towards the line of startled spectators. I regained my balance, involuntarily holding Vaughan's shoulder, as the motorcycle and its driver sailed over the bonnet of the car and struck the windshield, then careened across the roof in a black mass of fragments. The car plunged ten feet back on its hawsers. It came to rest astride the rails. The bonnet, windshield and roof had been crushed by the impact. Inside the cabin, the lopsided family lurched across each other, the decapitated torso of the front-seat woman passenger embedded in the fractured windshield.

The engineers waved to the crowd reassuringly and moved towards the motorcycle, which lay on its side fifty yards behind the car. They began to pick up the sections of the cyclist's body, tucking the legs and head under their arms. Shavings of fibreglass from its face and shoulders speckled the glass around the test car like silver snow, a death confetti.

The loudspeaker addressed the crowd again. I tried to follow the commentator's words, but my brain failed to translate the sounds. The ugly and violent impact of this simulated crash, the rupture of metal and safety glass, and the deliberate destruction of expensively engineered artefacts, had left me lightheaded.

Helen Remington held my arm. She smiled at me, nodding encouragingly as if urging a child across some mental hurdle. 'We can have a look at it again on the Ampex. They're showing it in slow-motion.'

The crowd was moving towards the trestle tables, voices lifting again in relieved chatter. I turned back, waiting for Vaughan to join us. He was standing among the empty seats, eyes still fixed on the wrecked car. Below his waistband a pool of semen darkened the crotch of his trousers.

Ignoring Helen Remington, who moved away from us with a faint smile, I stared at Vaughan, uncertain what to say to him. Faced with this junction of the crashed car, the dismembered mannequins and Vaughan's exposed sexuality, I found myself moving through a terrain whose contours led inside my skull towards an ambiguous realm. I stood behind

Vaughan, staring at his muscular back, hard shoulders swinging under his black jacket.

Beside the Ampex machine the visitors were watching the motorcycle as it crashed once again into the saloon car. Sections of the collision were replayed in slow motion. In a dream-like calm, the front wheel of the motorcycle struck the fender of the car. As the rim collapsed, the tyre sprung inwards upon itself to form a figure of eight. The tail of the machine rose into the air. The mannequin, Elvis, lifted himself from his seat, his ungainly body at last blessed by the grace of the slow-motion camera. Like the most brilliant of all stunt men, he stood on his pedals, legs and arms fully stretched. His head was raised with its chin forwards in a pose of almost aristocratic disdain. The rear wheel of the motorcycle lifted into the air behind him, and seemed about to strike him in the small of the back, but with great finesse the rider detached his feet from the pedals and inclined his floating body in a horizontal posture. His hands were still attached to the handlebars, now moving away from him as the cycle somersaulted. The metering coils severed one wrist, and he launched himself into a horizontal dive, head raised so that his face became a prow, bearing its painted wound areas towards the oncoming windshield. His chest struck the bonnet of the car, grazing its polished cellulose like a surfboard.

Already, as the vehicle moved back under the impact of the first collision, the four occupants of the car were themselves moving towards the second collision. Their smooth faces pressed on into the advancing windshield as if eager to see the chest glider soaring up the bonnet of the car. Both the driver and his woman passenger rolled forwards to meet the windshield, touching it with the crowns of their lowered heads at the same moment as the motorcyclist's profile struck the glass. A fountain of spraying crystal erupted around them, through which, as if in celebration, their figures were taking up ever more eccentric positions. The motorcyclist continued on his horizontal path through the emblazoned windshield, his face torn away by the centrally mounted driving mirror. His left arm detached itself at the elbow as it struck the windshield pillar, and was swept up through the fountain of glass to join the debris chasing the inverted body of the motorcycle three feet above his spine. His right arm moved through the fractured windshield, losing first its hand on the guillotine of the near-side windshield wiper, and then its forearm against the face of the front-seat woman passenger, taking with it her right cheekbone. The motorcyclist's body slewed gracefully to one side in an elegant slalom, his hips striking the right-hand windshield pillar, buckling it at the central welding point. His legs rotated around the car, shin-bones striking the central door pillar.

Above him, the inverted motorcycle fell on to the car's roof. Its handlebars passed through the empty windshield and decapitated the front-seat passenger. The front wheel and chromium fork assembly plunged through the roof, the whiplashing drive chain severing the cyclist's head as he swept past. The pieces of his disintegrating body rebounded off the rear wheel-housing of the car and passed over the ground in the haze of broken safety glass which fell like ice from the car, as if it had been defrosted after a long embalming. Meanwhile, the driver of the car had rebounded off the collapsing steering wheel and was sliding beneath the column into the lower compartment of the car. His decapitated wife, hands raised prettily in front of her neck, rolled against the instrument panel. Her detached head bounced off the vinyl seat covering and passed between the torsos of the children in the rear seat. Brigitte, the smaller of the two children, lifted her face to the roof of the car and raised her hands in a polite gesture of alarm as her mother's head struck the rear window and cannonaded around the car before exiting through the left-hand door.

The car slowly came to rest, continuing to heave itself laboriously off the ground. The four passengers subsided into the glass-embroidered cabin space. Their signalling limbs, busy with an encyclopedia of unheeded semaphores, settled again into a crudely human posture. Around them, the fountain of frosted glass moved away for the last time.

The audience of thirty or so visitors stared at the screen, waiting for something to happen. As we watched, our own ghostly images stood silently in the background, hands and faces unmoving while this slow-motion collision was re-enacted. The dream-like reversal of roles made us seem less real than the mannequins in the car. I looked down at the silk-suited wife of a Ministry official standing beside me. Her eyes watched the film with a rapt gaze, as if she were seeing herself and her daughters dismembered in the crash.

The visitors wandered away to the tea tent. I followed Vaughan towards the crashed car. He stepped between the chairs, spitting his chewing-gum on to the grass. I knew that he had been even more affected by the test crash and the slow-motion film than myself. Helen Remington watched us, sitting alone among the chairs. Vaughan stared down at the shattered car, almost about to embrace it. His hands roved along the torn bonnet and roof, the muscles of his face opening and shutting like manacles. He bent down and peered into the cabin, scanning each of the mannequins. I waited for him to say something to them, my eyes moving from the dented curvatures of the bonnet and fenders to the cleft of Vaughan's buttocks. The destruction of this motor-car and its occupants seemed, in turn, to sanction the sexual penetration of Vaughan's body; both were conceptualized acts abstracted from all feeling, carrying any ideas or emotions with which we cared to freight them.

Vaughan scraped the flaking fibreglass from the driver's face. He wrenched the door open and edged his thigh on to the seat, one hand holding the distorted steering wheel.

'I've always wanted to drive a crashed car.'

I took the remark to be a joke, but Vaughan appeared to mean it seriously. Already he was calmer, as if this act of violence had drained some of the tensions from his body, or pre-empted whatever violent behaviour he had suppressed for so long.

'All right,' Vaughan announced, dusting the fibreglass from his hands. 'We'll leave now – I'll give you a lift.' When I hesitated he said, 'Believe me, Ballard, one car-crash looks like another.'

Was he aware that I was duplicating in my mind a series

of sexual postures between Vaughan and myself, Helen Remington and Gabrielle which would re-enact the death-ordeals of the mannequins and the fibreglass motor-cyclist? In the urinal beside the car-park Vaughan deliberately exposed his half-erect penis as he stood well back from the stall, flicking out the last drops of urine on to the tiled floor.

Once away from the Laboratory he recovered all his aggressiveness, as if his appetite was quickened by the passing cars. He rolled the heavy car along the access road to the motorway, holding the battered bumpers a few feet behind any smaller vehicle until it moved out of his way.

I tapped the instrument panel. 'This car – a ten-year-old Continental. I take it that you see Kennedy's assassination as a special kind of car-crash?'

'The case could be made.'

'But why Elizabeth Taylor? Driving around in this car, aren't you putting her in some danger?'

'Who from?'

'Seagrave – the man's half out of his mind.'

I watched him drive along the last stretches of the motorway, making no effort to slacken his speed despite the warning signs.

'Vaughan – has she ever been in a car-crash?'

'Not a major crash – it means that everything lies in the future for her. With a little forethought she could die in a unique vehicle collision, one that would transform all our dreams and fantasies. The man who dies in that crash with her . . .'

'Does Seagrave appreciate this?'

'In his own way.'

We approached a major trunk roundabout. For almost the first time since we had left the Road Research Laboratory Vaughan applied the brakes. The heavy car swayed and went into a long right-hand slide which carried it across the path of a taxi already making its way around the island. Flooring the accelerator, Vaughan swerved in front of it, tyres screaming over the blaring horn of the taxi. He shouted through his open window at the driver and pressed on towards the narrow canyon of the northbound slip road.

As we settled down Vaughan reached behind him and lifted a briefcase off the back seat.

'I've been testing people for the programme with these questionnaires. Tell me if I've left anything out.'

14

As the heavy car moved through the London-bound traffic I began to read the questionnaires which Vaughan had prepared. The subjects who had completed the forms represented a cross-section of Vaughan's world: two computer programmers from his former laboratory, a young dietitian, several airport stewardesses, a medical technician at Helen Remington's clinic, as well as Seagrave and his wife Vera, the television producer and Gabrielle. From the brief curriculum vitae elicited from each subject I saw, as I expected, that they had all at some time been involved in a minor or major automobile crash.

In each questionnaire the subject was given a list of celebrities from the worlds of politics, entertainment, sport, crime, science and the arts, and invited to devise an imaginary car-crash in which one of them might die. Scanning the list offered, I saw that most of the figures were still alive; a few were dead, some of these in autocrashes. The names gave the impression of having been picked at random from a quick recall of newspaper and magazine headlines, television newscasts and documentaries.

By contrast, the choice of wounds and death-modes available showed all the benefits of an exhaustive and lingering research. Almost every conceivable violent confrontation between the automobile and its occupants was listed: mechanisms of passenger ejection, the geometry of kneecap and hip-joint injuries, deformation of passenger compartments in head-on and rear-end collisions, injuries sustained in accidents at roundabouts, at trunk-road intersections, at the junctions between access roads and motorway intersections, the telescoping mechanisms of car-bodies in front-end collisions, abrasive injuries formed in roll-overs, the amputation of limbs by roof assemblies and door sills during roll-over, facial injuries caused by dashboard and window trim, scalp and cranial injuries caused by rear-view mirrors and sun-visors, whiplash injuries in rear-end collisions, first and second-degree burns in accidents involving the rupture and detonation of fuel tanks, chest injuries caused by steering column impalements, abdominal injuries caused by faulty seat-belt adjustment, second-order collisions between front-seat and rear-seat passengers, cranial and spinal injuries caused by ejection through windshields, the graded injuries to the skull caused by variable windshield glasses, injuries to minors, both children and infants in arms, injuries caused by prosthetic limbs, injuries caused within cars fitted with invalid controls, the complex self-amplifying injuries of single and double amputees, injuries caused by specialist automobile accessories such as record players, cocktail cabinets and radio-telephones, the injuries caused by manufacturers' medallions, safety belt pinions and quarter-window latches.

Lastly came that group of injuries which had clearly most preoccupied Vaughan – genital wounds caused during automobile accidents. The photographs which illustrated the options available had clearly been assembled with enormous care, torn from the pages of forensic medical journals and textbooks of plastic surgery, photocopied from internally circulated monographs, extracted from operating theatre reports stolen during his visits to Ashford Hospital.

As Vaughan turned the car into a filling station courtyard the scarlet light from the neon sign over the portico flared across these grainy photographs of appalling injuries: the breasts of teenage girls deformed by instrument binnacles, the partial mammoplastics of elderly housewives carried out by the chromium louvres of windshield assemblies, nipples sectioned by manufacturers' dashboard medallions; injuries to male and female genitalia caused by steering wheel shrouds, windshields during ejection, crushed door pillars, seat springs and handbrake units, cassette player instrument toggles. A succession of photographs of mutilated penises, sectioned vulvas and crushed testicles passed through the flaring light as Vaughan stood by the girl filling-station attendant at the rear of the car, jocularly talking to her about her body. In several of the photographs the source of the wound was indicated by a detail of that portion of the car which had caused the injury: beside a casualty ward photograph of a bifurcated penis was an inset of a handbrake unit; above a close-up of a massively bruised vulva was a steering-wheel boss and its manufacturer's medallion. These unions of torn genitalia and sections of car body and instrument panel formed a series of disturbing modules, units in a new currency of pain and desire.

The same conjunctions, all the more terrifying when they seemed to evoke the underlying elements of character, I saw in the photographs of facial injuries. These wounds were illuminated like medieval manuscripts with the inset details of instrument trim and horn bosses, rear-view mirrors and dashboard dials. The face of a man whose nose had been crushed lay side by side with a chromium model-year emblem. A young coloured woman with sightless eyes lay on a hospital couch, a rear-view mirror inset beside her, its glassy stare replacing her own vision.

Comparing the completed questionnaires, I noticed the differing accident modes selected by Vaughan's subjects. Vera Seagrave's choices had been made at random, as if she had barely distinguished in her mind between windshield ejection, roll-over and head-on collisions. Gabrielle had emphasized facial injuries. Most disturbing of all the replies were Seagrave's – in the crashes he devised the only wounds his hypothetical victims suffered were severe genital injuries. Alone among Vaughan's subjects, Seagrave had selected a small target gallery of five film actresses, ignoring the politicians, sportsmen and television personalities whom Vaughan had listed. On these five women – Garbo, Jayne Mansfield, Elizabeth Taylor, Bardot and Raquel Welch – Seagrave had built an abattoir of sexual mutilation.

Horns sounded ahead of us. We had reached the first heavy traffic in the approaches to the western suburbs of

London. Vaughan drummed impatiently on the steering wheel. The scars on his mouth and forehead formed a clear hatchwork in the afternoon light, the marking areas of a future generation of wounds.

I turned the pages of Vaughan's questionnaires. The photographs of Jayne Mansfield and John Kennedy, Camus and James Dean had been marked in coloured crayons, pencil lines circled around their necks and pubic areas, breasts and cheekbones shaded in, section lines across their mouths and abdomens. Jayne Mansfield stepped from her car in a studio publicity still, left leg on the ground, right thigh raised to reveal the maximum of its inner surface. Her breasts were thrust forward, below an engaging come-on smile, and almost touched the canted door pillar of the wrap-around windshield. One of the interviewees, Gabrielle, had marked imaginary wound sites on her left breast and exposed thigh, a section line in coloured crayon across her throat, outlining those parts of the car which would marry with her body. The free areas around these photographs were covered with annotations in Vaughan's scrawled handwriting. Many ended with a question mark, as if Vaughan were speculating about alternative death modes, accepting some as plausible and rejecting others as too extreme. A faded agency picture of the car in which Albert Camus had died was elaborately re-worked, the dashboard and windshield marked with the words 'nasal bridge', 'soft palate', 'left zygomatic arch'. An area in the lower section of the instrument panel was reserved for Camus' genital organs, the dials covered with cross-hatching and provided at the left margin with a key: 'glans penis', 'scrotal septum', 'urethral canal', 'right testicle'. The fractured windshield opened on to the crushed bonnet of the car, an arcade of fractured metal revealing the engine and radiator, together covered by a long V-shaped swathe in a dotted white tint: 'Semen'.

At the conclusion of the questionnaire the last of Vaughan's victims appeared. Elizabeth Taylor stepped from her chauffeured limousine outside a London hotel, smiled across her husband's shoulder from the depths of a rear seat.

Thinking of this new algebra of leg-stance and wound area which Vaughan was calculating, I searched her thighs and kneecaps, the chromium door frames and cocktail cabinet lids. I assumed that either Vaughan or his volunteer subjects would have mounted her body in any number of bizarre postures, like a demented stunt driver, and that the cars in which she moved would become devices for exploiting every pornographic and erotic possibility, every conceivable sex-death and mutilation.

Vaughan's hand took the file from me and returned it to his briefcase.

The traffic had come to a halt, the access lanes to Western Avenue jammed by the first rush-hour traffic exiting from the city. Vaughan leaned against the window-sill, fingers raised to his nostrils as if clinging to the last odour of semen on their tips. The warning headlamps of the oncoming traffic, and the overhead lights of the expressway, the emblematic signals and destinations, lit up the isolated face of this hunted man at the wheel of his dusty car. I looked out at the drivers of the cars alongside us, visualizing their lives in the terms Vaughan had defined for them. For Vaughan they were already dead.

Six lanes wide, the traffic edged forward to the Western Avenue interchange, in this huge evening rehearsal of its own death. Red tail-lights flared like fireflies around us. Vaughan was holding passively to the rim of his steering wheel, staring with an expression of defeat at the fading passport photograph of an anonymous middle-aged woman clipped to the ventilation duct of the instrument binnacle. As two women walked along the road verge, cinema usherettes about to go on duty in their green braided uniforms, Vaughan sat up and scanned their faces, his eyes intent as a waiting criminal's.

As Vaughan stared at them I looked down at his semen-stained trousers, excited by this automobile marked with mucus from every orifice of the human body. Thinking of the photographs in the questionnaires, I knew that they defined the logic of a sexual act between Vaughan and myself. His long thighs, hard hips and buttocks, the scarred muscles of his stomach and chest, his heavy nipples together invited the countless injuries waiting among the protruding toggles and instrument heads of the car interior. Each of these imaginary wounds was the model for the sexual union of Vaughan's skin and my own. The deviant technology of the car-crash provided the sanction for any perverse act. For the first time, a benevolent psychopathology beckoned towards us, enshrined in the tens of thousands of vehicles moving down the highways, in the giant jetliners lifting over our heads, in the most humble machined structures and commercial laminates.

Using his horn, Vaughan forced the drivers in the slower lanes to back up and let him across on to the hard shoulder. Once free, he set off towards the parking apron of a supermarket built on an elevated deck across the expressway. He peered at me solicitously.

'You've had a hard afternoon, Ballard. Buy yourself a drink in the bar. I'll take you for a drive.'

15

WERE THERE ANY limits to Vaughan's irony? When I returned from the bar he was leaning against the window-sill of the Lincoln, rolling the last of four cigarettes with the hash kit kept in a tobacco bag in the dashboard locker. Two sharp-faced airport whores, barely older than schoolchildren, were arguing with him through the window.

'Where the hell do you think you were going?' Vaughan took from me the two wine bottles I had bought. He rolled the cigarettes on to the instrument binnacle, then resumed his discussion with the young women. They were arguing in an abstract way about time and price. Trying to ignore their voices, and the massed traffic moving below the supermarket, I watched the aircraft taking off from London Airport across the western perimeter fence, constellations of green and red lights that seemed to be shifting about large pieces of the sky.

The two women peered into the car, sizing me up in a one-second glance. The taller of the two, whom Vaughan had already assigned to me, was a passive blonde with unintelligent eyes focused three inches above my head. She pointed to me with her plastic handbag.

'Can he drive?'

'Of course – a few drinks always make a car go better.'

Vaughan twirled the wine bottles like dumb-bells, herding the women into the car. As the second girl, with short black hair and a boy's narrow-hipped body, opened the passenger door, Vaughan handed a bottle to her. Lifting her chin, he put his fingers in her mouth. He plucked out the knot of gum and flicked it away into the darkness. 'Let's get rid of that – I don't want you blowing it up my urethra.'

Adjusting myself to the unfamiliar controls, I started the engine and crossed the forecourt to the slip road. Above us, along Western Avenue, the traffic stream edged its way towards London Airport. Vaughan opened a wine bottle and passed it to the blonde sitting beside me in the front seat. He lit the first of the four cigarettes he had rolled. Already one elbow was between the dark-haired girl's thighs, raising her skirt to reveal her black crotch. He drew the cork from the second bottle and pressed the wet end against her white teeth. In the rear-view mirror I could see her avoiding Vaughan's mouth. She inhaled the cigarette smoke, her hand resting on Vaughan's groin. Vaughan lay back, inspecting her small features with a detached gaze, looking her body up and down like an acrobat calculating the traverses and impacts of a gymnastic feat involving a large amount of complex equipment. With his right hand he opened the zip of his trousers, then arched his hips forward to free his penis. The girl held it in one hand, the other steadying the wine bottle as I let the car surge away from the traffic lights. Vaughan unbuttoned her shirt with his scarred fingers and brought out her small breast. Examining the breast, Vaughan gripped the nipple between thumb and forefinger, extruding it forward in a peculiar manual hold, as if fitting together a piece of unusual laboratory equipment.

Brake-lights flared twenty yards ahead of me. Horns sounded from the line of cars in the rear. As their headlamps pulsed I moved the shift lever into drive and pressed the accelerator, jerking the car forward. Vaughan and the girl rolled back against the rear seat. The cabin was lit only by the instrument dials, and by the headlamps and tail-lights in the crowded traffic lanes around us. Vaughan had freed both the girl's breasts, nursing them with his palm. His scarred lips sucked at the thick smoke from the crumbling butt of the cigarette. He took the wine bottle and raised it to her mouth. As she drank he lifted her legs so that her heels rested on the seat, and began to move his penis against the skin of her thighs, drawing it first across the black vinyl and then pressing the glans against her heel and ankle bone, as if testing the possible continuity of these two materials before taking part in a sexual act involving both the car and this young woman. He lay against the rear seat, left arm stretched above the girl's head, embracing this slab of oversprung black vinyl. His hand was raised at right-angles to his forearm, measuring out the geometry of the chromium roof sill, while his right hand moved down the girl's thighs and cupped her buttocks. Squatting there with her heels under her buttocks, the girl opened her thighs to expose her small pubic triangle, the labia open and protruded. Through the smoke lifting from the ashtray Vaughan studied the girl's body in a good-humoured way.

Beside him, the girl's small, serious face was lit by the headlamps of the cars creeping forwards in the traffic files. The damp, inhaled smoke of burnt resin filled the interior of the car. My head seemed to float on these fumes. Somewhere ahead, beyond these immense lines of nearly stationary vehicles, was the illuminated plateau of the airport, but I felt barely able to do more than point the large car along the centre lane. The blonde woman in the front seat offered me a drink from the wine bottle. When I declined she leaned her head against my shoulder, giving a playful touch to the steering wheel. I put my arm around her shoulder, aware of her hand on my thigh.

I waited until we stopped again, and adjusted the driving mirror so that I could see into the rear seat. Vaughan had moved his thumb into the girl's vagina, forefinger into her rectum, as she sat back with her knees against her shoulders, drawing mechanically at the second of the cigarettes.

His left hand took the girl's breast, his ring- and forefingers propping up the nipple like a miniature crutch. Holding these elements of the girl's body in his formalized pose, he began to rock his hips back and forth, driving his penis into the girl's hand. When she tried to move his fingers from her vulva Vaughan knocked her hand away with his elbow, holding the fingers securely in her body. He straightened his legs, rotating himself around the passenger compartment so that his hips rested on the edge of the seat. Braced on his left elbow, he continued to work himself against the girl's hand, as if taking part in a dance of severely stylized postures that celebrated the design and electronics, speed and direction of an advanced kind of automobile.

This marriage of sex and technology reached its climax as the traffic divided at the airport overpass and we began to move forwards in the northbound lane. As the car travelled for the first time at twenty miles an hour Vaughan drew his fingers from the girl's vulva and anus, rotated his hips and inserted his penis in her vagina. Headlamps flared above us as the stream of cars moved up the slope of the overpass. In the rear-view mirror I could still see Vaughan and the girl, their bodies lit by the car behind, reflected in the black trunk of the Lincoln and a hundred points of the interior trim. In the chromium ashtray I saw the girl's left breast and erect nipple. In the vinyl window gutter I saw deformed sections of Vaughan's thighs and her abdomen forming a bizarre anatomical junction. Vaughan lifted the young woman astride him, his penis entering her vagina again. In a triptych of images reflected in the speedometer, the clock and revolution counter, the sexual act between Vaughan and this young woman took place in the hooded grottoes of these luminescent dials, moderated by the surging needle of the speedometer. The jutting carapace of the instrument panel and the stylized sculpture of the steering column shroud reflected a dozen images of her rising and falling buttocks. As I propelled the car at fifty miles an hour along the open deck of the overpass Vaughan arched his back and lifted the young woman into the full glare of the headlamps behind us. Her sharp breasts flashed within the chromium and glass cage of the speeding car. Vaughan's strong pelvic spasms coincided with the thudding passage of the lamp standards anchored in the overpass at hundred-yard intervals. As each one approached his hips kicked into the girl, driving his penis into her vagina, his hands splaying her buttocks to reveal her anus as the yellow light filled the car. We reached the end of the overpass. The red glow of brake-lights burned the night air, touching the images of Vaughan and the young woman with a roseate light.

Controlling the car, I drove down the ramp towards the traffic junction. Vaughan changed the tempo of his pelvic motion, drawing the young woman on top of himself and extending her legs along his own. They lay diagonally across the rear seat, Vaughan taking first her left nipple in his mouth, then the right, his finger in her anus, stroking her rectum to the rhythm of the passing cars, matching his own movements to the play of light sweeping transversely across the roof of the car. I pushed away the blonde girl lying against my shoulder. I realized that I could almost control the sexual act behind me by the way in which I drove the car. Playfully, Vaughan responded to different types of street furniture and road-side trim. As we left London Airport, heading inwards towards the city on the fast access roads, his rhythm became faster, his hands under the girl's buttocks forcing her up and down as if some scanning device in his brain was increasingly agitated by the high office blocks. At the end of the orgasm he was almost standing behind me in the car, legs outstretched, head against the rear seat, hands propping up his own buttocks as he carried the girl on his hips.

Half an hour later I had turned back to the airport and stopped the car in the shadows of the multi-storey car-park facing the Oceanic Terminal. The girl at last managed to pull herself from Vaughan, who lay exhausted against the rear seat. Clumsily, she reassembled herself, remonstrating with Vaughan and the drowsy blonde in the front seat. Vaughan's semen ran down her left thigh on to the black vinyl of the seat. The ivory globes searched for the steepest gradient to the central sulcus of the seat.

I stepped from the car and paid the two women. When they had gone, carrying their hard loins back to the neon-lit concourses, I waited beside the car. Vaughan was staring at the terraced cliff of the car-park, his eyes following the canted floors, as if trying to recognize everything that had passed between himself and the dark-haired girl.

Later, Vaughan explored the possibilities of the car-crash in the same calm and affectionate way that he had explored the limits of that young prostitute's body. Often I watched him lingering over the photographs of crash fatalities, gazing at their burnt faces with a terrifying concern, as he calculated the most elegant parameters of their injuries, the junctions of their wounded bodies with the fractured windshield and instrument assemblies. He would mimic these injuries in his own driving postures, turning the same dispassionate eyes on the young women he picked up near the airport. Using their bodies, he recapitulated the deformed anatomies of vehicle crash victims, gently bending the arms of these girls against their shoulders, pressing their knees against his own chest, always curious to see their reactions.

16

THE WORLD WAS beginning to flower into wounds. From the window of my office at the film studios I watched Vaughan seated in his car in the centre of the parking lot. Most of the staff were leaving for home, taking their cars one by one from the files around Vaughan's dusty limousine. He had driven into the studios an hour earlier. After Renata pointed him out to me I managed successfully to ignore him, but the steady subtraction of the other vehicles from the parking lot soon focused all my attention on this isolated car at the centre. In the three days since our visit to the Road Research Laboratory he had come to the studios each afternoon – ostensibly to see Seagrave, but his real motive was to force me to arrange his formal introduction to the film actress. At an uncertain moment the previous afternoon, after meeting him at a filling station on Western Avenue, I had agreed to help him, well aware that I was no longer able to throw Vaughan off. Without any effort now, he was able to follow me all day, for ever waiting for me at the airport entrances, in the forecourts of filling stations, almost as if I were unconsciously steering myself into his path.

His presence had affected my driving, and I guessed that I was really waiting to be involved in a second accident, this time under Vaughan's eyes. Even the giant aircraft taking off from the airport were systems of excitement and eroticism, punishment and desire waiting to be inflicted on my body. The massive traffic jams on the motorways seemed to suffocate the air, and I nearly believed that Vaughan himself had conjured these vehicles on to the exhausted concrete as part of some elaborate psychological test.

When Renata had gone Vaughan stepped from his car. I watched him walk across the parking lot to the entrance of the offices, wondering why he had chosen me – already I could see myself driving a target vehicle on a collision course with either Vaughan or some victim of his choice.

Vaughan walked through the outer offices, glancing to left and right at the enlarged sales photographs of automobile radiator grilles and windshield assemblies. He was wearing the same stale jeans he had unrolled around his hard buttocks during his sex-act as I drove the car. His lower lip had developed a small ulcer which he had opened by chewing on it. I stared with a peculiar fascination at this miniature orifice, aware of his extending sexual authority over me, an authority partly won by the accident memorialized in the scarred contours of his face and chest.

'Vaughan, I'm exhausted. It's been an effort to move in and out of this office, let alone chase up a producer I barely know. Anyway, the chance of her actually completing one of your questionnaires is nil.'

'Let me give it to her.'

'I know, you'll probably charm her . . .'

Vaughan was standing with his back to me, broken eyetooth gnawing away at the ulcer. My hands, apparently detached from the rest of my body and brain, hesitated in the air, wondering how to embrace his waist. Vaughan turned towards me, a reassuring smile on his scarred mouth, posed at its best diagonal profile as if I were auditioning him for his new television series. He spoke in an oblique and distracted voice, as if he had been clouded by the hash he was smoking. 'Ballard, she's central to the fantasies of all the subjects I've tested. There's a limited amount of time, though you're too obsessed with yourself to realize it. I need her responses.'

'Vaughan, the likelihood of her being killed in a car-crash is remote. You'll have to follow her around until doomsday.'

Standing behind Vaughan, I stared down at the cleft between his buttocks, wishing that these display photographs of car fenders and windshield sections could form themselves into a complete automobile, in which I could take his body in my hands, like that of some vagrant dog, and anneal its wounds within this arcade of possibilities. I visualized these sections of radiator grilles and instrument panels coalescing around Vaughan and myself, embracing us as I pulled the belt from its buckle and eased down his jeans, celebrating in the penetration of his rectum the most beautiful contours of a rear-fender assembly, a marriage of my penis with all the possibilities of a benevolent technology.

'Vaughan . . .'

He was looking down at a display photograph of the actress leaning against a motor-car. He had taken a pencil from my inkwell, and was shading in portions of the actress's body, ringing her armpits and cleavage. He stared almost sightlessly at the photographs, cigarette forgotten on the edge of an ashtray. A dank odour rose from his body, an amalgam of rectal mucus and engine coolant. His pencil cut heavier grooves in the picture. The shaded areas had begun to perforate under his more and more savage slashes, blows with the broken pencil point that punctured the cardboard backing. He marked in points of the motor-car interior, stabbing at the protruding areas of steering assembly and instrument panel.

'Vaughan!' I put my arm around his shoulder. His body was shaking towards an orgasm, the edge of his left hand against his groin in a karate-like hold, as if he were trying to injure himself, working away through the cloth at his erect penis as his right hand moved across the disfigured photographs.

With an effort, Vaughan straightened himself, leaning against my arm. He stared at the mutilated pictures of the screen actress, surrounded by the impact points and wound areas he had marked for her death.

Uneasily, I lowered my arm from Vaughan's shoulder. His hard stomach was marked by a fretwork of scars. On his right hip the scars formed a mould waiting for my fingers, the templates of a caress imprinted years earlier in some forgotten automobile pile-up.

Controlling the phlegm in my throat, I pointed to the scars, five notches that described a loose circle above his iliac crest. Vaughan watched me without comment as my fingers reached to within a few inches of his skin. A gallery of scars marked his thorax and abdomen. His right nipple had been severed and re-sectioned incorrectly, and was permanently erect.

We walked through the evening light towards the car-park. Along the northbound motorway embankment the sluggish traffic moved like blood in a dying artery. Two cars were parked in front of Vaughan's Lincoln in the empty parking lot: a police patrol car and Catherine's white sports saloon. One policeman was inspecting the Lincoln, peering through the dusty windows. The other stood beside Catherine's car, questioning her.

The policemen recognized Vaughan and signalled to him. Thinking that they had come to question me about my growing homo-erotic involvement with Vaughan, I turned away guiltily.

Catherine walked over to me as the policemen spoke to Vaughan.

'They want to question Vaughan about an accident near the airport. Some pedestrian – they think he was run over intentionally.'

'Vaughan isn't interested in pedestrians.'

As if taking their cue from this, the policemen walked back to their car. Vaughan watched them go, head raised like a periscope as if scanning something over the surface of their minds.

'You'd better drive him,' Catherine said as we walked towards Vaughan. 'I'll follow in my car. Where is yours?'

'At home. I couldn't face all this traffic.'

'I'd better come with you.' Catherine peered into my face, as if squinting through the window of a diving helmet. 'Are you sure you can drive?'

Waiting for me, Vaughan reached into the rear seat of his car for a white sweat-shirt. As he took off his denim jacket the falling light picked out the scars on his abdomen and chest, a constellation of white chips that circled his body from the left armpit down to his crotch. The handholds of complex sex acts had been created by the cars in which he had deliberately crashed for my future pleasure, of strange postures in the back and front seats of cars, peculiar acts of sodomy and fellatio I would perform as I moved across his body from one hand-hold to the next.

17

WE HAD ENTERED an immense traffic jam. From the junction of the motorway and Western Avenue to the ascent ramp of the flyover the traffic lanes were packed with vehicles, windshields leaching out the molten colours of the sun setting above the western suburbs of London. Brake-lights flared in the evening air, glowing in the huge pool of cellulosed bodies. Vaughan sat with one arm out of the passenger window. He slapped the door impatiently, pounding the panel with his fist. To our right the high wall of a double-decker airline coach formed a cliff of faces. The passengers at the windows resembled rows of the dead looking down at us from the galleries of a columbarium. The enormous energy of the twentieth century, enough to drive the planet into a new orbit around a happier star, was being expended to maintain this immense motionless pause.

A police car sped down the descent lane of the flyover, head-lamps flashing, the rotating blue light on its roof flicking at the dark air like a whip. Above us, on the crest of the ascent lane, two policemen steered the traffic stream from the nearside kerb. Warning tripods set up on the pavement flashed a rhythmic 'Slow . . . Slow . . . Accident . . . Accident . . .' Ten minutes later, when we reached the eastern end of the flyover, we could see the accident site below. Lines of cars moved past a circle of police spotlights.

Three cars had collided at the junction of the eastern descent ramp of the flyover and Western Avenue. Around them a police car, two ambulances and a breakdown truck formed a loose corral. Firemen and police engineers worked on the vehicles, oxy-acetylene torches flaring against door and roof panels. A crowd was gathering on the sidewalks, and on the pedestrian bridge that spanned Western Avenue the spectators leaned elbow to elbow on the metal rail. The smallest of the cars involved in the accident, a yellow Italian sports car, had been almost obliterated by a black limousine with an extended wheelbase which had skidded across the central reservation. The limousine had returned across the concrete island to its own lane and struck the steel pylon of a route indicator, crushing its radiator and nearside wheel housing, before being hit in turn by a taxi joining the flyover from the Western Avenue access road. The head-on collision into the rear end of the limousine, followed by roll-over, had crushed the taxi laterally, translating its passenger cabin and body panels through an angle of some fifteen degrees. The sports car lay on its back on the central reservation. A squad of police and firemen were jacking it on to its side, revealing two bodies still trapped inside the crushed compartment.

Beside the taxi, the three passengers lay in a group, blankets swathing their chests and legs. First-aid men worked on the driver, an elderly man who sat upright against the rear fender of his car, face and clothes speckled with drops of blood, like an unusual disease of the skin. The limousine's passengers still sat in the deep cabin of their car, their identities sealed behind the starred internal window.

We passed the accident site, edging forward in the line of cars. Catherine had half hidden herself behind the front seat. Her steady eyes followed the skid lines and loops of bloodstained oil that crossed the familiar macadam like the choreographic codes of a complex gun battle, the diagram of an assassination attempt. Vaughan, by contrast, leaned out of the window, both arms ready as if about to seize one of the bodies. In some recess or locker in the rear seat he had found a camera, which now swung from his neck. His eyes were racing over the three crashed vehicles, as if he were photographing every detail with his own musculature, in the white retinas of the scars around his mouth, memorializing every bent fender and broken bone in a repertory of rapid grimaces and droll expressions. For almost the first time since I met him he was completely calm.

Siren whining, a third ambulance drove down the oncoming lane. A police motorcyclist cut in front of us and slowed to a halt, signalling me to wait and allow the ambulance to pass. I stopped the car and switched off the engine, looking over Catherine's shoulder at the grim tableau. Ten yards from us was the crushed limousine, the body of the young chauffeur still lying on the ground beside it. A policeman stared at the blood netting like a widow's veil around his face and hair. Three engineers worked with crowbars and cutting equipment at the rear doors of the limousine. They severed the jammed door mechanism and pulled back the door to expose the passengers trapped inside the compartment.

The two passengers, a pink-faced man in his fifties wearing a black overcoat, and a younger woman with a pale, anaemic skin, still sat upright in the rear seat. Their heads were held forward, staring together at the policemen and hundreds of spectators like two minor royalties at a levée. A policeman pulled away the travelling rug that covered their legs and waists. This single motion, exposing the bare legs of the young woman and the splayed feet of the older man, apparently broken at the ankles, immediately transformed the entire scene. The woman's skirt had ridden up around her waist, and her thighs lay apart as if she were deliberately exposing her pubis. Her left hand held the window strap, the white glove marked with blood from her small fingers. She gave the policeman a weak smile, like a partially disrobed queen beckoning a courtier to touch her private parts. Her companion's coat was flared to reveal the full length of his black trousers and patent shoes. His right thigh was extended like a dancehall instructor's in a tango glide. As he turned to the young woman, one hand searching for her, he slipped sideways off the seat, his ankles kicking at the clutter of leather valises and broken glass.

The traffic stream moved on. I started the engine and eased the car forwards. Vaughan raised the camera to his eye, lowering it from sight when an ambulance attendant tried to knock it from his hands. The pedestrian bridge passed overhead. Half out of the car, Vaughan peered at the scores of legs pressed against the metal railings, then opened the door and dived out.

As I pulled the Lincoln on to the verge he was running back to the pedestrian bridge, darting in and out of the cars.

We followed Vaughan back to the accident site. Hundreds of faces pressed at the windows of the cars moving down the flyover. Spectators stood three deep on the sidewalks and central reservation, crowded together against the wire mesh fence that separated the roadway embankment from the nearby shopping precinct and housing estate. The police had given up any attempt to disperse this enormous crowd. One group of engineers worked on the crushed sports car, prying at the metal roof which had been flattened on to the heads of the occupants. The passengers from the taxi were carried on stretchers to an ambulance. The dead chauffeur of the limousine lay with a blanket over his face, while a doctor and two ambulance men climbed into the rear compartment.

I looked round at the crowd. A considerable number of children were present, many lifted on their parents' shoulders to give them a better view. The revolving police beacons moved across the watching faces as we climbed the embankment to the wire mesh fence. None of the spectators showed any signs of alarm. They looked down at the scene with the calm and studied interest of intelligent buyers at a leading bloodstock sale. Their relaxed postures implied a shared understanding of the most subtle points, as if they all realized the full significance of the displacement of the limousine's radiator grille, the distortion of the taxi's body frame, the patterns of frosting on its shattered windshield.

Pushing amiably between Catherine and myself on the embankment was a thirteen-year-old boy in a cowboy suit. He chewed steadily on a piece of gum, watching the last of the taxi passengers being lifted on to a stretcher. A policeman with a broom scattered lime on the blood-smeared concrete beside the sports car. With careful strokes, as if frightened of working out the complex human arithmetic of these injuries, he swept the darkening clots against the verge of the central reservation.

More spectators strolled across the common from the shopping precinct. They climbed through a break in the wire fence. Together we watched as the two occupants of the limousine were eased through the canted door of their car. Clearly the most vivid erotic fantasies would be moving through our minds, of imaginary acts of intercourse performed with enormous decorum and solicitude upon the bloodstained loins of this young woman while she lay within her car, as the members of her audience stepped forward and entered the broken compartment of the limousine, each placing his penis within her vagina, seeding the infinite futures that would flower from the marriage of violence and desire.

Around me, down the entire length of Western Avenue, along both ramps of the flyover, stretched an immense congestion of traffic held up by the accident. Standing at the centre of this paralysed hurricane, I felt completely at ease, as if my obsessions with the endlessly multiplying vehicles had at last been relieved.

Vaughan, by contrast, seemed to have lost interest in the accident. Holding his camera above his head, he pushed roughly through the spectators making their way down the bridge. Catherine watched him jump the last six steps and dart among the tired police. Her clear interest in Vaughan, her eyes avoiding my own but fixed continually on his scarred face as she held tightly to my arm, neither surprised nor upset me. Already I sensed that the three of us had yet to make the most of this crash, play its quickening possibilities into our own lives. I was thinking of the scars on my own body and on Vaughan's, handholds for our first embraces, and of the wounds on the bodies of the survivors of the crash behind us, contact points for all the sexual possibilities of their futures.

The last of the ambulances drove away, its siren wailing. The spectators returned to their cars, or climbed the embankment to the break in the wire fence. An adolescent girl in a denim suit walked past us, her young man with an arm around her waist. He held her right breast with the back of his hand, stroking her nipple with his knuckles. They stepped into a beach buggy slashed with pennants and yellow paint and drove off, horn hooting eccentrically. A burly man in a truck-driver's jacket helped his wife up the embankment, a hand on her buttocks. This pervasive sexuality filled the air, as if we were members of a congregation leaving after a sermon urging us to celebrate our sexualities with friends and strangers, and were driving into the night to imitate the bloody eucharist we had observed with the most unlikely partners.

Catherine leaned against the rear body panel of the Lincoln, crotch pressed against the chromium fin moulding. She kept her head away from me.

'Are you going to drive? You're all right, aren't you?'

I stood with my feet apart, hands on my breast bone, inhaling the floodlit air. I could feel my wounds again, cutting through my chest and knees. I searched for my scars, those tender lesions that now gave off an exquisite and warming pain. My body glowed from these points, like a resurrected man basking in the healed injuries that had brought about his first death.

I knelt by the nearside front wheel of the Lincoln. Streaks of a black gelatinous material smeared the fender and wheel housing, marking the muddied disc of the whitewall tyre. I touched the gummy residues with my fingers. A heavy dent marked the wheel housing, the same deformation produced on my own car some two years earlier when I had been hit by a German shepherd dog running blindly across a street. I had stopped a hundred yards ahead and walked back to find two schoolgirls vomiting into their hands over the dying dog.

I pointed to the smears of blood. 'You must have hit a dog – the police may impound the car while they have the blood analysed.'

Vaughan knelt beside me and inspected the bloodstains, nodding sagely. 'You're right, Ballard – there's an all-night car-wash in the airport service area.'

He held the door open for me, his steady eyes without any show of hostility, as if calmed and relaxed by the accident we had passed. I sat behind the wheel, waiting for him to walk around the car and sit beside me, but he pulled open the rear door and climbed in with Catherine.

As we set off, his camera landed on the front seat. Its invisible silver memories of pain and excitement distilled themselves on their dark reel as, behind me, Catherine's most sensitive mucous surfaces quietly discharged their own quickening chemicals.

We drove westwards towards the airport. I watched Catherine in the rear-view mirror. She sat in the centre of the rear seat, elbows forward on her knees, looking over my shoulder at the speeding lights of the expressway. At the first traffic lights, when I glanced at her, she smiled at me reassuringly. Vaughan sat like a bored gangster behind her, his left knee leaning against her thigh. One hand rubbed his groin absent-mindedly. He stared at the nape of her neck, running his eyes along the profiles of her cheek and shoulder. That Catherine should choose Vaughan, whose manic style summed up everything she found most unnerving, struck me as perfectly logical. The multiple car-crash we had seen had sprung the same traps in her mind as in mine.

At the north-west airport entrance I turned the car into the service area. On this peninsula between the perimeter fence and the access roads to Western Avenue was an encampment of car-hire firms, all-night cafeterias, air-freight offices and filling stations. The evening air was crossed by the navigation lights of airliners and maintenance vehicles, by the thousands of headlamps flowing along Western Avenue and the flyover. The jarring light across Catherine's face made her seem part of this midsummer nightmare, true creature of the electric air.

A line of cars waited their turn to pass through the automatic car-wash. In the darkness the three nylon rollers drummed against the sides and roof of a taxi parked in the washing station, water and soap solution jetting from the metal gantries. Fifty yards away, the two night attendants sat in their glass cubicle beside the deserted fuel pumps, reading their comic books and playing a transistor radio. I watched the rollers sweeping across the taxi. Hidden inside the cabin as the soapy water sluiced across the windows, the off-duty driver and his wife were invisible and mysterious mannequins.

The car ahead advanced a few yards. Its brake-lights illuminated the interior of the Lincoln, covering us with a pink sheen. Through the driving mirror I saw that Catherine was leaning against the rear seat. Her shoulder was pressed tightly into Vaughan's. Her eyes were fixed on Vaughan's chest, at the scars around his injured nipples shining like points of light.

I edged the Lincoln forward a few feet. Behind me lay a block of darkness and silence, a condensed universe. Vaughan's hand moved across a surface. I went through the pretence of withdrawing the car's radio aerial. The accident below the flyover, in a position almost symmetrically opposite to my own, and the thudding of the rollers had preempted my responses. The possibilities of a new violence, even more exciting for only touching my mind rather than my nerve endings, was reflected in the deformed sheen of the chromium window pillar beside my wrist, the dented panels of the Lincoln's hood. I thought of Catherine's past infidelities, liaisons always visualized in my mind but never observed.

An attendant left the pay-box and walked to the cigarette machine beside the lubrication bay. His reflection in the wet concrete merged with the lights of the cars passing along the expressway. The water jetted from the metal gantry across the car in front of us. The soap stream hit the bonnet and windshield, hiding two air hostesses and a steward in its liquid glaze.

When I turned around I saw that Vaughan was holding in his cupped hand my wife's right breast.

* * *

I eased the car forward into the empty bay, concentrating on the controls. The last liquid dripped from the stationary rollers in front of me. I wound down my window and searched in my pockets for the coins. The plump meridian of Catherine's breast jutted forwards in Vaughan's hand, the nipple inflated between his fingers as if about to feed a platoon of eager male mouths, the lips of countless lesbian secretaries. He stroked the nipple gently, brushing the supernumerary nipples, no larger than delicious warts, with the ball of his thumb. Catherine looked down at this breast with rapt eyes, as if seeing it for the first time, fascinated by its unique geometry.

Our car was alone in the washing bay. Around us the forecourt was deserted. Catherine lay back with her legs apart, her mouth raised to Vaughan, who touched it with his lips, laying each scar in turn against her mouth. I felt that this act was a ritual devoid of ordinary sexuality, a stylized encounter between two bodies which recapitulated their sense of motion and collision. Vaughan's postures, the way in which he held his arms as he moved my wife across the seat, lifting her left knee so that his body was in the fork between her thighs, reminded me of the driver of a complex vehicle, a gymnastic ballet celebrating a new technology. His hands explored the back of her thighs in a slow rhythm, holding her buttocks and lifting her exposed pubis towards his scarred mouth without touching it. He was arranging her body in a series of positions, carefully searching the codes of her limbs and musculature. Catherine seemed still only half aware of Vaughan, holding his penis in her left hand and sliding her fingers towards his anus as if performing an act divorced from all feeling. She touched his chest and shoulders with her right hand, exploring the patterns of scars on his skin, handholds which his crashes had designed specifically for this sexual act.

A voice shouted. Cigarette in hand, one of the attendants was standing in the wet darkness, beckoning to me like the flight commander of an aircraft carrier. I inserted my coins in the pay slot and closed the window. Water jetted on to the car, clouding the windows and shutting us into its interior, lit only by the lights from the instrument panel. Within this blue grotto Vaughan lay diagonally across the rear seat. Catherine knelt across him, skirt rolled around her waist, holding his penis in both hands, her mouth no more than an inch away from his. The distant headlamps, refracted through the soap solution jetting across the windows, covered their bodies with a luminescent glow, like two semi-metallic human beings of the distant future making love in a chromium bower. The gantry engine began to drum. The rollers pounded across the bonnet of the Lincoln and roared forwards to the windshield, driving the soap solution into a whirlwind of froth. Thousands of bubbles burst across the windows. As the rollers drummed against the roof and doors, Vaughan began to drive his pelvis upwards, almost lifting his buttocks off the seat. With clumsy hands Catherine settled her vulva over his penis. In the mounting roar of the rollers around us she and Vaughan rocked together, Vaughan holding her breasts with his palms as if trying to force them into a single globe. At his orgasm Catherine's gasps were drowned by the roar of the car-wash.

The gantry retreated to its start position. The machine switched itself out of circuit. The rollers hung limply in front of the clear glass of the windshield. The last of the detergent-stained water ran through the darkness to the drainage vents. Sucking at the air through his scarred lips, Vaughan lay back exhausted, staring at Catherine with confused eyes. He watched her raise her cramped left thigh, a movement I remembered her making a hundred times with me. Her breasts were bruised by Vaughan's fingers, the marks forming a pattern like crash injuries. I wanted to reach out and care for them, helping them into their next sexual act, steering her nipples into Vaughan's mouth, guiding his penis into her small rectum, along the guidelines provided by the diagonal seat vents that pointed towards her perineum. I wanted to adjust the contours of her breasts and hips to the roofline of the car, celebrating in this sexual act the marriage of their bodies with this benign technology.

I opened the window and inserted more coins into the cash meter. As the water jetted on to the streaming panes

Vaughan and my wife began to make love again. Catherine held his shoulders, staring at his face with possessive eyes, a dishevelled lover. She brushed her blonde hair from her cheeks, eager to get to Vaughan's body again. Vaughan laid her against the rear seat, opened her thighs and began to stroke her pubis, his middle finger searching for her anus. He leaned towards her on one hip, placing Catherine and himself in the postures of the injured diplomat and the young woman whom we had seen sitting together in the cabin of the crashed limousine. He lifted her on to him, pressing his penis frontally into her vagina, one hand under her right armpit, the other below her buttock, in the same handholds that the ambulance men had used to lift the young woman from the car.

As the rollers drummed over our heads Catherine looked into my eyes in a moment of complete lucidity. Her expression showed both irony and affection, an acceptance of a sexual logic we both recognized and had prepared ourselves for. I sat quietly in the front seat as the white soap sluiced across the roof and doors like liquid lace. Behind me, Vaughan's semen glistened on my wife's breasts and abdomen. The rollers drummed and battered at the car; the streams of water and soap solution jetted over its now immaculate body. Each time the machine completed its cycle I wound down my window and pushed more coins into the pay slot. The two attendants watched us from their glass kiosk, the faint music of the transistor radio sounding into the night air as the gantry returned to its start position.

Catherine cried out, a gasp of pain cut off by Vaughan's strong hand across her mouth. He sat back with her legs across his hips, slapping her with one hand as the other forced his flaccid penis into her vagina. His face was clamped in an expression of anger and distress. Sweat poured from his neck and chest, soaking the waist-band of his trousers. The blows from his hand raised blunted weals on Catherine's arms and hips. Exhausted by Vaughan, Catherine hung to the rear seat behind his head. As his penis jerked emptily into her bruised vulva, Vaughan sank back against the seat. Already he had lost interest in the whimpering young woman pulling herself into her clothes. His scarred hands explcred the worn fabric of the seat, marking in semen a cryptic diagram: some astrological sign or road intersection.

As we drove away from the car-wash, the rollers dripped silently in the darkness. Around the car an immense pocl of white bubbles subsided into the wet concrete.

18

NO TRAFFIC MOVED along the expressway. For the first time since my release from hospital the streets were empty, as if the exhausted sexual acts between Vaughan and Catherine had banished these vehicles for ever. As I drove towards our apartment house in Drayton Park the street-lamps illuminated Vaughan's sleeping face in the rear of the car, scarred mouth lying open like a child's against the sweat-soaked seat. His face seemed drained of all aggressiveness, as if the semen he had voided into Catherine's vulva had carried with it his sense of crisis.

Catherine sat forward, freeing herself from Vaughan. She touched my shoulder in a gesture of domestic affection. In the driving mirror I saw the weals on her cheek and neck, the bruised mouth that deformed her nervous smile. These disfigurements marked the elements of her real beauty.

When we reached the apartment house Vaughan was still asleep. Catherine and I stood in the darkness beside the immaculate car, its polished hood like a black shield. I took Catherine's arm to steady her, holding her bag in my hand. As we walked towards the entrance across the worn gravel Vaughan pulled himself from the rear seat. Without looking back at us he climbed unsteadily behind the steering wheel. I expected him to drive off in a roar of noise, but he started the engine and slipped away silently.

In the elevator I held Catherine closely, loving her for the blows Vaughan had struck her body. Later that night, I explored her body and bruises, feeling them gently with my lips and cheeks, seeing in the rash of raw skin across her abdomen the forcing geometry of Vaughan's powerful physique. My penis traced the raw symbols that his hands and mouth had left across her skin. I knelt over her as she lay diagonally across the bed, her small feet resting on my pillow, one hand over her right breast. She watched me with a calm and affectionate gaze as I touched her body with the head of my penis, marking out the contact points of the imaginary automobile accidents which Vaughan had placed on her body.

The next morning, I drove to the studios at Shepperton, revelling in the movement of the traffic around me, free at last to enjoy the lanes of speeding vehicles. Along the elegant motion sculpture of the concrete highway the coloured carapaces of the thousands of cars moved like the welcoming centaurs of some Arcadian land.

Vaughan was already waiting for me in the studio car-park, the Lincoln parked in my own space. The scars on his abdomen shone in the morning sunlight, a few inches from my fingers as they rested on the door-sill. A white areole of dried vaginal mucus circled the vent of his jeans, marking where my wife's vulva had pressed against his groin.

Vaughan opened the driver's door of the Lincoln for me. As I took my seat behind the steering wheel I realized that I now wanted to spend as much time as possible with him. He sat facing me, one arm along the seat behind my head, his heavy penis pointing towards me in the crotch of his jeans. I now felt the elements of a true affection for Vaughan, elements of jealousy, love and pride. I wanted to touch his body, holding his thigh as we drove in the same way that I had held Catherine's when we first met, letting my hand rest on his hip as we walked to and from the car.

As I turned the ignition switch, Vaughan said, 'Seagrave has gone.'

'Where? They've finished the crash sequence here.'

'God only knows. He's driving around in a wig and leopard-skin coat. He may start following Catherine.'

I abandoned my office. On that first day we drove for hours along the motorways in search of Seagrave, listening to the police and ambulance broadcasts on Vaughan's VHF radio. Vaughan listened to the accident reports, readying his cameras in the rear seat.

As the evening light lay over the last traffic jams of the day Vaughan came completely awake. I drove him to his apartment, a large single-roomed studio on the top floor of a block overlooking the river north of Shepperton. The room was filled with discarded electronic equipment – electric typewriters, a computer terminal, several oscilloscopes, tape recorders and cine-cameras. Bales of electric cable were heaped on the unmade bed. The shelves and walls were packed with scientific textbooks, incomplete runs of technical journals, science-fiction paperbacks and reprints of his own papers. Vaughan had furnished the apartment without any interest – the selection of chromium and vinyl chairs looked as if they had been seized at random from a suburban department-store window.

Above all, the apartment was dominated by Vaughan's evident narcissism – the walls of the studio, bathroom and kitchen were covered with photographs of himself, stills from his television programmes, half-plate prints from newspaper photographers, polaroid snapshots of himself on location, enjoying the attentions of the make-up lady, gesturing at the producer for the photographer's benefit. All these photographs dated back to the time before Vaughan's accident, as if the subsequent years marked a temporal no-zone, a period whose urgencies went beyond vanity. Yet, as he moved around the apartment, taking a shower and changing his clothes, Vaughan was self-consciously absorbed in these fading images, straightening their curling corners as if frightened that when they finally vanished his own identity would also cease to matter.

I saw this attempt at tagging himself, to fix his identity by marking it upon some external event, as we drove along the expressways that evening. Listening to his radio, Vaughan lay in the front passenger seat beside me, lighting the first of his cigarettes. The fresh scent of his well-showered body was overlaid, first, by the smell of hash and then by the tang of Vaughan's semen moistening the crotch of his trousers as we passed the first of the automobile crashes. As I drove the car through the network of back streets to the next accident site, my head invaded by the burning resin, I thought of Vaughan's body in the bathroom at his apartment, the powerful hose of his penis jutting from his hard groin. The scars on his knees and thighs were like miniature rungs, handholds on this ladder of desperate excitements.

By the early hours of the morning we had seen three car-crashes. Inside my fuddled head I assumed that we were still trying to track down Seagrave, but I knew that Vaughan had lost interest in the stunt-driver. After the third of these crashes, when the police and ambulance attendants had left, and the last all-night truck driver had returned to his vehicle, Vaughan finished his cigarette and walked unsteadily across the oil-slick concrete to the motorway embankment. A heavy saloon car driven by a middle-aged woman dentist had skidded through the railings and overturned in the abandoned allotment garden below. I followed Vaughan and watched from the ruptured balustrade as he climbed down to the now upended car. Vaughan walked through the knee-deep grass around the car, and picked up a piece of white chalk discarded by the police. With his hands he felt the sharp edges of the fractured glass and metalwork, pressing against the crushed roof and hood panels. Resting for a moment, he urinated in the darkness against the still warm radiator grille, sending a cloud of vapour into the night air. He stared down at his half-erect penis, looking back at me in a muddled way as if asking me to help him identify this strange organ. He placed it against the right-hand front wing of the car, and with the chalk drew its outline on the black cellulose. He inspected this thoughtfully and, satisfied, moved around the car, marking the profile of his penis on the doors and fractured windows, on the trunk lid and rear fender. Carrying his penis in his hand to shield it from the sharp metal, Vaughan climbed into the front seat and began to draw the outline of his penis against the instrument panel and centre arm-rest, marking out the erotic focus of a crash or sex act, celebrating the marriage of his own genitalia and the skull-shattered dashboard binnacle against which this middle-aged woman dentist had died.

For Vaughan the smallest styling details contained an organic life as meaningful as the limbs and sense organs of the human beings who drove these vehicles. He would stop me at traffic lights and stare for minutes at the junction of a wiper-blade mounting and windshield assembly in a parked car. The body contours of American saloons and European sports cars, with their subordination of function to gesture, delighted Vaughan. We would follow a new Buick or Ferrari for half an hour, as he studied every detail of body trim and rear deck moulding. Several times we were stopped by police for hanging about a parked Lamborghini owned by a well-to-do Shepperton publican as Vaughan obsessively photographed the exact rake of the windshield pillars, the jut of a headlamp visor, the flare of a wheel housing. He was obsessed with the design of chromium accents on fender louvres, stainless-steel body-sill mouldings, windshield-wiper cowl panels, hood locks and door latches.

He would saunter through the parking lots of the Western Avenue supermarkets as if strolling around a beach colony, fascinated by the high-rise fenders of a Corvette being reversed out by a young housewife. The front and rear air spoilers plunged Vaughan into a trance of recognition, as if he were seeing again some paradise bird. Often, as we drove along the motorways, Vaughan gestured me across the lane marker lines, positioning the Lincoln so that the exact profile of a passing coupé roofline shone in the speeding sunlight in front of us, savouring the perfect proportions of an abbreviated rear deck assembly. The equations between the styling of a motor-car and the organic elements of his body Vaughan mimed continually in his own behaviour. Following an Italian concept car with truncated rear fenders Vaughan's gestures towards the airport whore sitting between us became stylized and exaggerated, mystifying this bored woman with his surging talk and shoulder movements.

For Vaughan, the colour-keyed interiors of the Lincoln and the other cars which he began to steal for an hour or so each evening exactly simulated the skin areas of the young whores whom he undressed as I drove along the darkened expressways. Their bare thighs modulated the panels of pastel vinyl; the deep-cone speakers recapitulated the contours of their sharp breasts.

I saw the interior of the motor-car as a kaleidoscope of illuminated pieces of the bodies of women. This anthology of wrists and elbow, thigh and pubis formed ever-changing marriages with the contours of the automobile. Once Vaughan and I drove along the perimeter highway to the south of the airport; I held the car carefully on the apex of the high-cambered surface, celebrating with Vaughan the exposed breast of a schoolgirl he had accosted near the studios. The two of us isolated the perfect geometry of this white pear drawn from her tunic in the motion of the car along the curved road surface.

Vaughan's body, with its unsavoury skin and greasy pallor, took on a hard, mutilated beauty within the elaborately signalled landscape of the motorway. The concrete buttresses along the base of the Western Avenue overpass, angular shoulders spaced at fifty-yard intervals, brought together the sections of Vaughan's scarred physique.

During the many weeks in which I acted as Vaughan's chauffeur, giving him money to pay the prostitutes and part-time whores who hung about the airport and its hotels, I watched Vaughan explore every byway of sex and the automobile. For Vaughan the motor-car was the sexual act's greatest and only true locus. With each of these women Vaughan explored a different sex act, inserting his penis in vagina, anus and mouth almost in reponse to the road along which we moved, the traffic density, the style of my driving.

At the same time it seemed to me that Vaughan was selecting certain sexual acts and positions in his mind for future use, the maximum sex act within the automobile. The clear equation he had made between sex and the kinaesthetics of the highway was in some way related to his obsessions with Elizabeth Taylor. Did he visualize himself in a sexual act with her, dying together in some complex car-crash? During the mornings and early afternoons he followed her from her hotel to the film studios. I did not tell him that our negotiations to feature the actress in our projected automobile commercial had fallen through. Vaughan's hands moved through small contortions as he waited for her to appear, fretting around the rear seat, almost as if his body was unconsciously miming in fast motion hundreds of acts of intercourse with her. I realized that he was assembling in disjointed form the elements of a conceptual sexual act involving the actress and the route she would take from the studios at Shepperton. His self-conscious gestures, the grotesque way in which he hung his arm out of the car, as if about to unscrew it and toss the bloody limb under the wheels of the car following us, the rictus of his mouth as he framed his lips around a nipple, seemed to be private rehearsals for a terrifying drama unfolding in his mind, the sex act he saw as the climax of his own death-collision.

During these last weeks Vaughan was determined to touch with his own sexuality the places of a secret itinerary, mapping with his semen the corridors of this future drama. Gradually, we came nearer to an open confrontation with the police. During the rush-hour one evening, Vaughan signalled me to wait at green traffic lights, deliberately blocking the line of cars behind us. Headlamps flashing, a police car pulled alongside us, the co-driver assuming from Vaughan's contorted position that we had been involved in a major accident. Covering the face of the girl beside him, a teenage supermarket cashier, Vaughan held himself in the posture of the injured ambassador we had seen taken from his crashed limousine. At the last moment, as the policeman stepped from his car, I ignored Vaughan's protest and accelerated forwards.

Tired of the Lincoln, Vaughan borrowed other cars from the airport parking lots, using a set of trade pass-keys which Vera Seagrave had given him. We let ourselves in and out of these day-parked vehicles, whose owners were in Paris, Stuttgart or Amsterdam, driving them back to their parking places in the evening when we had finished with them. By this time I was unable to rally myself and make an effort to stop Vaughan. As obsessed with his hard body as he himself was with the bodies of automobiles, I found myself locked into a system of beckoning violence and excitement, made up of the motorway and traffic jams, the cars we stole and Vaughan's discharging sexuality.

During this last period with Vaughan I saw that the women he brought to the car each evening had begun to resemble more and more closely the colouring and figure of the film actress. The dark-haired schoolgirl resembled the young Elizabeth Taylor, while the other women represented her at successively older stages.

19

VAUGHAN, GABRIELLE AND myself visited the motor show at Earls Court. Calm and gallant, Vaughan steered Gabrielle through the crowd, parading his scarred face as if these wounds were a sympathetic response to Gabrielle's crippled legs. Gabrielle swung herself among the hundreds of cars displayed on their stands, their chromium and cellulosed bodies gleaming like the coronation armour of an archangelic host. Pivoting about on her heels, Gabrielle seemed to take immense pleasure from these immaculate vehicles, placing her scarred hands on their paintwork, rolling her injured hips against them like an unpleasant cat. She provoked a young salesman on the Mercedes stand to ask her to inspect a white sports car, relishing his embarrassment when he helped her shackled legs into the front seat. Vaughan whistled in admiration at this.

We moved through the stands and revolving cars, Gabrielle heeling and toeing herself among the motor industry executives and show-girls. My eyes were fixed on her leg brace, on her deformed thighs and knees, her swinging left shoulder, these portions of her body that seemed to beckon towards the immaculate machines on their revolving stands, inviting them to confront her wounds. As she climbed into the cabin of a small Japanese sedan her bland eyes saw my uninjured body in the same glaucous light as these geometrically perfect machines. Vaughan guided her from one car to the next, helping her on to the stands, into the cockpits of styling department exercises, specialist concept cars, carriage-trade limousines in whose rear seats she sat like the hostile queen of this overactive technarchy.

‘Walk with Gabrielle, Ballard,’ Vaughan urged me. ‘Hold her arm. She’d like you to.’

Vaughan encouraged me to take his place. When he slipped away, on the pretext that he had seen Seagrave, I helped Gabrielle to inspect a succession of invalid cars. I talked in over-formal terms to the demonstrators about the installation of auxiliary controls, brake treadles and hand-operated clutch levers. All the while I stared at those parts of Gabrielle’s body reflected in this nightmare technology of cripple controls. I watched her thighs shifting against each other, the jut of her left breast under the strap of her spinal harness, the angular bowl of her pelvis, the hard pressure of her hand on my arm. She gazed back at me through the windshield, playing with the chromium clutch treadle as if hoping that something obscene might happen.

Gabrielle showed no hostility to Vaughan for this, but it was I who first made love to her, in the rear seat of her small car, surrounded by the bizarre geometry of the invalid controls. As I explored her body, feeling my way among the braces and straps of her underwear, the unfamiliar planes of her hips and legs steered me into unique culs-de-sac, strange declensions of skin and musculature. Each of her deformities became a potent metaphor for the excitements of a new violence. Her body, with its angular contours, its unexpected junctions of mucous membrane and hairline, detrusor muscle and erectile tissue, was a ripening anthology of perverse possibilities. As I sat with her by the airport fence in her darkened car, her white breast in my hand lit by the ascending airliners, the shape and tenderness of her nipple seemed to rape my fingers. Our sexual acts were exploratory ordeals.

As she drove towards the airport I watched her handle the unfamiliar controls. The complex of inverted treadles and clutch levers of the car had been designed for her – implicitly, I guessed, for her first sexual act. Twenty minutes later, as I embraced her, the scent of her body mingled with the showroom odour of mustard leatherette. We had turned off near the reservoirs to watch the aircraft landing. As I pressed her left shoulder against my chest I could see the contoured seat which had been moulded around her body, hemispheres of padded leather that matched the depressions of her brace and backstraps. I slipped my hand around her right breast, already colliding with the strange geometry of the car's interior. Unexpected controls jutted from beneath the steering wheel. A cluster of chromium treadles was fastened to a steel pivot clamped to the steering column. An extension on the floor-mounted gear lever rose laterally, giving way to a vertical wing of chromium metal moulded into the reverse of a driver's palm.

Aware of these new parameters, the embrace of this dutiful technology, Gabrielle lay back. Her intelligent eyes followed her hand as it felt my face and chin, as if searching for my own missing armatures of bright chromium. She lifted her left foot so that the leg brace rested against my knee. In the inner surface of her thigh the straps formed marked depressions, troughs of reddened skin hollowed out in the forms of buckles and clasps. As I unshackled the left leg brace and ran my fingers along the deep buckle groove, the corrugated skin felt hot and tender, more exciting than the membrane of a vagina. This depraved orifice, the invagination of a sexual organ still in the embryonic stages of its evolution, reminded me of the small wounds on my own body, which still carried the contours of the instrument panel and controls. I felt this depression on her thigh, the groove worn below her breast under her right armpit by the spinal brace, the red marking on the inside of her right upper arm – these were the templates for new genital organs, the moulds of sexual possibilities yet to be created in a hundred experimental car-crashes. Behind my right arm the unfamiliar contours of the seat pressed against my skin as I slipped my hand towards the cleft between her buttocks. The interior of the car was in shadow, concealing Gabrielle's face, and I avoided her mouth as she lay back against the head-rest. I lifted her breast in my palm and began to kiss the cold nipple, from which a sweet odour rose, a blend of my own mucus and some pleasant pharmaceutical compound. I let my tongue rest against the lengthening teat, and then moved away and examined the breast carefully. For some reason I had expected it to be a detachable latex structure, fitted on each morning along with her spinal brace and leg supports, and I felt vaguely disappointed that it should be made of her own flesh. Gabrielle was sitting forward against my shoulder, a forefinger feeling the inside of my lower lip, her nail against my teeth. The exposed portions of her body were joined together by the loosened braces and straps. I played with her bony pubis, feeling through the scanty hair over her crotch. As she sat passively in my arms, lips moving in a minimal response, I realized this bored and crippled young woman found that the nominal junction points of the sexual act – breast and penis, anus and vulva, nipple and clitoris – failed to provide any excitement for us.

Through the fading afternoon light the airliners moved across our heads along the east-west runways of the airport. The pleasant surgical odour from Gabrielle's body, the tang of the mustard leatherette, hung in the air. The chromium controls reared in the shadows like the heads of silver snakes, the fauna of a metal dream. Gabrielle placed a drop of spit on my right nipple and stroked it mechanically, keeping up the small pretence of this nominal sexual link. In return, I stroked her pubis, feeling for the inert nub of her clitoris. Around us the silver controls of the car seemed a *tour de force* of technology and kinaesthetic systems. Gabrielle's hand moved across my chest. Her fingers found the small scars below my left collar bone, the imprint of the outer quadrant of the instrument binnacle. As she began to explore this circular crevice with her lips I for the first time felt my penis thickening. She took it from my trousers, then began to explore the other wound-scars on my chest and abdomen, running the tip of her tongue into each one. In turn, one by one, she endorsed each of these signatures, inscribed on my body by the dashboard and control surfaces of my car. As she stroked my penis I moved my hand from her pubis to the scars on her thighs, feeling the tender causeways driven through her flesh by the handbrake of the car in which she had crashed. My right arm held her shoulders, feeling the impress of the contoured leather, the meeting points of hemispherical and rectilinear geometries. I explored the scars on her thighs and arms, feeling for the wound areas under her left breast, as she in turn explored mine, deciphering together these codes of a sexuality made possible by our two car-crashes.

My first orgasm, within the deep wound on her thigh, jolted my semen along this channel, irrigating its corrugated ditch. Holding the semen in her hand, she wiped it against the silver controls of the clutch treadle. My mouth was fastened on the scar below her left breast, exploring its sickle-shaped trough. Gabrielle turned in her seat, revolving her body around me, so that I could explore the wounds of her right hip. For the first time I felt no trace of pity for this crippled woman, but celebrated with her the excitements of these abstract vents let into her body by sections of her own automobile. During the next few days my orgasms took place within the scars below her breast and within her left armpit, in the wounds on her neck and shoulder, in these sexual apertures formed by fragmenting windshield louvres and dashboard dials in a high-speed impact, marrying through my own penis the car in which I had crashed and the car in which Gabrielle had met her near-death.

I dreamed of other accidents that might enlarge this repertory of orifices, relating them to more elements of the automobile's engineering, to the ever-more complex technologies of the future. What wounds would create the sexual possibilities of the invisible technologies of thermonuclear reaction chambers, white-tiled control rooms, the mysterious scenarios of computer circuitry? As I embraced Gabrielle I visualized, as Vaughan had taught me, the accidents that might involve the famous and beautiful, the wounds upon which erotic fantasies might be erected, the extraordinary sexual acts celebrating the possibilities of unimagined technologies. In these fantasies I was able at last to visualize those deaths and injuries I had always feared. I visualized my wife injured in a high-impact collision, her mouth and face destroyed, and a new and exciting orifice opened in her perineum by the splintering steering column, neither vagina nor rectum, an orifice we could dress with all our deepest affections. I visualized the injuries of film actresses and television personalities, whose bodies would flower into dozens of auxiliary orifices, points of sexual conjunction with their audiences formed by the swerving technology of the automobile. I visualized the body of my own mother, at various stages of her life, injured in a succession of accidents, fitted with orifices of ever greater abstraction and ingenuity, so that my incest with her might become more and more cerebral, allowing me at last to come to terms with her embraces and postures. I visualized the fantasies of contented paedophiliacs, hiring the deformed bodies of children injured in crashes, assuaging and irrigating their wounds with their own scarred genital organs, of elderly pederasts easing their tongues into the simulated anuses of colostomized juveniles.

Every aspect of Catherine at this time seemed a model of something else, endlessly extending the possibilities of her body and personality. As she stepped naked across the floor of the bathroom, pushing past me with a look of nervous distraction; as she masturbated in the bed beside me in the mornings, thighs splayed symmetrically, fingers grovelling at her pubis as if rolling to death some small venereal snot; as she sprayed deodorant into her armpits, those tender fossas like mysterious universes; as she walked with me to my car, fingers playing amiably across my left shoulder – all these acts and emotions were ciphers searching for their meaning among the hard, chromium furniture of our minds. A car-crash in which she would die was the one event which would release the codes waiting within her. Lying in bed beside Catherine, I would slide my hand into the natal cleft between her buttocks, lifting and moulding each of these white hemispheres, these plenums of the flesh that contained all the programmes of dreams and genocides.

I began to think about Catherine's death in a more calculated way, trying to devise in my mind an even richer exit than the death which Vaughan had designed for Elizabeth Taylor. These fantasies were part of the affectionate responses exchanged between us as we drove along the motorway together.

20

BY THIS TIME I was certain that if the screen actress never died in a car-crash, Vaughan had created all the possibilities of her death. From these hundreds of miles and sexual acts, Vaughan was selecting certain needed elements: a section of the Western Avenue flyover, examined through my own accident and the death of Helen Remington's husband, marked in a sexual notation by an act of oral copulation with a seventeen-year-old schoolgirl; the off-side fender of a black American limousine, marked by the pressure of Catherine's arm against the left door-sill and celebrated by the sustained erection of a middle-aged prostitute's nipple; the actress herself stepping from her car and stumbling briefly against the half-open window, her grimace recorded by Vaughan through the zoom lens of his cine-camera; elements of accelerating cars, changing traffic lights, swaying breasts, varying road surfaces, clitorises held gently like botanical specimens between thumb and forefinger, the stylization of a thousand actions and postures as he drove – together these were stored in Vaughan's mind, ready to be recalled and fitted into whatever weapon of assassination he devised. Vaughan questioned me repeatedly about the actress's sexual life, about which I knew nothing, urging me to enlist Catherine in a literature search of defunct movie magazines. Many of his sexual acts were clearly models for what he imagined her own to be within the automobile.

However, Vaughan had already worked out the imaginary sexual acts within the automobile of a host of famous personalities – politicians, Nobel prizewinners, international athletes, astronauts and criminals – just as he had already conceived their deaths. As we strolled together through the airport parking lots, searching for a car to borrow, Vaughan would cross-examine me about the ways in which Marilyn Monroe or Lee Harvey Oswald would probably have had intercourse in their cars, Armstrong, Warhol, Raquel Welch . . . their choice of vehicle and model year, their postures and favourite erogenous zones, the freeways and autostradas of Europe and North America along which they moved in Vaughan's mind, their bodies funded by their limitless sexualities, love, tenderness and eroticism.

'. . . Monroe masturbating, or Oswald, say – left- or right-handed, which would you guess? And what instrument panels? Was orgasm reached more quickly with a recessed or overhanging binnacle? Vinyl colour-contouring, windshield glass, these are factors. Garbo and Dietrich, there's a place for the gerontological approach. The special involvement of at least two of the Kennedys with the automobile . . .' Always he deliberately side-stepped into self-parody.

However, during my last days with Vaughan his obsessions with the crashed car became increasingly disordered. His fixation on the screen actress and the sex-death he had devised for her seemed to make him all the more frustrated when this hoped-for death failed to occur. Instead of driving along the motorway we sat in a deserted parking lot behind my apartment house in Drayton Park, watching the leaves of the plane trees carried through the falling light across the wet macadam. For hours Vaughan listened to the police and ambulance broadcasts, his long body fretting as he flicked at the overloaded ashtray, stuffed with reefer stubs and an old sanitary tampon. Caring for him, I wanted to stroke his scarred thighs and abdomen, offering him the automobile injuries carried by my own body in place of those imaginary wounds he wished upon the actress.

The crash that I most feared – after Vaughan's own death, already a coming reality in my mind – took place on the Harlington clearway three days later. As the first garbled references to the multiple injuries of the screen actress,

Elizabeth Taylor, were made on the police broadcasts, and cancelled shortly afterwards, I knew whose death-ordeal we were about to witness.

Vaughan sat patiently beside me as I pushed the Lincoln westwards to the accident site. He stared with resigned eyes at the white façades of the plastics factories and tyre warehouses along the clearway. He listened to the details of the three-vehicle collision on the police frequency, steadily turning up the volume as if wanting to hear the final confirmation broadcast at full crescendo.

We reached the accident site at Harlington half an hour later, and parked on the grass verge below the overpass. Three cars had collided in the centre of a high-speed intersection. The first two vehicles – a customized fibreglass sports car and a silver Mercedes coupé – had struck each other in a right-angle collision, ripping away their nearside wheels and crushing their engine compartments. The fibreglass sports car, an anthology of every bulbous and fin-shaped motif of the 1950s, had then been hit in the rear by a chauffeur-driven government saloon. Shaken but uninjured, the young woman driver in her green uniform was helped from her vehicle, which had buried its bonnet in the rear end of the sports car. Sections of tattered fibreglass lay around the crushed fuselage, like discarded styling exercises in a designer's studio.

The driver of the sports car lay dead in his cockpit, as two firemen and a police constable worked to free him from the buckled overhang of the instrument panel. The woman's leopard-skin coat which he was wearing had been torn back to expose his crushed chest, but his white platinum hair was still neatly held together by a nylon hair-net. On the seat beside him, like a dead cat, lay a black wig. Seagrave's slim and exhausted face was covered with shattered safety glass, as if his body were already crystallizing, at last escaping out of this uneasy set of dimensions into a more beautiful universe.

Only five or six feet away from him, the woman driver of the silver Mercedes coupé lay sideways across her seat below the broken windshield. The crowd of spectators pressed around and over the two cars, almost toppling the ambulance men trying to lift the woman from her crushed driving compartment. From a policeman pushing past with a blanket I heard her name, that of a former television presenter, several years past her bloom but still an occasional performer on panel games and late-night talk shows. As she was propped into a half-sitting position I recognized her face, pallid and drained now like an old woman's. A lacework of dried blood hung from her chin, forming a dark bib. As she was placed on a stretcher, the spectators stared respectfully at the injuries to her thighs and lower abdomen, making way for her when she was carried to the ambulance.

Two women in headscarves and tweed coats were pushed aside. Arms outstretched, Vaughan plunged between them. His eyes seemed to be out of focus. He seized one of the handles already held by an attendant, and swept along with it to the ambulance. The woman was lifted into the back of the vehicle, breathing jerkily through the crust of blood over her nose. I nearly shouted to the police, convinced from the agitated way in which Vaughan bent over the recumbent woman that he was about to draw his penis and use it to free her blood-filled mouth passage. Assuming from his overwrought state that Vaughan was some kind of relative, the attendants stood back for him, but a policeman who recognized Vaughan punched him in the chest with the palm of his hand and shouted to him to move along.

Vaughan hovered around the closing doors, ignoring the constable, then made off through the crowd in a sudden swerve, his bearings lost for the moment. He forced his way to the crushed fibreglass sports car and looked down uncertainly at Seagrave's body, dressed in its coronation armour of fractured glass, a suit of lights like a dead matador's. His hands gripped the windshield pillar.

Confused and shaken by the stunt-man's death and the tags of the film actress's clothing – themselves the props of a calculated collision – still lying around the car, I followed Vaughan through the spectators. He wandered blankly around the silver Mercedes, eyes fixed on the bloodstains smeared across the seat and instrument panel, examining every piece of the strange litter that had materialized from nowhere after the crash. His hands made small movements through the air, marking out the trajectories of the internal impacts within the car as Seagrave struck it, the mechanical moments of the second collision between this minor television personality and her instrument panel.

Later, I realized what had most upset Vaughan. This was not Seagrave's death, but that in his collision, still wearing Elizabeth Taylor's wig and costume, Seagrave had pre-empted that real death which Vaughan had reserved for himself. In his mind, from that accident onwards, the film actress had already died. All that remained now for Vaughan was to constitute the formalities of time and place, the entrances of her flesh to a wedding with himself already celebrated across the bloody altar of Seagrave's car.

We walked back to the Lincoln. Vaughan opened the passenger door, staring at me as if he had never seen me clearly before.

'Ashford Hospital.' He motioned me on. 'They'll take Seagrave there when they've cut him loose.'

'Vaughan . . .' I tried to think of some means of calming him. I wanted to touch his thigh, press the knuckles of my left hand against his mouth. 'You've got to tell Vera.'

'Who?' Vaughan's eyes cleared momentarily. 'Vera – she knows already.'

He drew from his pocket a grimy square of silk scarf. He spread it carefully on the seat between us. Lying in the centre was a triangle of bloodstained grey leather, the drying blood still a bright carmine. Experimentally, Vaughan touched the blood with his fingertips, brought it up to his mouth and tasted the tacky fragments. He had cut the piece from the front seat of the Mercedes, where the blood from the woman's abdominal wounds had flowed between her legs.

Mesmerized, Vaughan stared at the fragment, prodding the stitched vinyl inlay that traversed the triangle from its apex. It lay between us like a saintly relic, the fragment of a hand or shinbone. For Vaughan this piece of leather, as delicious and as poignant as the stains on the gusset of a shroud, contained all the special magic and healing powers of a modern martyr of the super-highways. These precious square inches had pressed against the vulva of the dying woman, stained with the blood that had flowed from her wounded genital orifice.

I waited for Vaughan at the entrance to the hospital. He ran towards the casualty department, ignoring the shout of a passing attendant. I sat in the car outside the gates, wondering if Vaughan had been waiting here with his camera when my own injured body was brought in. At this moment the injured woman was probably dying, her blood pressure falling, organs heavy with uncirculated fluid, a thousand stagnant arterial deltas forming an ocean bar that blocked the rivers of her bloodstream. I visualized her lying on a metal bed in the emergency ward, her bloodied face and shattered nasal bridge like the mask worn at an obscene halloween, the initiation rite into one's own death. I visualized the graphs that recorded the falling temperatures of her rectum and vagina, the steepening gradients of nerve function, the last curtains of her dying brain.

Along the pavement a traffic policeman walked towards the car, clearly recognizing the Lincoln. When he saw me behind the wheel he moved on, but for a moment I had relished being identified with Vaughan and the uncertain images of crime and violence that were forming in the eyes of the police. I thought of the crashed cars at the collision site, of Seagrave dying during a last acid trip. In the moment of her collision with this deranged stunt-driver the television actress celebrated her last performance, marrying her body with the stylized contours of the instrument panel and windshield, her elegant posture with the violent conjunctions of colliding door panels and bulkheads. I visualized the accident filmed in slow motion, like the simulated collisions we had seen at the Road Research Laboratory. I saw the actress colliding with her instrument panel, the steering column buckling under the weight of her heavy-breasted thorax; her slim hands, familiar from a hundred panel games, feinting with the razor-sharp louvres of the ashtray and instrument clusters; her self-immersed face, idealized in a hundred close-ups, three-quarter profile lit by the most flattering light densities, striking the upper rim of the steering wheel; her nasal bridge crushed, upper incisors driven back through her gums into her soft palate. Her mutilation and death became a coronation of her image at the hands of a colliding technology, a celebration of her individual limbs and facial planes, gestures and skin tones. Each of the spectators at the accident site would carry away an image of the violent transformation of this woman, of the complex of wounds that fused together her own sexuality and the hard technology of the automobile. Each of them would join his own imagination, the tender membranes of his mucous surfaces, his groves of erectile tissue, to the wounds of this minor actress through the medium of his own motor-car, touching them as he drove in a medley of stylized postures. Each would place his lips on those bleeding apertures, lay his own nasal septum against the lesions of her left hand, press his eyelids against the exposed tendon of her forefinger, the dorsal surface of his erect penis against the ruptured lateral walls of her vagina. The automobile crash had made possible the final and longed-for union of the actress and the members of her audience.

This last period with Vaughan is inseparable in my mind from the excitement I felt as I thought about these imaginary deaths, the exhilaration of being close to Vaughan and wholly accepting his logic. Curiously, Vaughan remained subdued and depressed, indifferent to his success in converting me into an eager disciple. As we ate lunch in a motorway cafeteria he fed his scarred mouth with amphetamine tablets, but these stimulants only touched him later in the day, when he recovered slightly. Was Vaughan losing his resolve? Already I felt the dominant partner in our relationship. Without needing any instruction from Vaughan, I listened to the police and ambulance frequencies, propelling the heavy car up and down the access roads in pursuit of the latest vehicle pile-up and collision.

Our behaviour together became increasingly stylized, as if we were some skilled partnership of surgeons, jugglers or comedians. Far from reacting with horror or revulsion now at the sight of these injured victims, sitting stunned on the grass beside their cars after an early afternoon fog patch, or pinned against their instrument panels, Vaughan and I felt a sense of professional detachment, in which the first workings of some kind of true involvement were revealed. My horror and disgust at the sight of these appalling injuries had given way to a lucid acceptance that the translation of these injuries in terms of our fantasies and sexual behaviour was the only means of re-invigorating these wounded and dying victims. Early that evening, after seeing a woman driver with severe facial injuries, Vaughan lay for ten minutes with his penis in the mouth of a middle-aged, silver-haired prostitute, almost choking her as she knelt across him. He held her head fiercely in his bands to prevent her from moving, until the spit dribbled from her mouth like a tap. Driving slowly around the darkening streets of the housing estates to the south of the airport, I watched over my shoulder as Vaughan moved this woman around the rear seat, steering her with his strong thighs. All his violence and anger had returned. After his orgasm the woman slumped against the seat. She let the semen drip on to the damp vinyl below Vaughan's testicles, gasping for breath as she wiped away the flecks of vomit from his penis. Staring at her face as she replaced her spilled bag, I saw the wounded face of the injured woman driver irrigated with Vaughan's semen. On the seat, and on Vaughan's thighs, on the hands of this middle-aged prostitute, the semen glimmered in opalescent drops, their colour changing from red to amber and green in the rhythm of the traffic lights, reflecting the thousands of lights in the night air as we sped along the expressway, the harsh phosphorescent tubes of the lamp standards, and the huge corona of light that hung over the airport. As I looked at the evening sky it seemed as if Vaughan's semen bathed the entire landscape, powering these thousands of engines, electric circuits and private destinies, irrigating the smallest gestures of our lives.

It was during this evening that I noticed the first of Vaughan's self-inflicted wounds. At a Western Avenue filling station he deliberately trapped his hand in the door of the car, mimicking the injuries to the arm of a young hotel receptionist involved in a side-swipe collision in the car-park of her hotel. Vaughan picked repeatedly at the scabs running across his knuckles. The scars on his knees, healed now for more than a year, were beginning to re-open. The points of blood seeped through the worn fabric of his jeans. Red flecks appeared on the lower curvature of the dashboard locker, on the lower rim of the radio console, and marked the black vinyl of the doors. Vaughan encouraged me to drive faster than the airport access roads allowed. When I braked sharply at the intersections he deliberately let himself slide against the instrument panel. Blood mingled with the dried semen on the seats, marking my own hands with dark points as I turned the wheel. His face was whiter than I had ever seen it, and he moved in bursts of exhausted nervousness around the cabin of the car, like an uncomfortable animal. This hyper-irritation reminded me of my own long recovery from a bad acid trip some years earlier, when I had felt for months afterwards as if a vent of hell had opened momentarily in my mind, as if the membranes of my brain had been exposed in some appalling crash.

21

MY LAST MEETING with Vaughan – the climax of a long punitive expedition into my own nervous system – took place a week later in the mezzanine lounge of the Oceanic Terminal. In retrospect, it seems ironic that this house of glass, of flight and possibility, should have been the departure point for our own lives and deaths. As he walked towards me through the chromium chairs and tables, his reflection multiplied in the glass wall-panels, Vaughan had never appeared more derelict and uncertain. His pock-marked face and haggard shamble through the passengers waiting for their flight-calls together gave him the look of an unsuccessful fanatic, doggedly holding together his spent obsessions.

He stood beside me at the bar when I rose to greet him, barely bothering to recognize me, as if I were some unfamiliar blur. His hands fretted at the bar, searching for a control surface, the points of fresh blood on his knuckles catching the light. During the previous six days I had waited restlessly in my office and apartment, watching the motorways through the windows, running down the elevator staircase whenever I thought that I had seen his car speeding past. I scrutinized the gossip columns of newspapers and film-trade magazines, trying to guess which screen star or political celebrity Vaughan might be following, assembling the elements of imaginary accidents in his mind. All the experiences of our weeks together had left me in a state of increasing violence, which I knew only Vaughan could resolve. In my fantasies, as I made love to Catherine, I saw myself in an act of sodomy with Vaughan, as if only this act could solve the codes of a deviant technology.

Vaughan waited as I ordered a drink for him, staring across

the runways at an airliner lifting into the air over the western perimeter of the airfield. He had telephoned me that morning, his voice barely recognizable, and suggested that we meet at the airport. Seeing him again, tracing the outlines of his buttocks and thighs in his worn trousers, the scars around his mouth and below his jaw angle, filled me with a hard, erotic excitement.

'Vaughan . . .' I tried to press the cocktail into his hands. He nodded without arguing. 'Try to sip it. Do you want some breakfast?'

Vaughan made no effort to touch the cocktail. He stared at me with his uncertain eyes, like a marksman calculating the distance of a target. He picked up a water jug, holding the sliding fluid between his hands. When he filled a dirty glass on the counter and drank thirstily, I realized that he was moving into the opening stages of an acid high. He was squeezing and flexing the palms of his hands, wiping his scarred mouth with his fingertips. I waited as he climbed these first gradients of excitation and alarm, eyes roving around the glass-enclosed mezzanine as he picked from the air the first motes of fused light and movement.

We walked to his car, double-parked alongside an airline coach. A few paces ahead of me, Vaughan moved like an over-careful dream-walker. He stared at different pieces of the sky, experiencing – as I myself remembered only too well – the first of those premonitory light changes that turn a brilliant summer noon into a leaden winter evening within the space of a second. Sitting in the passenger seat of the Lincoln, Vaughan eased his shoulders into the upholstery, as if laying out his wounds. He watched me fumble with the ignition, a faint smile mocking me for all the eagerness I had shown in pursuing him, and yet accepting now his own failure and my authority over him.

As I started the engine Vaughan laid his bandaged palm across my thigh. Surprised by this physical contact between us, I thought at first that Vaughan was trying to reassure me. He lifted his hand to my mouth, and I saw the dented silver cube in his fingers. I unwrapped the foil and placed the sugar cube on my tongue.

We left the airport through the exit tunnel, crossed Western Avenue and ascended the upward ramp of the interchange. For twenty minutes I drove along the Northolt expressway, holding the car in the centre lane and letting the faster traffic overtake us on either side. Vaughan lay back, right cheek resting against the cool seat, his arms limply at his sides. Now and then his hands contracted, arms and legs flexing involuntarily. Already I could feel the first effects of the acid. My palms felt cool and tender; wings were about to grow from them and lift me into the speeding air. An icy nimbus was gathering around the roof of my skull, like the clouds that form in the hangars of spacecraft. I had taken an acid trip two years earlier, a paranoid nightmare during which I had let a Trojan horse into my mind. As Catherine tried helplessly to calm me she had appeared in my eyes as a hostile and predatory bird. I had felt my brains sliding on to the pillow through the hole she had pecked in my skull. I remembered crying like a child and hanging from her arm, begging her not to leave me as my body shrank to a naked membrane.

With Vaughan, by contrast, I felt at ease, confident of his affection for me, as if he were deliberately guiding me along this expressway which he had created for me alone. The other cars passing us were present through an enormous act of courtesy on his part. At the same time, I was sure that everything around me, the growing extension of the LSD through my body, was part of some ironic intention of Vaughan's, as if the excitement suffusing my mind hovered between hostility and affection, emotions which had become interchangeable.

We joined the fast westward sweep of the outer circular motorway. I moved the car into the slow lane as we turned around the central drum of the interchange, accelerating when we gained the open deck of the motorway, traffic speeding past us. Everywhere the perspectives had changed. The concrete walls of the slip road reared over us like luminous cliffs. The marker lines diving and turning formed a maze of white snakes, writhing as they carried the wheels of the cars crossing their backs, as delighted as dolphins.

The overhead route signs loomed above us like generous dive-bombers. I pressed my palms against the rim of the steering wheel, pushing the car unaided through the golden air. Two airport coaches and a truck overtook us, their revolving wheels almost motionless, as if these vehicles were pieces of stage scenery suspended from the sky. Looking around, I had the impression that all the cars on the highway were stationary, the spinning earth racing beneath them to create an illusion of movement. The bones of my forearms formed a solid coupling with the shift of the steering column, and I felt the smallest tremors of the road-wheels magnified a hundred times, so that we traversed each grain of gravel or cement like the surface of a small asteroid. The murmur of the transmission system reverberated through my legs and spine, echoing off the plates of my skull as if I myself were lying in the transmission tunnel of the car, my hands taking the torque of the crankshaft, my legs spinning to propel the vehicle forwards.

The daylight above the motorway grew brighter, an intense desert air. The white concrete became a curving bone. Waves of anxiety enveloped the car like pools of heat off summer macadam. Looking down at Vaughan, I tried to master this nervous spasm. The cars overtaking us were now being super-heated by the sunlight, and I was sure that their metal bodies were only a fraction of a degree below their melting points, held together by the force of my own vision, and that the slightest shift of my attention to the steering wheel would burst the metal films that held them together and break these blocks of boiling steel across our path. By contrast, the oncoming cars were carrying huge cargoes of cool light, floats loaded with electric flowers being transported to a festival. As their speeds increased I found myself drawn into the fast lane, so that the oncoming vehicles were moving almost straight towards us, enormous carousels of accelerating light. Their radiator grilles formed mysterious emblems, racing alphabets that unravelled at high speed across the road surface.

Exhausted by the effort of concentrating on the traffic and holding the cars around us in their lanes, I took my hands off the wheel and let the car press on. In a long and elegant swerve the Lincoln crossed the fast lane. The tyres roared against the concrete verge, lashing the windshield with a storm of dust. I lay back helplessly, my body exhausted. In front of me I saw Vaughan's hand on the wheel. He sat across me, one knee up on the instrument panel, steering the car within inches of the central reservation. An oncoming truck sped towards us in the adjacent fast lane. Vaughan removed his hand from the wheel and gestured towards it, suggesting that I drive the Lincoln across the central reservation and straight into the truck.

Distracted by Vaughan's physical presence as he leaned against me, I held the wheel again, steering the car down the fast lane. Vaughan's body was a collection of loosely coupled planes. The elements of his musculature and personality were suspended a few millimetres apart, floating beside me in this pressure-free zone like the contents of an astronaut's capsule. I watched the cars approaching us, unable to grasp more than a fraction of the thousands of messages which their wheels and headlamps, windshields and radiator grilles were flashing at me.

I remembered my first journey home from Ashford Hospital after my accident. The brightness of the traffic, the nervous perspectives of the motorway embankments and the vehicle lanes along Western Avenue, had anticipated this acid vision, as if my wounds had flowered into these paradisial creatures, celebrating the unity of my crash and this metallized Elysium. As Vaughan urged me again to crash the car into the vehicles approaching us, I was tempted to obey him, making no effort to answer the teasing pressure of his hand. An airline coach sped towards us, its silver hull irradiating all six lanes of the motorway, bearing down on us like an alighting archangel.

I held Vaughan's wrist in my hand. The dark hairs of his pallid forearm, the scar tissue on the knuckles of his ring and index fingers, were now irrigated with a harsh beauty. Taking my eyes off the road, I clasped Vaughan's hand in my own, trying to close my eyes to the fountain of light that poured through the windshield of the car from the vehicles approaching us.

An armada of angelic creatures, each surrounded by an immense corona of light, was landing on the motorway on either side of us, sweeping down in opposite directions. They soared past, a few feet above the ground, landing everywhere on these endless runways that covered the landscape. I realized that all these roads and expressways had been built by us unknowingly for their reception.

Leaning across me, Vaughan steered the car through the flight paths. As we changed direction, horns and tyres screamed around us. Vaughan controlled the wheel, like a parent guiding an exhausted child. I held the rim passively in my hands, following the pathway of the car down a slip road.

We stopped below an overpass, the front fender of the Lincoln rolling on to the concrete palisade that divided the motorway embankment from the edge of an abandoned wrecker's yard. I listened to the last music of the engine before I switched off the ignition, and lay back in my seat. In the screen of the rear-view mirror I watched the cars climbing the access ramp on to the motorway behind us, eager arrivals at this aerial carnival. They sailed along the road surface above our heads to join the aircraft Vaughan had watched for so many months. As I gazed at the distant causeways of the northern circular motorway I could see that everywhere these metallized creatures were soaring through the sunlight, ascending from the traffic jams that had locked them together.

Around me the interior of the car glowed like a magician's bower, the light within the compartment becoming darker and brighter as I moved my eyes. The instrument dials irradiated my skin with their luminous needles and numerals. The carapace of the instrument binnacle, the inclined planes of the dashboard panel, the metal sills of the radio and ashtrays gleamed around me like altarpieces, their geometries reaching towards my body like the stylized embraces of some hyper-cerebral machine.

In the breaker's yard a testudo of abandoned cars lay together in the ever-changing light, their outlines shifting as if some time-wind were blowing across them. Strips of rusting chrome leaked into the overheated air, patches of intact cellulose bled away into the crown of light that covered the yard. The spurs of deformed metal, the triangles of fractured glass, were signals that had lain unread for years in this shabby grass, ciphers translated by Vaughan and myself as we sat with our arms around each other in the centre of the electric storm moving across our retinas.

I stroked Vaughan's shoulder, remembering the terror in which I had clung to my wife. Yet Vaughan, for all his harshness, was a wholly benevolent partner, the eye of this illumination of the landscape around us. Taking his hand, I pressed his palm against the medallion of the horn boss, an aluminized emblem which had always irritated me. I felt the indentation in his white skin, remembering the triton-shaped bruise in the palm of the dead Remington as he lay across my bonnet, remembering the pink grooves in my wife's skin left by her underwear, the imprints of imaginary wounds, as she changed in her department store cubicle, remembering the exciting crevices and sulci of Gabrielle's crippled body. One by one, I moved Vaughan's hand across the glowing dials of the instrument panel, pressing his fingers against the sharp toggles, the projecting lances of the direction indicator and gear shift.

At last I let his hand rest on my penis, reassured by its firm pressure on my testicles. I turned towards Vaughan, floating with him on the warm amnion of illuminated air, encouraged by the stylized morphology of the automobile's interior, by the hundreds of radiant gondolas soaring along the motorway above our heads. As I embraced him, Vaughan's body seemed to slide up and down in my arms, the muscles of his back and buttocks becoming hard and opaque as I felt the changing planes. I held his face in my hands, feeling the porcelain smoothness of his cheeks, and touched with my fingers the scars on his lips and cheeks. Vaughan's skin seemed to be covered with scales of metallic gold as the points of sweat on his arms and neck fired my eyes. I hesitated at finding myself wrestling with this ugly golden creature, made beautiful by its scars and wounds. I moved my mouth across the scars on his lips, feeling with my tongue for those familiar elements of long-vanished dashboards and windshields.

Vaughan loosened his leather jacket, exposing the re-opened wounds that marked his chest and abdomen, a deranged drag queen revealing the leaking scars of an unsuccessful trans-sexual surgery. I lowered my head to his chest, pressing my cheek against the bloody profiles of a collapsing steering wheel, the collision points of an instrument panel. I ran my lips along his left collar-bone, and sucked at his scarred nipple, feeling the re-sectioned areola between my lips. I moved my mouth down his abdomen to his damp groin, marked with blood and semen, a faint odour of a woman's excrement clinging to the shaft of his penis. A zodiac of unforgotten collisions illuminated Vaughan's groin, and one by one I explored these scars with my lips, tasting the blood and urine. With my fingers I touched the scar on his penis, then felt the glans within my mouth. I loosened Vaughan's bloodstained trousers. His naked buttocks were like a pubertal youth's, as unscarred as a child's. The nerves in my legs and arms began to jump with irritation, my limbs flexing themselves in a series of nervous spasms. I crouched behind Vaughan, forcing his thighs against my own. The jutting carapace of the instrument binnacle presided over the dark cleft between his buttocks. With my right hand I parted his buttocks, feeling for the hot vent of his anus. For several minutes, as the cabin walls glowed and shifted, as if trying to take up the deformed geometry of the crashed cars outside, I laid my penis at the mouth of his rectum. His anus opened around the head of my penis, settling itself around the shaft, his hard detrusor muscles gripping my glans. As I moved in and out of his rectum the light-borne vehicles soaring along the motorway drew the semen from my testicles. After my orgasm I lifted myself slowly from Vaughan, holding his buttocks apart with my hands so as not to injure his rectum. Still parting his buttocks, I watched my semen leak from his anus across the fluted ribbing of the vinyl upholstery.

Sitting together, we were washed by the light flowing in every direction across the landscape. I held my arm around Vaughan as he slept, watching as the fountain pouring from the radiator grilles of the crashed cars twenty yards away gradually faded. A profound sense of calm presided over my body, composed partly of my love for Vaughan, and partly of my feelings of tenderness towards the metal bower in which we sat. When Vaughan woke, exhausted and still half asleep, he leaned his naked body against me. His face was pallid, eyes exploring the contours of my arms and chest. Together we showed our wounds to each other, exposing the scars on our chests and hands to the beckoning injury sites on the interior of the car, to the pointed sills of the chromium ashtrays, to the lights of a distant intersection. In our wounds we celebrated the re-birth of the traffic-slain dead, the deaths and injuries of those we had seen dying by the roadside and the imaginary wounds and postures of the millions yet to die.

22

FLIES CRAWLED ACROSS the oil-smeared windshield, vibrating against the glass. The chains of their bodies formed a blue veil between myself and the traffic moving along the motorway. I turned on the windshield wipers, but the blades swept through the flies without disturbing them. Vaughan lay back on the seat beside me, trousers open around his knees. The flies crawled in thick clumps across his blood-smeared chest, festering on his pallid stomach. They formed an apron of pubic hair that reached from his limp testicles to the scars along his diaphragm. The flies covered Vaughan's face, hovering around his mouth and nostrils as if waiting for the rancid liquors distilled from the body of a corpse. Vaughan's eyes were open and alive, watching me as his head lay against the seat with a calm gaze. I tried to brush the flies from his face, thinking that they must irritate him, and saw that my hands and arms, the interior of the car, were covered with the insects.

The steering wheel and instrument panel were alive with this retinal horde. Ignoring Vaughan's raised hand, I opened the driver's door. Vaughan tried to stop me. His exhausted face was raised in a warning gesture, a rictus of alarm and concern, as if frightened of what I might find in the open air. I stepped on to the roadway, mechanically brushing these motes of optical irritation from my hands and arms. I had entered an abandoned world. The stones in the road surface cut unevenly into the soles of my shoes, discarded there after the passage of a hurricane. The concrete walls of the overpass were drained and grey, like the entrance to a hypogeum. The cars moving in a desultory way along the road above me had shed their cargoes of light, and clattered down the highway like the dented instruments of a fugitive orchestra.

But as I turned, the sunlight against the concrete walls of the overpass formed a cube of intense light, almost as if the stony surface had become incandescent. I was sure that the white ramp was a section of Vaughan's body, and that I was one of the flies crawling across him. Afraid to move for fear of burning myself against this luminous surface, I put my hands on the roof of my skull, holding the soft brain tissue in place.

Abruptly, the light faded. Vaughan's car sank into the darkness below the bridge. Everything had become drab again. The air and light were exhausted. I stepped into the road, moving away from the car, aware of Vaughan's uncertain arm reaching for me. I walked along the palisade to the weed-grown entrance of the breaker's yard. Above me, the cars on the motorway moved like motorized wrecks, paintwork worn and blunted. Their drivers sat stiffly behind their wheels, overtaking the airline coaches filled with mannequins dressed in meaningless clothing.

An abandoned car, its engine and wheels removed, sat on its axles in a layby below the overpass. I opened the door on its rusting hinges. A confetti of fragmented glass covered the front passenger seat. For the next hour I sat there, waiting for the acid to wear its way through my nervous system. Crouching over the mud-streaked instrument panel of this hollow wreck, I tightened my knees against my chest wall, flexing the muscles of my calves and arms, trying to squeeze the last micro-drops of this insane irritant from my body.

The termites had gone. The light changes became less frequent, and the air over the motorway steadied itself. The last silver and golden sprays sank back into the deserted wrecks in the breaker's yard. The distant motorway embankments resumed their blurred outlines. Irritable and exhausted, I pushed back the door and stepped from the car. The nodes of glass scattered on the ground glinted like pieces of discredited coinage.

An engine started with a roar. As I stepped into the road from the layby I was briefly aware of a heavy black vehicle accelerating towards me from the shadow of the overpass where Vaughan and I had lain together. Its white-walled tyres tore through the broken beer bottles and cigarette packs in the gutter, mounted the narrow kerb and hurtled on towards me. Knowing now that Vaughan would not stop for me, I pressed myself against the concrete wall of the layby. The Lincoln swerved after me, its right-hand front fender striking the rear wheel housing of the abandoned car in which I had sat. It swung away, ripping the open passenger door from its hinges. A column of exploding dust and torn newspaper rose into the air as it slid sideways across the access road. Vaughan's bloodied hands whirled at the steering wheel. The Lincoln re-mounted the kerb on the far side of the access road. It crushed a ten-yard section of the wooden palisade. The rear wheels regained their traction on the road surface and the car swung away on to the motor road above.

I walked to the abandoned car and leaned against the roof. The passenger door had been crushed into the front fender, the deformed metal welded together by the impact. Thinking of Vaughan's scar-tissue, fused together in the same way along these arbitrary seams, contours of sudden violence, I retched emptily over a pool of acid mucus. As the Lincoln crushed the palisade Vaughan had looked back, his hard eyes calculating if he could make a second pass at me. Shreds of torn paper eddied through the air around me, pasting themselves at various points against the crushed door panels and radiator hood.

23

GLASS AEROPLANES CLIMBED into the sky above the airport. Through the brittle air I watched the traffic move along the motorway. The memories of the beautiful vehicles I had seen soaring down the concrete lanes transformed these once-oppressive jams and tail-backs into an endless illuminated queue, patiently waiting for some invisible slip road into the sky. From the balcony of my apartment I gazed across the landscape below, trying to find this paradisial incline, a mile-wide gradient supported on the shoulders of two archangelic figures, on to which all the traffic in the world might flow.

In these strange days, as I recovered from my acid trip and my near-death afterwards, I remained at home with Catherine. Sitting here, my hands in a familiar grip on the arms of the chair, I watched the metallized plain below for any sign of Vaughan. The traffic moved sluggishly along the crowded concrete lanes, the roofs of the vehicles forming a continuous carapace of polished cellulose. The after-effects of the LSD had left me in a state of almost disturbing calm. I felt detached from my own body, as if my musculature were suspended a few millimetres from the armature of bones, the two joined together only by the few wound points which had been alerted when I flexed my legs and arms during the acid trip. For days afterwards segments of the experience returned intact, and I would see the cars on the motorway wearing their coronation armour, soaring along the causeways on wings of fire. The pedestrians in the streets below wore their suits of lights, as if I were a solitary visitor in a city of matadors. Catherine would move behind me like some electric nymph, a devotional creature guarding my gestures of excitement with her calm presence.

At less happy moments the sluggish delirium and queasy perspectives of the grey overpass would return, the damp hypogeum at whose mouth I had seen the thousands of flies festering on the instrument panel of the car, on Vaughan's buttocks as he lay back watching me with his trousers around his knees. Terrified by these brief re-enactments, I held Catherine's hands as she pressed my shoulders, trying to convince myself that I was sitting with her by a sealed window in my own apartment. Often I asked her what period of the year it was. The light changes within my retina moved the seasons without warning.

One morning, when Catherine had left me alone to take her last flying lesson, I saw her aircraft above the motorway, a glass dragonfly carried by the sun. It seemed to hang motionlessly over my head, the propeller rotating slowly like a toy aircraft's. The light poured from its wings in a ceaseless fountain.

Below her, the cars soaring along the motorway marked on the plain of the landscape all the possible trajectories of her flight, laying down the blueprints of our coming passage through heaven, the transits of a technology with wings. I thought of Vaughan, covered with flies like a resurrected corpse, watching me with a mixture of irony and affection. I knew that Vaughan could never really die in a car-crash, but would in some way be re-born through those twisted radiator grilles and cascading windshield glass. I thought of the scarred white skin over his abdomen, the heavy pubic hair that started on the upper slopes of his thighs, his tacky navel and unsavoury armpits, his crude handling of women and automobiles, and his submissive tenderness towards myself. Even as I had placed my penis in his rectum Vaughan had known he would try to kill me, in a final display of his casual love for me.

Catherine's car sat in the drive below the bedroom window. The paintwork along the left-hand side had been marked in some minor collision.

'Your car – ?' I held her shoulders. 'Are you all right?'

She leaned against me, as if memorializing the image of this collision into our body pressures. She took off her flying jacket. Both of us had now made our separate love to Vaughan.

'I wasn't driving – I'd left the car in the parking lot at the airport.' She reached out and held my elbows in her hands. 'Could it have been deliberate?'

'One of your suitors?'

'One of my suitors.'

She must have been frightened by this meaningless assault on the car, but she watched me examine it with a calm gaze. I felt the abrasions on the left-hand door and body panels, and explored with my hand the deep trench that ran the full length of the car from the crushed tail-light to the front headlamp. The imprint of the other car's heavy front bumper was clearly marked on the rear wheel guard, the unmistakable signature of Vaughan's Lincoln. I felt the curved groove, as clear as the rounded cleft between Vaughan's hard buttocks, as well-formed as the tight annulus of his anus which I could still feel on my penis during my erections.

Had Vaughan deliberately followed Catherine, striking her parked car in a first gesture of courtship? I looked at her pale skin and firm body, thinking of Vaughan's car hurtling towards me among the concrete pillars of the overpass. Like Seagrave, I would have died in an acid death-out.

I opened the passenger door, beckoning Catherine into the seat.

'Let me drive – the light is clear now.'

'Your hands. Are you ready yet?'

'Catherine – ' I took her arm. 'I need to drive again before it all goes.'

She held her bare arms across her breasts, and peered into the interior of her car, as if searching for the flies which I had described to her.

I wanted to show her to Vaughan.

I started the engine and turned out of the courtyard. As I accelerated, the perspectives of the street swerved around me, leaning away from me as if streamlining themselves. Near the supermarket, a young woman in a plastic coat glowed with cerise light as she crossed the road. The motion of the car, its attitude and geometry, had undergone a marked transformation, as if they had been purged of all accretions of the familiar and sentimental. The surrounding street furniture, the shop-fronts and passers-by were illuminated by the motion of the car, the intensity of the light they emitted regulated by the passage of the vehicle I was driving. At the traffic lights I looked across the seat at Catherine. She sat with one hand on the window-sill. The colours of her face and arms revealed themselves in their clearest and richest forms, as if each blood cell and pigment granule, the cartileges of her face, were real for the first time, assembled by the movement of this car. The skin of her cheeks, the indicator signs guiding us on to the motorway, the cars parked on the roof of the supermarket, were clarified and defined, as if some immense deluge had at last receded, leaving everything isolated for the first time, like the features of a lunar landscape, a still-life arranged by a demolition squad.

We drove southwards along the motorway.

'The traffic – where is everyone?' I realized that the three lanes were almost deserted. 'They've all gone away.'

'I'd like to go back – James!'

'Not yet – it's only beginning . . .'

I thought of this image of an empty city, with an abandoned technology left to its own devices, as we drove down the access road where Vaughan had tried to kill me a few days earlier. In the waste lot beyond the damaged palisade the group of abandoned cars lay in the blanched light. I drove past the scarred concrete abutment towards the dark cavern of the overpass, where Vaughan and I had embraced each other among the concrete pillars, listening to the traffic drumming overhead. Catherine gazed up at the cathedral-like vaults of the overpass, like a succession of empty submarine pens. I stopped the car and turned towards her. Without thinking, I took up the posture in which I had sodomized Vaughan. I looked down at my own thighs and abdomen, visualizing Vaughan's buttocks lifted high against my hips, remembering the tacky texture of his anus. By some paradox, this sex act between us had been devoid of all sexuality.

All that afternoon we drove along the expressways. The endless highway systems along which we moved contained the formulas for an infinity of sexual bliss. I watched the cars leaving the flyover. Each of them carried on its roof a piece of the sun.

'Are you looking for Vaughan?' Catherine asked.

'In a manner of speaking.'

'You're no longer frightened of him.'

'Are you?'

'He's going to kill himself.'

'I knew that after Seagrave died.'

I watched her staring at the traffic sweeping down the flyover towards us as we waited on a slip road below Western Avenue. I wanted Vaughan to see her. Thinking of the long dents that scarred the side of Catherine's car, I wanted to expose them to Vaughan, encouraging him to take Catherine again.

At a concourse filling station we saw Vera Seagrave talking to a girl at the pumps. I turned into the forecourt. Vera's strong-hipped body, with its hard-working breasts and buttocks, was dressed in a heavy leather jacket, as if she were about to leave on an Antarctic expedition.

At first she failed to recognize me. Her firm eyes cut across me to Catherine's elegant figure, as if suspicious of her cross-legged posture in the open cockpit of the sports car with its lacerated bodywork.

'Are you leaving?' I pointed to the suitcases in the rear seat of Vera's car. 'I'm trying to find Vaughan.'

Vera finished her questioning of the girl attendant, completing some arrangement for the boarding of her small son. Still staring at Catherine, she stepped into her car.

'He's following his film actress. The police are after him – an American serviceman was killed on the Northolt overpass.'

I put my hand on the windshield, but she switched on the windshield wipers, almost cutting the knuckle of my wrist. Explaining everything, she said: 'I was with him in the car.'

Before I could stop her she had moved towards the exit and turned into the fast evening traffic.

Catherine telephoned me from her office the next morning to say that Vaughan had followed her to the airport. As she spoke in her calm tones I carried the telephone to the window. Watching the cars edge along the motorway, I felt my penis stiffening. Somewhere below me, among those thousands of vehicles, Vaughan was waiting at an intersection.

'He's probably looking for me,' I told her.

'I've seen him twice – this morning he was waiting for me in the entrance to the car-park.'

'What did you say?'

'Nothing. I'll get in touch with the police.'

'No, don't.'

Talking to her, I found myself slipping into the same erotic reverie in which I sometimes used to question Catherine about the flight instructor she lunched with, drawing one detail after another about some small amorous encounter, a brief act of intercourse. I visualized Vaughan waiting for her at quiet intersections, following her through car-washes and traffic detours, moving ever closer to an intense erotic junction. The drab streets were illuminated by the passage of their bodies during this exquisitely prolonged mating ritual.

Unable to stay any longer in the apartment while this courtship was taking place, I drove my car to the airport. From the roof of the multi-storey car-park next to the air-freight building I waited for Vaughan to appear.

As I expected, Vaughan was waiting for Catherine at the junction of Western Avenue and the flyover. He made no attempt to conceal himself from either of us, pushing his heavy car bluntly into the passing traffic stream. Apparently uninterested in Catherine or myself, Vaughan lay against his door-sill, almost asleep at the wheel as he surged forward when the lights changed. His left hand drummed across the rim of the steering wheel, as if reading the road's braille in its rapid tremors. Following these rippling contours inside his head, he swerved the Lincoln to and fro across the road surface. His heavy face was fixed in a rigid mask, his scarred cheeks clamped rigidly around his mouth. He cut in and out of the traffic lanes, surging ahead in the fast lane until he was abreast of Catherine and then sliding back behind her, allowing other cars to cut between them and then taking up a watchful position in the slow lane. He began to mimic Catherine's driving, her trim shoulders and high chin, her incessant use of the brake pedal. Their harmonized brake-lights moved down the expressway like the dialogue of a long-married couple.

I sped along behind them, flashing my headlamps at any cars in my way. We reached the ramp of the flyover. As Catherine climbed the ramp, forced to slow down behind a line of fuel tankers, Vaughan accelerated sharply, turning left at the junction. I raced after him, winding through the round-abouts and intersections which the flyover spanned. We jumped a set of traffic lights as the airport traffic closed towards us. Somewhere over our heads Catherine moved along the open deck of the flyover.

Vaughan cut through the afternoon traffic, throwing on his brakes at the last moment, rolling his car on to its off-side wheels as he circled the roundabouts at speed. A hundred yards behind him, I raced down the straight towards the descent ramp. Vaughan stopped at the junction, waiting as the fuel tankers thundered past. As Catherine's small sports car appeared he surged forward.

Swerving after him, I waited for Vaughan to collide with Catherine. His car moved forward across the marker lines on a collision course. But at the last moment he pulled away, fading across the traffic stream behind her. He lost himself beyond the roundabout on the northward carriageway. Watching him, as I struggled to catch up with Catherine, I had a last glimpse of a battered front fender, cracked headlamps flashing at a bullish truck-driver.

Half an hour later, in the basement garage of my apart-ment house, I felt with my hand the imprint of Vaughan's car in the body panels of Catherine's sports car, the rehearsal-marks of a death.

These rehearsals for a union between Vaughan and Catherine continued during the following days. Twice Vera Seagrave telephoned me to ask if I had seen Vaughan, but I insisted that I had not left the apartment. She told me that the police had removed Vaughan's photographs and equipment from the dark-room at her house. Astonishingly, they seemed unable to catch Vaughan.

Catherine never referred to Vaughan's pursuit of her. Between us we now maintained an ironic calm, the same stylized affection we showed to each other at parties whenever she or I was openly taking another lover. Did she understand Vaughan's real motives? At the time, even I failed to realize that she was merely a stand-in during an elaborate rehearsal for another and far more important death.

Day by day Vaughan followed Catherine around the expressways and airport perimeter roads, sometimes waiting for her in the damp cul-de-sac adjacent to our drive, at other times appearing like a spectre in the high-speed lane of the overpass, his battered car tilted over on its near-side springs. I watched him waiting for her at various intersections, clearly testing in his mind the possibilities of different accident modes: head-on collisions, side-impacts, rear-end collisions, roll-over. During this time I felt a gathering euphoria, the surrender to an inevitable logic that I had once resisted, as if I were watching my own daughter in the early stages of a burgeoning love affair.

Often I would stand on the grass verge of the embankment by the western descent ramp of the flyover, knowing that this was Vaughan's favourite zone, and watch him lunge forward after Catherine as she swept by in the evening rush hour.

Vaughan's car was becoming increasingly battered. The right-hand fender and doors were marked with impact points scored deep into the metal, a rusting fretwork that turned more and more white, as if revealing a skeleton below.

Waiting behind him in a traffic jam on the Northolt expressway, I saw that two of the rear windows had been broken.

Further damage continued. A body panel detached itself from the off-side rear wheel housing and the front bumper hung from the chassis pinion, its rusting lower curvature touching the ground as Vaughan cornered.

Hidden behind his dusty windshield, Vaughan sat hunched over his steering wheel as he travelled at speed along the motorway, unaware of his car's dents and impacts, like the self-inflicted wounds of a distressed child.

Still uncertain whether Vaughan would try to crash his car into Catherine's, I made no attempt to warn her. Her death would be a model of my care for all the victims of air-crashes and natural disasters. As I lay beside Catherine at night, my hands modelling her breasts, I visualized her body in contact with various points of the Lincoln's interior, rehearsing for Vaughan the postures she might assume. Aware of this coming collision, Catherine had entered an entranced room within her mind. Passively, she allowed me to move her limbs into the positions of unexplored sex acts.

As Catherine slept, a battered car moved below us along the deserted avenue. The total stillness of the streets below made the entire city seem deserted. In that brief lull before dawn when no aircraft took off from the airport the only sound we could hear was the kicking exhaust box of Vaughan's car. From the kitchen window I saw Vaughan's grey face, leaning against the cracked quarter window, marked by a deep weal that crossed his forehead like a bright leather band. For a moment I felt that all the aircraft he had watched rising from the airport had now left. After Catherine and I had gone he would be finally alone, marauding the empty city in his derelict car.

Uncertain whether to wake Catherine, I waited for half an hour, and then dressed and went down to the forecourt. Vaughan's car was parked under the trees in the avenue. The dawn light shone bleakly on the dusty paintwork. The seats were covered with oil and grime, and in the rear the remnants of a torn tartan blanket lay across a greasy pillow. I guessed from the broken bottles and food cans on the floor that Vaughan had been living in the car for several days. In an evident burst of anger he had slashed at the instrument panel, bludgeoning several of the dials and the upper lip of the binnacle. Torn plastic housings and chrome strips hung over the light toggles.

The ignition keys hung from the switch. I looked up and down the avenue, trying to see if Vaughan were waiting behind one of the trees. I walked around the car, and pushed the broken body panels into place with my hand. As I worked, the front off-side tyre slowly flattened itself to the ground.

Catherine came down and watched me. We walked through the clearing light to the entrance. As we crossed the gravel a car's engine roared in the garage. A polished silver car, which I recognized immediately as my own, hurtled up the ramp towards us. Catherine cried out, tripping over her feet, but before I could take her arm the car had swerved around us and plunged through the sliding gravel into the street. Through the dawn air its engine sounded a cry of pain.

24

I SAW NO more of Vaughan. Ten days later he died on the flyover as he tried to crash my car into the limousine carrying the film actress whom he had pursued for so long. Trapped within the car after it jumped the rails of the flyover, his body was so disfigured by its impact with the airline coach below that the police first identified it as mine. They telephoned Catherine while I was driving home from the studios at Shepperton. When I turned into the forecourt of my apartment house I saw Catherine pacing in a light-headed way around the rusting hulk of Vaughan's Lincoln. As I took her arm she stared through my face at the dark branches of the trees over my head. For a moment I was certain that she had expected me to be Vaughan, arriving after my death to console her.

We drove towards the flyover in Catherine's car, listening to the news broadcast on the radio of the film actress's escape. We had heard nothing of Vaughan since he had taken my car from the garage. Increasingly I was convinced that Vaughan was a projection of my own fantasies and obsessions, and that in some way I had let him down.

Meanwhile, the Lincoln lay abandoned in the avenue. Without Vaughan's presence, it rapidly disintegrated. As the leaves from the autumn trees settled on the roof and bonnet, sinking through the broken windows into the passenger compartment, the car sank on the flat tyres. Its derelict condition, the loosened body panels and fenders invited the hostility of passers-by. A gang of youths smashed the windshield and kicked in the headlamps.

When we reached the accident site below the flyover I felt

that I was visiting, incognito, the place of my own death. Not far from here, my own accident had taken place in a car identical to the vehicle in which Vaughan had died. A massive tail-back of traffic blocked the flyover, and we left the car in a garage forecourt and walked towards the revolving accident beacons half a mile ahead. A brilliant evening sky lit the entire landscape, exposing the roofs of the cars caught in the hold-up, as if we were all waiting to embark on a voyage into the night. Overhead, the airliners moved like observation planes sent up to supervise the progress of this vast migration.

I watched the people in the cars, peering through their windshields as they adjusted the frequencies of their car radios. I seemed to recognize them all, guests at the latest of an unending series of road parties which we had attended together during the previous summer.

At the accident site, under the high deck of the flyover, at least five hundred people had gathered on every verge and parapet, drawn there by the news that the film actress had narrowly missed her death. How many of the people there assumed that she had already died, taking her place in the pantheon of auto-disaster victims? On the descent ramp of the flyover the spectators stood three deep along the rising balustrade, staring down at the police cars and ambulances at the junction with Western Avenue. The crushed roof of the airline coach rose above the heads.

I held Catherine's arm, thinking of the mock attempts Vaughan had made upon her at this junction. In the glare of the arc-lights my car lay beside the coach. Its wheels were still inflated, but the rest of the car was unrecognizable, as if impacted from all directions, internally and externally. Vaughan had been travelling along the open deck of the flyover at the car's maximum speed, trying to launch himself into the sky.

The last of the passengers was carried from the upper deck of the coach, but the spectators' eyes were fixed, not on these human victims, but on the deformed vehicles at the centre of the stage. Did they see within them the models for their own future lives? The isolated figure of the screen actress stood beside her chauffeur, a hand raised to her neck as if shielding herself from the image of the death she had so narrowly avoided. The police and ambulance men, the crush of spectators squeezing themselves between the parked police cars and ambulances, were careful to leave a clear space around her.

On the roofs of the police cars the warning lights revolved, beckoning more and more passers-by to the accident site, across the recreation grounds from the high-rise apartment blocks in Northolt, from the all-night supermarkets on Western Avenue, from the lines of traffic moving past the flyover. Lit by the arc-lights below, the deck of the flyover formed a proscenium arch visible for miles above the surrounding traffic. Across the deserted side-streets and pedestrian precincts, the concourses of the silent airport, the spectators moved towards this huge stage, drawn there by the logic and beauty of Vaughan's death.

On our last evening, Catherine and I visited the police pound to which the remains of my car had been taken. I collected the gate key from the officer at the station, a sharp-eyed young man whom I had already seen when he had supervised the removal of Vaughan's car from the street outside our apartment house. I was sure that he realized that Vaughan had been planning his attempted crash into the film actress's limousine for many months, assembling the materials of this collision from the stolen cars and the photographs of couples in intercourse.

Catherine and I walked down the lines of seized and abandoned vehicles. The pound was in darkness, lit only by the street-lights reflected in the dented chromium. Sitting together in the rear seat of the Lincoln, Catherine and I made brief, ritual love, her vagina drawing off a small spurt of semen after a short throe, her buttocks held tightly in my hands as she sat across my waist. I made her kneel across me as my hand gathered the semen flowing from her vulva.

Afterwards, the semen in my hand, we walked among the

cars. The beams of small headlamps cut across our knees. An open sports car had stopped beside the gatehouse. Two women sat behind the windshield, peering into the darkness, the driver turning the car until the headlamps illuminated the remains of the dismembered vehicle in which Vaughan had died.

The woman in the passenger seat stepped out and paused briefly by the gates. Watching her from the darkness as Catherine straightened her clothes, I recognized Dr Helen Remington. Gabrielle sat at the controls of the car. That they should be drawn here for a last glimpse of what remained of Vaughan seemed appropriate. I visualized them touring the car-parks and expressways marked in their minds by Vaughan's obsessions, celebrated now in the gentle embraces of this woman doctor and her crippled lover. I was glad that Helen Remington was becoming ever more perverse, finding her happiness in Gabrielle's scars and injuries.

When they had gone, Helen's arm on Gabrielle's shoulder as she reversed away, Catherine and I moved among the cars. I found that I was still carrying the semen in my hand. Reaching through the fractured windshields and passenger windows around me, I marked my semen on the oily instrument panels and binnacles, touching these wound areas at their most deformed points. We stopped at my own car, the remains of its passenger compartment sleek with Vaughan's blood and mucilage. The instrument panel was covered with a black apron of human tissue, as if the blood had been sprayed on with a paint gun. With the semen in my hands I marked the crushed controls and instrument dials, defining for the last time the contours of Vaughan's presence on the seats. The imprint of his buttocks seemed to hover among the creases of these deformed seats. I spread my semen over the seat, and then marked the sharp barb of the steering column, a bloodied lance rising from the deformed instrument panel.

Catherine and I stood back, watching these faint points of liquid glisten in the darkness, the first constellation in the new zodiac of our minds. I held Catherine's arm around my waist as we wandered among the derelict cars, pressing her fingers against the muscles of my stomach wall. Already I knew that I was designing the elements of my own car-crash.

Meanwhile, the traffic moves in an unceasing flow along the flyover. The aircraft rise from the runways of the airport, carrying the remnants of Vaughan's semen to the instrument panels and radiator grilles of a thousand crashing cars, the leg stances of a million passengers.

P.S.

Ideas, interviews & features . . .

About the author

About the book

Read on

The Sage of Shepperton:

A biographical profile

JAMES GRAHAM BALLARD, whose father ran a textile firm in Shanghai, was born in Shanghai General Hospital on 15 November 1930. Following the bombing of Pearl Harbor in 1941 and the Japanese invasion of China, Ballard and his family were interned in a detention camp for three years. Later the basis for his acclaimed autobiographical novel *Empire of the Sun* (1984), this incarceration, along with his formative years in Shanghai, underscores much of Ballard's imaginative output. His first major novel, *The Drowned World* (1962), a vision of London inundated by a primeval swamp, was as much an exorcism of childhood memories of the Yangtze as it was a compelling account of an imminent environmental apocalypse. Similarly many of the leitmotifs in his work – the drained swimming pools, abandoned buildings, wasted landscapes and wrecked cars – can be traced back to Shanghai. 'One of the things I took from my wartime experiences,' he has said, 'was that reality was a stage set . . . the comfortable day-to-day life, school, the home where one lives and all the rest of it . . . could be dismantled overnight.' And our capacity to engender catastrophe and the ease with which the veneer of civilization can slip away have preoccupied Ballard throughout his career.

The Drowned World was followed by two further 'cataclysmic' novels, *The Drought* (1964) and *The Crystal World* (1966), to form what has been described as a loose trilogy. To an extent, Ballard came relatively late to the novel. He initially rose to prominence as an author of short stories for science fiction magazines like *Science Fantasy* and *New Worlds*. He continued to be a prolific story writer and many of the themes, obsessions and even characters subsequently found in his novels often have analogues or first outings in the shorter works. ('Almost all of my novels,' he wrote in 2001, 'were first hinted at in short stories.')

Ballard had begun to write fiction as a medical student at Cambridge. One of his early stories, in his words, a 'Hemingwayesque effort called "The Violent Noon"', was joint winner of the university's annual fiction prize in 1951. The award convinced him to abandon medicine for literature, but the study of anatomy was another invaluable component in Ballard's creative arsenal. ('I do think,' he has maintained, 'that novelists should be like scientists, dissecting the cadaver.') It would, however, be another five years before he had a story accepted for publication.

During that period he attended Queen Mary College in London and worked as an advertising copywriter and sold encyclopedias door to door, before, significantly for his direction as a writer, signing up for a short commission with the RAF. Stationed at a NATO flight-training base in Moose Jaw, Saskatchewan, Canada and hungry for anything to read, Ballard ▶

“'I do think,' Ballard has maintained, 'that novelists should be like scientists, dissecting the cadaver.'”

The Sage of Shepperton

(continued)

◀ fell upon the science fiction magazines in the airbase's cafeteria. At that point, he had read very little science fiction. Although bored by the interplanetary yarns that dominated the field, he immediately responded to the vitality – and possibilities – of the genre. As he told Robert McCrum of the *Observer* in 2006, here was 'a fiction that was about the present day that owed nothing to aping past models . . . a fiction about advertising, the media landscape, television, the threat of nuclear war'.

His first forays into SF, the tales 'Prima Belladonna' and 'Escapement', were published in *Science Fantasy* and *New Worlds* respectively in December 1956. And in his own words, he 'never looked back'. Although many of his stories in the late 1950s fall more easily within conventional science fiction, it is a mark of Ballard's unique take on the form that he met with resistance from many of its devotees. 'Most readers,' he has claimed, 'saw me as an interloper, a sort of virus that had got into the cell of science fiction.' While consistently championing it as 'the authentic literature of the twentieth century', Ballard argued that the true domain of science fiction post-Sputnik was not outer but 'inner' space. This was a cosmos of the unconscious – and far more terrifying for being about the human condition now or nearly now. 'The biggest developments of the immediate future will take place, not on the Moon or Mars, but on Earth,' he maintained in 1962. Adding, memorably, that 'the only truly alien planet is Earth'.

Shortly before that, Ballard's first novel, *The Wind from Nowhere* (1961), had appeared. Written in ten days for £300, it has long been disowned by its author, who dismissed it as 'just a piece of hack work' in 1975. The book, however, has its admirers. The novelist Toby Litt selected it in a round-up of forgotten literary treasures for the *Observer* in 2007. And whatever shortcomings it holds for its creator, the novel is, perhaps, most intriguing for containing elements, including the setting of its opening scene (the Great West Road) and its protagonist's name (Maitland), that reappear in *Crash* (1973) and its near sequel, *Concrete Island* (1974).

It was in a review of the latter that his friend and contemporary Michael Moorcock astutely compared Ballard to a Surrealist painter. He works, Moorcock wrote, 'with a large vocabulary of images that he transmutes and re-uses over and over again to accomplish his various literary intentions, in pursuit of a recognizable range of moral concerns'. The emphasis on Ballard's morality here is far from accidental. Moorcock was writing in the direct aftermath of *Crash*, a novel that remains controversial to this day. But the importance of the visual arts and especially the Surrealists, cited in an author profile for *New Worlds* back in 1956, cannot be stressed enough. One of Ballard's closest friends for many years was the artist Eduardo Paolozzi. And he has said that '*Crash* to ►

❛ SF was 'a fiction that was about the present day that owed nothing to aping past models . . . a fiction about advertising, the media landscape, television, the threat of nuclear war'. ❜

The Sage of Shepperton
(continued)

◀ some extent' was composed 'as a visual experience, marrying elements in the book that make sense primarily as visual constructs'.

Foreshadowing *Crash* though were a series of fragmentary short stories, or 'condensed novels', subsequently collected in *The Atrocity Exhibition* (1971). Produced in the latter half of the 1960s, and mainly published in the literary quarterly *Ambit* and in *New Worlds* (then under Moorcock's stewardship), they marked a noticeable change in direction and a significant darkening in tone. Sex, violence and celebrity were by now Ballard's main preoccupations and the experimental 'cut-up' novels of William Burroughs an inspiration.

This shift in focus, however, came in direct response to a personal tragedy, the death of his wife Mary in 1964, and the increasing turbulence of those times. 'From my point of view,' Ballard has said, 'the sixties started in 1963 with the assassination of President Kennedy – his death and the Vietnam War presided over the whole of the sixties. Those two events, transmitted through television and mass communications, overshadowed the whole decade – a sort of institutionalized disaster area.'

In *The Kindness of Women* (1991), the autobiographical sequel to *Empire of the Sun*, his protagonist narrator, Jim, effectively voices Ballard's own opinion when he notes that 'the media landscape of the 1960s was a laboratory designed specifically to cure me of all my obsessions. Violence and pornography provided a kit of desperate measures that might give meaning both to Miriam's death and the unnumbered victims of the war in China.' (Miriam is the name of the character closely modelled on Ballard's own wife.) And in 1996 Ballard said, 'I think *Crash* is, in a way, my most autobiographical novel, notwithstanding *Empire of the Sun* . . . *Crash* is an autobiographical novel in the sense that it is about my inner life, my imaginative life. It is true to that interior life, not the life I have actually led.'

Although none of his books would ever be quite as extreme as *Crash*, its immediate successors *Concrete Island* and *High-Rise* were similarly bold dissections of the psychopathology of the contemporary urban landscape. And while Ballard again moved on from what Martin Amis later described as this 'concrete and steel period', he continued to probe the darker recesses of the human psyche. From his suburban home in Shepperton, he produced fictions that constantly melded provocative cultural analysis with outrageous, and sometimes shockingly prescient, prediction. Whether chronicling barbarism in a seemingly idyllic upmarket resort in *Cocaine Nights* (1996) or, more recently, positing the notion of a middle-class revolution in the mordantly witty *Millennium People* (2003), Ballard has been ceaselessly alert to the inherent horrors and absurdities of the modern world. He remains a true visionary, and one of the greatest writers of this or indeed any age. ■

‘*Crash* is an autobiographical novel in the sense that it is about my inner life, my imaginative life. It is true to that interior life, not the life I have actually led.’

The Road to *Crash*

Like many of Ballard's other novels, the seeds for *Crash* were sown in a short story or, in effect, the series of stories that were eventually published as *The Atrocity Exhibition* (or *Love and Napalm: Export USA*). Described by Will Self as representing 'the zenith of the experimental novel in English' and as 'a profound and disquieting book' by William Burroughs, *The Atrocity Exhibition* is composed of seemingly disconnected, almost shard-like tales, some made up of short listed paragraphs. Full of extreme imagery and, as its author admits, 'rather obsessive sexual fantasies about the prominent figures of the day', it strove, in its fragmentary structure, to emulate the confused (and confusing) messages of news broadcasts, advertising billboards, television commercials and technical manuals. In an author's note readers were advised to 'simply turn the pages until a paragraph catches your eye'.

The arrival of the internet, with its unending stream of overlapping text and pornographic images, has, as Ballard comments in his memoir *Miracles of Life* (2008), made this experimental novel 'a good deal more accessible' and, arguably, less outrageous than it once was. But in 1970 it was greeted with outright dismay in some quarters.

In America, the entire first print run by Doubleday was pulped just before publication. Idly flicking through an advance copy, the firm's head, Nelson

Doubleday, had hit upon the story 'Why I Want to Fuck Ronald Reagan'. Prophetic in its suggestion that Reagan, then the governor of California, would become the president of the United States, the piece had already attracted the attention of the police in Britain. (The Unicorn Bookshop in Brighton, who originally published the story in pamphlet form in 1968, had their premises raided and were charged with obscenity.) Doubleday, a close friend of Reagan's, immediately moved to kill the book. His intervention meant that *The Atrocity Exhibition* would not appear in the States until 1972. Paul Theroux, reviewing it for the *New York Times* when it did, called it 'a cold-blooded fantasy of aberrant proportions', declaring it 'a horrible book'.

One of the key stories in *The Atrocity Exhibition* was 'Crash!' A meditation on celebrity road fatalities and the erotic possibilities of the car crash, it was the gene from which the novel later sprang. Before embarking on the novel, however, Ballard took advantage of an offer to stage an exhibition at the Art Laboratory in London. To test his 'deviant thesis' that there was an unconscious link between sex and the car crash, he filled this gallery with wrecked vehicles. For the opening night a model was hired to interview guests in the nude. Arriving at the gallery though, and seeing the cars, she would only agree to appear topless. 'A significant response', as Ballard later wrote. The evening, which descended into drunken mayhem, seemed to ►

❛ One of the key stories in *The Atrocity Exhibition* was 'Crash!', it was the gene from which the novel later sprang. ❜

The Road to *Crash*

(continued)

◀ confirm his thesis only too well and he set about writing the novel in 1970.

Confronted with an early, and much longer, draft of *Crash*, a reader for his publisher famously sent a note that ran: 'This author is beyond psychiatric help. Do not publish.' It is to their enormous credit that they did not heed this advice. But the novel was intended to disturb. 'I wanted to write a book in which there was nowhere to hide,' he told David Pringle in 1975. 'I wanted the reader, once I'd got him inside the book, never to lose sight of the subject matter. As long as he continued reading he was face to face with the subject matter. It would have been easy to write a conventional book about car crashes in which it was quite clear that the author was on the side of sanity, justice and against injuring small children, deaths on the road, bad driving, etc. What could be easier? I chose to completely accept the demands of the subject matter, which was to provoke the reader by saying that car crashes are good for you, you thoroughly enjoy them, they make your sex life richer, they represent part of the marriage between sex, the human organism, and technology.'

This was, as he commented in 1984, an '*extreme hypothesis*', one that he advanced for readers to draw their own 'moral and psychological conclusions' from. That the novel's narrator, however, bore his name, and the object of Vaughan's psychotic desires – Elizabeth Taylor – was similarly a 'real' person, blurred the polite distinction

> *Crash* is not a cautionary tale. *Crash* is what it appears to be. It is a psychopathic hymn.

between exploring ideas in a work of fiction and their possible advocacy beyond it. It was Ballard's refusal to impose a traditional moral or message that was especially disquieting.

In the years since the book's publication Ballard has offered a few caveats. Writing in the introduction that appears in this edition, he states that 'the ultimate role of *Crash* is cautionary'. But in 1994, he confessed to Will Self that '*Crash* is not a cautionary tale. *Crash* is what it appears to be. It is a psychopathic hymn.' But, he argued, 'It is a psychopathic hymn which has a point.' In 1973, the precise nature of that point certainly eluded some of its earliest reviewers. ■

DID YOU KNOW?

Two weeks after completing the novel, Ballard was involved in a car crash when the front tyres of his Ford Zephyr had a blow-out at the foot of Chiswick Bridge. Luckily he emerged unscathed.

What the Papers Said in 1973

'I didn't read any of the reviews of *Crash* . . . There didn't seem any point after the reviews of *The Atrocity Exhibition* – nobody read the book.' J. G. BALLARD

As viewers of the popular time-travelling television series *Life on Mars* have recently been reminded, 1973 was, in some respects, a far more conservative time than now. Here are some of the stunned reactions to Ballard's novel from the period, an era when three-day weeks continued to blight the land.

' *Crash* is, hands down, the most repulsive book I've yet to come across. '

'*Crash* is, hands down, the most repulsive book I've yet to come across. *Sport Illustrated* coverage of the round-robin eliminations at Ravensbruck would be somewhat less freakish. And as reader, I promise you, only a virtuoso foulness can turn my stomach. (As person, I faint when someone serves medium-rare London broil.) J. G. Ballard choreographs a crazed, morbid roundelay of dismemberment and sexual perversion. *Crash* is well written; credit given where due. But I could not, in conscience, recommend it. Indeed I most cordially advise against. Believe me, no one needs this sort of protracted and gratuitous anguish: except perhaps those who think quadruple amputees are chic.'

New York Times, September 1973

'Ballard has a brilliant reputation but this novel's obsession with sado-masochism via deliberate car-crashing is repellent. The fact that he writes well makes it creepier.'

The Times, June 1973

'. . . the tone of this book is neither gloating nor priapic; the glazed monotony of its descriptions and the deadpan singlemindedness of its attitudes aren't designed to convert or excite the reader, merely to transmit the chilling isolation of the psychopath. Granted this generous rationale, however, *Crash* remains heavily flawed: loose construction, a perfunctory way with minor characters, and a lot of risible overwriting make it hard not to see the book as just an exercise in vicious whimsy.'

MARTIN AMIS, *Observer*, July 1973

❛ Ballard has a brilliant reputation but this novel's obsession with sado-masochism via deliberate car-crashing is repellent. ❜

Autopia
by J. G. Ballard

THINK OF THE twentieth century – what key image most sums it up in your mind? Neil Armstrong standing on the moon? Winston Churchill giving the V-sign? A housewife in a supermarket loading her trolley with brightly coloured food packs? A television commercial? For me, none of these. If I were asked to condense the whole of the present century into one mental picture I would pick a familiar everyday sight: a man in a motor car, driving along a concrete highway to some unknown destination. Almost every aspect of modern life is there, both for good and for ill – our sense of speed, drama, aggression, the worlds of advertising and consumer goods, engineering and mass manufacture, and the shared experience of moving together through an elaborately signalled landscape.

We spend a large part of our lives in the car, and the experience of driving involves many of the experiences of being a human being in the 1970s, a focal point for an immense range of social, economic and psychological pressures. I think the twentieth century reaches its purest expression on the highway. Here we see all too clearly the speed and violence of our age, its strange love affair with the machine and, conceivably, with its own death and destruction.

What is the real significance in our lives of this huge metallized dream? Is the car, in more senses than one, taking us for a ride? Increasingly, the landscape of the twentieth century is being created by and for the car, a development which people all over the world are beginning to rebel against. They look with horror at Los Angeles – nicknamed Autopia, Smogville and Motopia – a city ruthlessly ruled by the automobile, with its air clouded by exhaust gases and its man-made horizons formed by the raised embankments of gigantic freeway systems.

In Britain the first motorways are already reaching across our cities. Many of them are motion sculptures of considerable grace and beauty, but they totally overpower the urban areas around and – all too often – below them. It may well be that these vast concrete intersections are the most important monuments of our urban civilization, the twentieth century's equivalent of the Pyramids, but do we want to be remembered in the same way as the slave armies who constructed what, after all, were monuments to the dead?

Sadly, despite the enormous benefits which the car has created, a sense of leisure, possibility, freedom and initiative, undreamt of by the ordinary man eighty-six years ago when Karl Benz built the world's first successful petrol-driven vehicle, the car has brought with it a train of hazards and disasters, from the congestion of city and countryside to serious injury and deaths of millions of people. The car crash is the most dramatic event in most people's lives apart from their own deaths and for many the two will coincide. Are we merely ►

‘The landscape of the twentieth century is being created by and for the car, a development which people all over the world are beginning to rebel against.’

Autopia

(continued)

◀ victims in a meaningless tragedy, or do these appalling accidents take place with some kind of unconscious collaboration on our part? Most of us when we drive our cars willingly accept a degree of risk for ourselves, our wives and our children which we would regard as criminally negligent in any other field – the wiring of an electrical appliance, say, or the design of a bridge or apartment block, the competence of a surgeon or midwife. Yet the rough equivalent of speeding on unchecked tyres along a fast dual carriageway at the end of a tiring day at the office is lying in a hot bath with a blazing three-bar electric fire balanced on the edge below a half-open window rattling in a rising gale. If we really feared the crash, most of us would be unable to look at a car, let alone drive one.

Drive, 1971

Squeezed into Somebody Else's Mould:

Ballard on the Big Screen

IN HIS MONOGRAPH on David Cronenberg's film *Crash*, Iain Sinclair wrote that 'Ballard's compacted novels of the 60s and early 70s read as much like storyboards for unmakeable films as auditions for future books.' And it is perhaps surprising, given the spare, intensely visual quality of so much of Ballard's writing and the successful transfer of novels like Ray Bradbury's *Fahrenheit 451* and Anthony Burgess's *A Clockwork Orange* to film, that so few adaptations of his works – compacted fictions, full novels and short stories alike – were undertaken at the time. In the late 1960s, when there was some interest in *The Drowned World*, Ballard had provided the story for the Hammer Horror picture *When Dinosaurs Ruled the Earth* (1970). (Ballard has written that he is glad that Hammer misspelled his name on the finished film's credits.)

But until Steven Spielberg brought *Empire of the Sun* to the big screen in 1987, Ballard's fictions remained effectively unfilmed.

Originally acquired on behalf of David Lean, Spielberg's movie, judged by some to be his best, is held in high esteem by Ballard himself. 'I liked the film. I think it is a very impressive piece of work,' he said in 2005. 'I see it not as the film of my book but a film in its own right.'

The film's success did not, however, instantly trigger a new wave of Ballard ►

> ‘In 1982, Ballard said, 'I am glad really that *Crash* has not been filmed . . . Because I can see myself beginning to believe the movie version – my own imagination deformed by the damned thing, squeezed into somebody else's mould.'’

Squeezed into Somebody Else's Mould

(continued)

◀ adaptations. Only very recently did Jonathan Weiss tackle the previously 'unmakeable' *The Atrocity Exhibition* (2000) and Solveig Nordlund film *Low-Flying Aircraft* (*Aparelho Voador a Baixa Altitude* 2002).

Though a short film of the story 'Crash!', directed by Harley Cokliss and starring Ballard and Gabrielle Drake (sister of the singer Nick) was broadcast on BBC2 in 1971, an actual movie of *Crash* the novel would have to wait until 1996.

Between 1973 and 1996, several attempts were made. A script by the artist, actor and poet Heathcote Williams, whose graffiti was as much a feature of Notting Hill in the 1970s as the Westway, did the rounds, apparently. And Nicholas Roeg, director of *Don't Look Now* and *The Man Who Fell to Earth*, was reputedly in the frame to film the book at one time.

Asked about any progress on a film by interviewers from *Re/Search* in 1982, Ballard said, 'I am glad really that *Crash* has not been filmed . . . Because I can see myself beginning to believe the movie version – my own imagination deformed by the damned thing, squeezed into somebody else's mould.'

Nearly a decade later, however, Ballard received what he believed was an 'excellent' script from David Cronenberg. Cronenberg, who as a teenager had submitted stories to science fiction magazines, albeit without success, was an ideal interpreter of Ballard's book. A filmmaker whose primary subjects have been frailty and decay and the capacity of technology to mutate the human form, he had, at that point, only just put a loose-limbed interpretation of one of Ballard's favourite novels, William Burroughs' *Naked Lunch*, before cinemagoers. (It was while filming *Naked Lunch*, in fact, that Cronenberg had first proposed making *Crash*.)

Cronenberg, naturally, made several changes to the book, not least its setting – with Ballard's approval, insistence possibly, he moved the action from west London to Toronto. (In an interview with Kevin Jackson in 1996, Ballard maintained that he told Cronenberg, 'Don't set it in England, set it in North America. That's the land of the automobile and of great highways, where the car has an iconic beauty.') He also provided a new and more conclusive ending, and excised media scientist Vaughan's murderous obsession with Elizabeth Taylor entirely. Despite these alterations, Cronenberg's film, which casts James Spader as Ballard, Deborah Unger as Catherine, Holly Hunter as Helen Remington and Elias Koteas as Vaughan, is enormously faithful to the spirit of the book.

Ballard pronounced it 'a masterpiece' and described it to Iain Sinclair as 'a most elegant and mysterious film', adding elsewhere that he felt the film merged 'seamlessly with the book'.

Crash was premiered at the 1996 Cannes Film Festival, where it received a Special Jury Prize 'For Originality, For Daring, ▶

❛ Ballard pronounced it 'a masterpiece' and described it to Iain Sinclair as 'a most elegant and mysterious film' ❜

Squeezed into Somebody Else's Mould

(continued)

◄ and For Audacity'. The film, however, was greeted with dismay by the *Evening Standard*'s film critic Alexander Walker, who reported that it was 'beyond the bounds of depravity'. On the day the film had its first screening in Britain at the London Film Festival, the front page of the *Daily Mail* sported an article headed 'Ban This Car Crash Sex Film'. Despite a concerted media campaign to have it banned, the British Board of Film Classification, having sought the advice of a QC and a psychologist and having held a screening for a group of disabled people, who it had been argued might be offended by the picture, eventually granted the film an 18 certificate. Westminster City Council, though, refused to allow the movie to be shown unless further cuts were made. With the result that, to this day, the film, which has since been released on video, dvd and broadcast on television, cannot be viewed in a cinema in London's West End. ■

Conclusions:
From Cult to Classic and Life Beyond the Page

AFTER WEATHERING ITS many controversies, the status of *Crash*, the novel, as a work of literature has only grown. Even some of those who dismissed the book back in 1973 have come round. As Martin Amis admitted in 2001, 'It took me a long time to get the hang of *Crash*, and of Ballard.' Reviewing Cronenberg's film for the *Independent on Sunday* in 1996, he wrote: 'The novel is indifferent to the passage of time and has lost nothing in twenty-five years. It is like a clinical case of chronic shock, confusedly welcomed by the sufferer.' In Amis's view, only 'in the stories collected under the title *Vermilion Sands* (1973) did he duplicate this glazed and melodious precision'. Ballard himself has called it his 'most important book'.

Ballard's influence has been profound and wide-ranging, affecting writers like Iain Sinclair and Will Self, who has confessed he only has to 'look at a few paragraphs of *Crash* to feel . . . in the presence of an extreme mind, a mind at the limits of dark imagination', and musicians like David Bowie, whose 'Always Crashing in the Same Car' from his 1976 album *Low* was inspired by Ballard's novel. As someone who confesses to not owning a hi-fi, Ballard has always expressed some amusement that his work should have been so readily adopted by rock stars. In the 1970s the term 'Ballardian' was frequently deployed in the pages of those now largely defunct ►

❛ Martin Amis wrote: 'The novel is indifferent to the passage of time and has lost nothing in twenty-five years. It is like a clinical case of chronic shock, confusedly welcomed by the sufferer.' ❜

Conclusions
(continued)

◄ music weeklies, the *NME*, *Melody Maker* and *Sounds*.

In his expansive history of the Sex Pistols, *England's Dreaming*, Jon Savage notes that for London punks in 1976, 'the big book . . . was *High Rise*'. 'After Ballard's *High Rise* and *Crash*,' he writes, 'it was possible to see high-rises as both appalling and vertiginously exciting.' The Westway, the locale of *Concrete Island*, would consequently provide the visual backdrop to many a punk band's photo shoot.

Several of the new wave artists that came to prominence in the aftermath of punk – Cabaret Voltaire, The Human League, Gary Numan and Ultravox – were avid admirers of Ballard. John Foxx, the former lead singer of Ultravox, penned a whole album, *Metamatic*, under the influence of *Crash*. Daniel Miller, aka The Normal, paid homage to the novel in the stark electronic number 'Warm Leatherette', later a hit for Grace Jones. And Joy Division's Ian Curtis pinched the title of *The Atrocity Exhibition* for a track on the band's 1980 album *Closer*. In Anton Corbijn's recent biopic, *Control*, a thumbed copy of *Crash* is shown nestling on the shelves of Curtis's Bowie poster-plastered teenage bedroom.

More recently, the Klaxons, winners of the 2007 Nationwide Mercury Music Prize, named their debut album after the Ballard short-story collection, *Myths of the Near Future*.

Such new tributes only show that Ballard's fictions are continuing to attract a fresh generation of readers. His relevance, in our fully technocratic age, has, if anything, only increased. Writing on the *Guardian*'s website in November 2007, Lee Rourke said of *Crash*, 'I can't think of a more prophetic novel written by a British writer in the last fifty years.' You'd be hard pushed to disagree with him. ■

‘Ballard's relevance, in our fully technocratic age, has, if anything, only increased.’

Have You Read?

Other books by J. G. Ballard

The Atrocity Exhibition
Ballard's prophetic, groundbreaking experimental novel is as brilliant and unnerving as ever and contains the story 'Crash!', an embryonic version of this novel.

Concrete Island
Almost a sister volume or near sequel to *Crash*, this mesmerizing novel tells the story of a 35-year-old architect, who, having crashed on the Westway while driving home from his London office, remains marooned on a traffic island. A heady, petrol-soaked twist on Defoe's *Robinson Crusoe*, it is a compelling exploration of isolation.

High-Rise
Within the concealing walls of an elegant forty-storey tower block, the affluent tenants are hellbent on an orgy of destruction. Cocktail parties degenerate into marauding attacks on 'enemy' floors and the once luxurious amenities become an arena for technological mayhem . . . In this classic visionary novel from 1975, human society slips into violent reverse as the inhabitants of the high-rise, driven by primal urges, recreate a world ruled by the laws of the jungle.

The Complete Short Stories, Volumes 1 and 2
Ballard's first stories were published in 1956. These volumes provide the reader with the chance to explore his complete shorter oeuvre and marvel at both his

development as a writer and his mastery of the form.

Empire of the Sun

Based on J. G. Ballard's own childhood, this is the extraordinary account of a boy's life in Japanese-occupied wartime Shanghai – a mesmerizing, hypnotically compelling novel of war, of starvation and survival, of internment camps and death marches. It blends searing honesty with a vivid picture of a world thrown utterly out of joint.

Cocaine Nights

When Charles Prentice arrives in Spain to investigate his brother's involvement in the death of five people in a fire in the upmarket coastal resort of Estrella de Mar, he gradually discovers that beneath the civilized, cultured surface of this exclusive enclave for Britain's retired rich there flourishes a secret world of crime, drugs and illicit sex. What starts as an engrossing mystery develops into a thrilling novel of ideas.

Millennium People

When a bomb goes off at Heathrow it looks like just another random act of violence to psychologist David Markham. But then he discovers that his ex-wife Laura is among the victims. Acting on police suspicions, he starts to investigate London's fringe protest movements, falling in with a shadowy group based in the comfortable Thameside

Have You Read?
(continued)

estate of Chelsea Marina. Led by a charismatic doctor, the group aims to rouse the docile middle classes to anger and violence, to free them from both the self-imposed burdens of civic responsibility and the trappings of a consumer society – private schools, foreign nannies, health insurance and overpriced housing. Markham, seeking the truth behind Laura's death, is swept up in a campaign that spirals rapidly out of control.

Kingdom Come
In this late masterpiece from Ballard, the Sage of Shepperton asks could consumerism turn into fascism?

Richard Pearson, unemployed advertising executive and life-long rebel, is driving out to Brooklands, a motorway town on the M25. A few weeks earlier his father was fatally wounded at the Metro Centre, a vast shopping mall in this apparently peaceful town, when a deranged mental patient opened fire on a crowd of shoppers. Richard suspects that there is more to his father's death than meets the eye, and a more sinister element lurks behind the pristine facades of the labyrinthine mall.

In this gripping, dystopian tour de force, J. G. Ballard presents an unsettling image of suburbia that reveals the darker forces at work beneath the gloss of consumerism.

If You Loved This,
You Might Like . . .

Naked Lunch
William Burroughs

Lord of the Flies
William Golding

Friday
Michel Tournier

Foe
J. M. Coetzee

Robinson
Muriel Spark

My Idea of Fun
Will Self

Robinson
Chris Petit

Falling Out of Cars
Jeff Noon

London Orbital
Iain Sinclair

Leadville: A Biography of the A40
Edward Platt

The Contortionist's Handbook
Craig Clevenger

Find Out More

Other books by J. G. Ballard

READ

Miracles of Life: Shanghai to Shepperton, an autobiography
In prose of characteristic precision and wit, Ballard here offers his own account of his extraordinary life, times and career.

The Kindness of Women
A sequel, in effect, to *Empire of the Sun*, this second autobiographical novel follows Jim Ballard as he moves from Shanghai to England, and from adolescence to middle age.

Crash
Iain Sinclair
In this monograph, which includes a lengthy and immensely illuminating interview with Ballard, Sinclair not only explores the relationship between Cronenberg's film and the novel but also the author's own connection to the narrator of the book, who carried his name, and much else besides. Idiosyncratic but highly recommended.

J. G. Ballard: Conversations
Edited by V. Vale
A fantastic collection of interviews that capture Ballard's thoughts on everything from the rise of the internet and the impact of 9/11 to the arrival of luxury gated communities and the meaning of Las Vegas.

J. G. Ballard: Quotes
Edited by V. Vale
A compendium of quotations from J. G. Ballard's fiction, articles and interviews, this book provides a panoramic tour of the author's views on life, work and the world.

WATCH

Empire of the Sun (1987)
Directed by Steven Spielberg
With a screenplay by Tom Stoppard, and starring a young Christian Bale as Jim, Spielberg's adaptation has the grace and grandeur of a David Lean epic, and is much admired by Ballard himself – who puts in a fleeting cameo appearance.

Crash (1996)
Directed by David Cronenberg
Cronenberg's film caused almost as much controversy on its release in the 1990s as the novel itself had in the 1970s. It is, however, a respectful treatment of the book, one that, importantly, received its author's glowing endorsement.

The Atrocity Exhibition (2000)
Directed by Jonathan Weiss
Mixing dramatic and documentary footage, Weiss's uncompromising version of Ballard's book brilliantly mimics the collage-like quality of that experimental novel.

Crash! (1971)
Directed by Harley Cokliss
Cokliss's short feature for BBC2, shot in a ►

Find Out More
(continued)

◀ multistorey car park in Watford and starring Ballard and Gabrielle Drake, can now be viewed on YouTube.

SURF

www.jgballard.com
A comprehensive website devoted to Ballard's life and works.

www.ballardian.com
A true web *Wunderkammer* of all things Ballard.